"Katie is a charming amateur sleuth, baking her way through murder and magic set against the enchanting backdrop of Savannah, Georgia."
—*New York Times* bestselling author Jenn McKinlay

"A smooth, accomplished writer who combines a compelling plot with a cast of interesting characters that are diverse and engaging . . . while the story's magical elements bring a fun, intriguing dimension to the genre." —*Kirkus Reviews*

"[A] promising series." —*Library Journal*

"With a top-notch whodunit, a dark magic investigator working undercover, and a simmering romance in the early stages, fans will relish this tale." —Gumshoe

"A tight mystery packed with charming characters and drool-worthy baked goods." —MyShelf.com

"Be warned—[this book] will work its spell on you, and you'll find yourself looking forward to more enchantment."
—Kings River Life Magazine

"An enchanting treat. . . . Well written, well put together, with characters that stay with you long after." —Lily Pond Reads

"Cates does a fantastic job of creating a magical atmosphere that is both believable and enchanting." —Debbie's Book Bag

DAISIES
FOR
INNOCENCE

❦

AN ENCHANTED
GARDEN MYSTERY

BAILEY CATTRELL

AN OBSIDIAN MYSTERY

OBSIDIAN
Published by New American Library,
an imprint of Penguin Random House LLC
375 Hudson Street, New York, New York 10014

This book is an original publication of New American Library.

First Printing, January 2016

For more information about Penguin Random House, visit penguin.com.

ISBN 978-0-451-47688-3

Printed in the United States of America
1 3 5 7 9 10 8 6 4 2

Penguin
Random
House

This book is dedicated to Jessica Wade

ACKNOWLEDGMENTS

I'm so grateful to the many people who helped this book come into being. Kim Lionetti provided great suggestions as well as being my staunch ally and friend. My brilliant and hardworking team at Penguin Random House takes a manuscript and makes it fit for public consumption—thanks to Jessica Wade, Isabel Farhi, Ashley Polikoff, Karen Haywood, and Danielle Dill. I also consider myself incredibly rich to have so many wonderful writers in my life, friends and colleagues who give me advice, encouragement, and are happy to chat about all things writing ad nauseam. They include (but are not limited to) Mark Figlozzi, Laura Pritchett, Laura Resau, and Bob Trott. Amy Lockwood told me about *The Elves of Lily Hill Farm*, which sparked the idea for the Enchanted Garden Mystery series, while Stacey Kollman inspired my interest in aromatherapy oh so many years ago. And from the genesis of the proposal to the words "The End," Kevin Brookfield has been my anchor and my wings— whichever I needed more.

CHAPTER 1

THE sweet, slightly astringent aroma of *Lavandula stoechas* teased my nose. I couldn't help closing my eyes for a moment to appreciate its layered fragrance drifting on the light morning breeze. Spanish lavender, or "topped" lavender—according to my gamma, it had been one of my mother's favorites. It was a flower that had instilled calm and soothed the skin for time eternal, a humble herb still used to ease headache and heartache alike. I remembered Gamma murmuring to me in her garden when I was five years old:

Breathe deeply, Elliana. Notice how you can actually taste the scent when you inhale it? Pliny the Elder brewed this into his spiced wine, and Romans used it to flavor their ancient sauces. In the language of flowers, it signifies the acknowledgment of love.

Not that I'd be using it in that capacity anytime soon.

But Gamma had been gone for over twenty years, and my mother had died when I was only four. Shaking my head, I returned my attention to the tiny mosaic pathway next to where I knelt. Carefully, I added a piece of foggy sea glass to the design. The path was three feet long and four inches wide, and led from beneath a tumble of forget-me-nots to a violet-colored fairy door set into the base of the east fence. Some people referred to them as "gnome doors," but whatever you called them, the decorative miniature garden phenomena were gaining popularity with adults and children alike. The soft green and blue of the water-polished, glass-nugget path seemed to morph directly from the clusters of azure flowers, curving around a lichen-covered rock to the ten-inch round door. I wondered how long it would take one of my customers to notice this new addition to the verdant garden behind my perfume and aromatherapy shop, Scents & Nonsense.

The rattle of the latch on the gate to my left interrupted my thoughts. Surprised, I looked up and saw Dash trotting toward me on his short corgi legs. His lips pulled back in a grin as he reached my side, and I smoothed the thick ruff of fur around his foxy face. Astrid Moneypenny—my best friend in Poppyville, or anywhere else, for that matter—strode behind him at a more sedate pace. Her latest foster dog, Tally, a Newfoundland mix with a graying muzzle, lumbered beside her.

"Hey, Ellie! There was a customer waiting on the boardwalk out front," Astrid said. "I let her in to look around. Tally, sit."

I bolted to my feet, the fairy path forgotten. "Oh, no. I totally lost track of time. Is it already ten o'clock?"

The skin around Astrid's willow-green eyes crinkled in a smile. They were a startling contrast to her auburn hair and freckled nose. "Relax. I'll watch the shop while you get cleaned up." She jammed her hand into the pocket of her hemp dress and pulled out a cookie wrapped in a napkin. "Snickerdoodles today."

I took it and inhaled the buttery cinnamon goodness. "You're the best."

Astrid grinned. "I have a couple of hours before my next gig. Tally can hang out here with Dash." She was a part-time technician at the veterinary clinic and a self-proclaimed petrepreneur—dog walker and pet sitter specializing in animals with medical needs. "But isn't Josie supposed to be working today?"

"She should be here soon," I said. "She called last night and left a message that she might be late. Something about a morning hike to take pictures of the wildflowers." I began gathering pruners and trowel, kneeling pad and weed digger into a handled basket. "They say things are blooming like crazy in the foothills right now."

Astrid turned to go, then stopped. Her eyes caught mine. "Ellie . . ."

"What?"

She shook her head. "It's just that you look so happy working out here."

I took in the leafy greenery, the scarlet roses climbing the north fence, tiered beds that overflowed with herbs and scented blooms, and the miniature gardens and doors tucked into surprising nooks and alcoves. A downy woodpecker rapped against the trunk of the oak at the rear of the lot, and two hummingbirds whizzed by on their way to drink from the handblown glass feeder near the back patio of Scents & Nonsense. An asymmetrical boulder hunkered in the middle of the yard, the words ENCHANTED GARDEN etched into it by a local stone carver. He'd also carved words into river rocks I'd placed in snug crannies throughout the half-acre space. The one next to where Dash had flopped down read BELIEVE. Mismatched rocking chairs on the patio, along with the porch swing hanging from the pergola, offered opportunities for customers to sit back, relax, sip a cup of tea or coffee, and nibble on the cookies Astrid baked up each morning.

"I am happy," I said quietly. More than that. *Grateful.* A sense of contentment settled deep into my bones, and my smile broadened.

"I'm glad things have worked out so well for you." Her smile held affection that warmed me in spite of the cool morning.

"It hasn't been easy, but it's true that time smooths a lot of rough edges." I rolled my eyes. "Of course, it's taken me nearly a year."

A year of letting my heart heal from the bruises of infidelity, of divorce, of everyone in town knowing my—and my ex's—business. In fact, perfect cliché that it was, everyone except me seemed to know Harris had been having an affair with Wanda Simmons, the owner of one of Poppyville's ubiquitous souvenir shops. Once I was out of the picture, though, he'd turned the full spectrum of his demanding personality on her. She'd bolted within weeks, going so far as to move back to her hometown in Texas. I still couldn't decide whether that was funny or sad.

I'd held my ground, however. Poppyville, California,

nestled near the foothills of the Sierra Nevada Mountains, was *my* hometown, and I wasn't about to leave. The town's history reached back to the gold rush, and tourists flocked to its Old West style; its easy access to outdoor activities like hiking, biking, and fly fishing; and to the small hot spring a few miles to the south.

After the divorce, I'd purchased a storefront with the money Harris paid to buy me out of our restaurant, the Roux Grill. The property was perfect for what I wanted: a retail store to cater to townspeople and tourists alike and a business that would allow me to pursue my passion for all things scentual. Add in the unexpected—and largely free—living space included in the deal, and I couldn't turn it down.

Sense & Nonsense was in a much sought after location at the end of Corona Street's parade of bric-a-brac dens. The kite shop was next door to the north, but to the south, Raven Creek Park marked the edge of town with a rambling green space punctuated with playground equipment, picnic tables, and a fitness trail. The facade of my store had an inviting, cottagelike feel, with painted shutters above bright window boxes and a rooster weathervane twirling on the peaked roof. The acre lot extended in a rectangle behind the business to the front door of my small-scale home, which snugged up against the back property line.

With a lot of work and plenty of advice from local nurserywoman Thea Nelson, I'd transformed what had started as a barren, empty lot between the two structures into an elaborate garden open to my customers, friends, and the occasional catered event. As I'd added more and more whimsical details, word of the Enchanted Garden had spread. I loved sharing it with others, and it was good for business, too.

"Well, it's nice to have you back, sweetie. Now we just have to find a man for you." Astrid reached down to stroke Tally's neck. The big dog gazed up at her with adoration, while I struggled to keep a look of horror off my face.

"Man?" I heard myself squeak. That was the last thing on my mind. Well, almost. I cleared my throat. "What about your love life?" I managed in a more normal tone.

She snorted. "I have plenty of men, Ellie. Don't you worry about me."

It was true. Astrid attracted men like milkweed attracted monarch butterflies. At thirty-seven, she'd never been married, and seemed determined to keep it that way.

"Astrid," I began, but she'd already turned on her heel so fast that her copper-colored locks whirled like tassels on a lamp shade. Her hips swung ever so slightly beneath the skirt of her dress, the hem of which skimmed her bicycle-strong calves as she returned to the back door of Scents & Nonsense to look after things. Tally followed her and settled down on the patio flagstones as my friend went inside. I saw Nabokov, the Russian blue shorthair who made it his business to guard the store day and night, watching the big dog through the window with undisguised feline disdain.

Basket in hand, I hurried down the winding stone pathway to my living quarters. "God, I hope she doesn't get it into her head to set me up with someone," I muttered around a bite of still-warm snickerdoodle.

Dash, trotting by my left heel, glanced up at me with skeptical brown eyes. He'd been one of Astrid's foster dogs about six months earlier. She'd told me he was probably purebred, but there was no way of knowing, as he'd been found at a highway rest stop and brought, a bit dehydrated but otherwise fine, to the vet's office where she worked. Of course, Astrid agreed to take care of him until a home could be found—which was about ten seconds after she brought him into Scents & Nonsense. I'd fallen hard for him, and he'd been my near constant companion ever since.

"Okay. It's possible, just possible, that it would be nice to finally go on an actual date," I said to him now. Leery of my bad judgment in the past, I'd sworn off the opposite sex since my marriage ended. But now that Scents & Nonsense wasn't demanding all my energy and time, I had to admit that a sense of loneliness had begun to seep into my evenings.

"But you know what they say about the men in Poppyville, Dash. The odds here are good, but the goods are pretty odd."

A hawk screeched from the heights of a pine in the open meadow behind my house. Ignoring it, Dash darted away to nose the diminutive gazebo and ferns beneath the ancient gnarled trunk of the apple tree. He made a small noise in the back of his throat and sat back on his haunches beside the little door I'd made from a weathered cedar shake and set into a notch in the bark. Absently, I called him back, distracted by how sun-warmed mint combined so nicely with the musk of incense cedar, a bright but earthy fragrance that followed us to my front door.

Granted, my home had started as a glorified shed, but it worked for a Pembroke Welsh corgi and a woman who sometimes had to shop in the boy's section to find jeans that fit. The "tiny house" movement was about living simply in small spaces. I hadn't known anything about it until my half brother, Colby, mentioned it in one of his phone calls from wherever he'd stopped his Westfalia van for the week. The idea had immediately appealed to my inner child, who had always wanted a playhouse of her very own, while my environmental side appreciated the smaller, greener footprint. I'd hired a contractor from a nearby town who specialized in tiny-house renovations. He'd made a ramshackle three-hundred-twenty-square-foot shed into a super-efficient living space.

There were loads of built-in niches, an alcove in the main living area for a television and stereo, extra foldout seating, a drop-down dining table, and even a desk that tucked away into the wall until needed. A circular staircase led to the sleeping loft above, which boasted a queen bed surrounded by cupboards for linens and clothing and a skylight set into the angled roof. The staircase partially separated the living area from the galley kitchen, and the practical placement of shelves under the spiraling steps made it not only visually stunning, but a terrific place to house my considerable library of horticulture and aromatherapy books.

Most of the year, the back porch, which ran the seventeen-foot width of the house, was my favorite place to hang out when not in the garden or Scents & Nonsense. It looked out on an expanse of meadow running up to the craggy foothills of Kestrel Peak. Our resident mule deer herd often congregated there near sunset.

After a quick sluice in the shower, I slipped into a blue cotton sundress that matched my eyes, ran fingers through my dark shoulder-length curls in a feeble attempt to tame them, skipped the makeup, and slid my feet into soft leather sandals. Dash at my heel, I hurried down the path to the shop. I inhaled bee balm, a hint of basil, lemon verbena, and . . . what was *that*?

My steps paused, and I felt my forehead wrinkle. I knew every flower, every leaf in this garden, and every scent they gave off. I again thought of my gamma, who had taught me about plants and aromatherapy—though she never would have used that word. She would have known immediately what created this intoxicating fragrance.

Check her garden journal. Though without more information it would be difficult to search the tattered, dog-eared volume in which she'd recorded her botanical observations, sketches, flower recipes, and lore.

A flutter in my peripheral vision made me turn my head, but where I'd expected to see a bird winging into one of the many feeders, there was nothing. At the same time, a sudden breeze grabbed away the mysterious fragrance and tickled the wind chimes.

Glancing down, I noticed the engraved river rock by the fairy path I'd been forming earlier appeared to have shifted.

For a second, I thought it read BEWARE.

My head whipped up as I wildly searched the garden. When I looked down again, the word BELIEVE cheerfully beckoned again.

Just a trick of the light, Ellie.

Still, I stared at the smooth stone for what felt like a long time. Then I shook my head and continued to the patio. After giving Tally a quick pat on the head, I wended my way between two rocking chairs and opened the sliding door to Scents & Nonsense.

Nabby slipped outside, rubbing his gray velvety self against my bare leg before he touched noses with Dash, threw Tally a warning look, and padded out to bask in the sunshine. A brilliant blue butterfly settled near the cat and opened its iridescent wings to the warming day. As I turned away, two more floated in to join the first. As the cat moved toward his preferred perch on the retaining wall, the butterflies wafted behind him like balloons on a string. It was funny—they seemed to seek him out, and once I'd seen two or three find him in the garden, I knew more blue wings would soon follow.

CHAPTER 2

INSIDE Scents & Nonsense, Astrid had brewed coffee and now stood behind the register chatting with a young woman. The customer sported straight blond hair and a T-shirt advertising Fat Tire beer. I poured my second mug of caffeine and opened the curtains over the big plateglass window that looked out onto the garden. Then I ducked behind the low counter on the east side of the shop, where I manufactured many of the Scents & Nonsense signature products.

I'd discovered early on that there was no way to tend the shop and make my perfumes, bath oils, and the rest unless I combined the two. It turned out that people were actually interested in watching me stir and pour and bottle and label. During working hours I made sure to stick with items that could be easily interrupted for long stretches, so I could take my time with patrons, answering their questions and finding them exactly what they wanted or needed. In addition, I could sample and mix custom perfumes right on the spot, which snagged me a few more sales from tourists who wandered in off the covered boardwalk intending to "just look."

"I need a gift for my mother-in-law," the customer said as I sidled up beside Astrid. "Tomorrow is her birthday, and she's downright impossible to shop for." Her mouth twitched ruefully for a second before her pleasant mask descended again. Her gaze went up to Astrid's five foot ten and back down to me, a full foot shorter.

Astrid's eyes flashed with humor as she put her palm on my shoulder. "Ellie can help you out, I guarantee."

I stepped forward, and my friend gracefully sidestepped and began to load a plate with snickerdoodles. Astrid loathed cooking of all kinds—except baking cookies. She'd gotten into the habit of whipping up a batch every morning and dropping them by the shop. Called it her "therapy." I wasn't about to ask her to stop, either. The woman wouldn't boil an egg on a bet, but she was a cookie-baking genius.

"Let me guess," I said to the customer. "Your mother-in-law either has everything—or doesn't want it."

Her lips turned down in a slight frown, but her shoulders relaxed a fraction. "Exactly! I thought I'd get her a candle or soap or something. Everyone has to bathe, right?" Her bright tone seemed a little forced.

"I certainly hope so," I teased. "What are her favorite scents?"

"I . . . I don't know. She used to like jasmine. But . . ." She trailed off, looking uncomfortable.

"But?" I prompted.

She shrugged. "Her husband passed away a while ago. She hasn't been the same since."

Sad. Sad for a long time. I felt the heavy weight of the unknown woman's grief settle someplace near my sternum.

"I have an idea." I came out from behind the counter and went to a shelf on the far wall. She followed with a curious expression. I selected a quart-sized, Mason-jar candle, unscrewed the top, and took a deep sniff. The tight sensation in my chest eased as the fragrances of strong essential oils filled my lungs. I held the jar out to the woman, who took a tentative whiff, then with widening eyes, a longer, deeper inhalation.

"Oh, that's wonderful. What is it?"

I explained. "Cedar." *For courage.* "Cinnamon." *For warmth and safety during times of change.* "And lemon." *Which in this combination would inspire clarity when things seem muddled.*

A smile widened on her face. "You know, I think she'll like it. A lot."

I nodded. "Personally, I find the scents of those oils quite uplifting." In fact, I'd developed that particular combination to help me get through the past year. Starting over at thirty-five could feel pretty scary at times.

She breathed in the scent again and nodded. "I'll take it. But I'd like to get her something else, too. Any suggestions?"

"You mentioned soap. I think this one might go over well." I reached for a creamy ecru bar packaged in cellophane to keep the volatile essential oils from dissipating into the dry California air.

"What's in it?" she asked.

I pulled the tiny stopper out of the blue glass tester bottle at the front of the display and handed it to her to smell. My sensitive nose could detect the combination from a foot and a half away. The remaining pressure in my chest eased, and I knew it was the right choice for her mother-in-law. "Bergamot and jasmine. Cheerful scents, happy scents. The jasmine is the high note, the most noticeable, and you said she's partial to it. The bergamot underlies it with subtle charm. I'd suggest a box of high-quality Earl Grey tea— which gets its distinct, citrus flavor from bergamot—and make up a little gift basket. Tessa at the tea room down the street has a nice selection of Earl Grey, and I have some unique baskets over here." I led the way to a selection of sturdy baskets crocheted from stiff multicolored twine. "If you want a little something more to fill out the basket, a couple of packets of rose bath salts would do the trick." Rose was a scent of deep compassion.

My customer's head bobbed. "That's a great idea. Oh, and I'll take a bar of that soap for myself." She blushed, then shrugged. "It smells heavenly, and I deserve a treat."

"Good for you," I said with a grin, and gathered her purchases.

The door swung open, and Josie Overland strode in, bouncing on the balls of her feet with each step. Her long brown ponytail swayed back and forth.

"Hi! Sorry I'm late! Oh, but golly, it's so gorgeous up on Kestrel right now!" Her sunburned nose wrinkled in delight, and she bounded into my small office to stow her backpack. "It'll just take me a sec to change out of these hiking clothes," she called.

I wrapped the gift basket items and rang up the sale. As the door closed behind the blond woman, Astrid came up and leaned her elbows on the counter. "You okay?"

"Sure. Why wouldn't I be?"

She quirked an eyebrow. "You know. That"—she waved her hand—"superpower you use to find the right scents for your customers."

"Ha! I wouldn't call it *that*," I said. "My sense of smell is just . . . fine-tuned, I guess. If that's a superpower then your ability to diagnose what's wrong with an animal, or the way Maria can know exactly what book someone at the library needs are superpowers, too."

"It's not the same, and you know it," Astrid said.

I said, "Everyone has something they're really good at. Or more than one thing. Some people just train and practice. It's no different from being a good dancer or talented baseball player."

I truly believed that, though to be honest, my senses of smell and empathy were a unique combination that gave me the ability to sometimes read what scents could help someone. It wasn't infallible, and some people I couldn't read at all, but it was so satisfying when I could truly make someone feel better. The first time it had happened, I'd given our neighbor, Mr. Finder, a sprig of lily of the valley because he'd looked tired.

I'd been three.

Later, Gamma had told me that Mr. Finder had been working double shifts at his job, but that my present had helped him feel better. Over time, my ability to decipher people had evolved into something I mirrored on a physical level.

Now Astrid shook her head. "Okay, call it whatever you want, but I saw your face. Was it bad?"

"Not too bad," I said. "And the fragrances took care of it. That's how I know."

"That you're giving people what they need?"

I dipped my chin. "Yes."

"But this was by proxy, you might say. How can you know how to help someone you've never met?"

I frowned and leaned against the counter. "I don't know. That doesn't happen very often." I shrugged. "Maybe it didn't this time, either. Maybe she was the one who needed help." I gestured toward the door where the customer had departed.

Astrid looked skeptical but didn't comment. Still, I pondered her question until Josie emerged from the office, her shorts and T-shirt replaced with white Capri pants, a coral blouse, and boat shoes. "Ready for work, boss! Where should I start?"

A STRID left to jog a German shepherd for some clients who wanted their baby to have her exercise while they were out of town. I started Josie on a labeling project, then called to let Inga Fowler know that the custom perfume she'd ordered was ready for pickup. She didn't answer, so I left a voice mail and settled in at the counter to make a list of errands.

The beginning of the week tended to be slower for retail shops in tourist-oriented towns like Poppyville. Josie came in for most of the day on Mondays and Tuesdays, which gave me the opportunity to do some of the other things life requires during regular business hours. I'd been happy when she'd applied for the part-time position, since she bartended at the Roux Grill, and I already knew she was a great employee.

"Let's see," I said under my breath. "Bank, grocery store, library. Stop by Thea's and get a bag of mushroom compost for the new herb bed. And Dash is almost out of cookies from Doggone Gourmet." I paused and tapped my pen on the counter, thinking.

The Greenstockings, a loose-knit group of independent businesswomen in Poppyville that Astrid and I belonged to, were meeting later in the Enchanted Garden. The name was based on the famous Bluestocking Society in eighteenth-century England, which was made up of intellectual women discussing culture and literature. The Greenstockings, however, got together to talk about marketing and business strategy. The "green" in our name was short for "greenbacks."

Astrid would bring cookies—naturally—and Gessie King had promised to bring her signature guacamole. Cynthia Beck, who owned Foxy Locksies Hair Studio, could always be counted on for wine.

I texted Thea Nelson, who assured me she'd be at the Greenstockings meeting.

I put my phone away and went back to my list of errands.

"Um, Ellie?" Josie's voice wavered from behind me.

I turned to look at her. She shuffled from one foot to the other in the doorway of the office.

"Can't find the labels for the milk bath?" I asked, ready to climb down from my stool.

She raised her hand to reveal a roll of yellow stickers. "They were right where you said they would be. But, um, I kind of need to . . ." She bit her lip. "I need to tell you something."

My brow knitted in concern. Josie was normally anything but tentative. "Sweetie, what is it?"

She took a deep breath, and her pale eyes opened wide as she seemed to brace herself. "I'm, uh . . ." She looked away. "Harris and I . . ."

I was vaguely aware of the pen dropping from my fingers. In the ensuing silence, it rolled to the edge of the counter and fell to the floor with a tiny clatter.

"What?" I asked stupidly.

"Harris asked me out to dinner about a month ago, and I said yes. We've been seeing each other pretty regularly ever since. God, Ellie, I'm so sorry!"

Slowly, I shook my head. "No need to be sorry. It's just—" I stopped myself. *It's just that you're ten years younger than he is. And he's your boss. And you're bright and positive and he's . . . Harris.* "I'm just surprised, is all."

She hung her head, her chestnut ponytail swooping down over her shoulder. "I should have said something earlier." She looked up again before her gaze shunted to the side. "It's not that we were trying to keep anything from you, Ellie. Like it was a secret or anything. It just sort of happened. I didn't know I'd end up liking him so much. I mean, I've worked at the Roux for a long time now, right?"

I forced a smile and nodded. She'd started bartending there two years ago when I was still running the place with Harris. At twenty-nine, two years might seem like a long time to her.

Come to think of it, two years still seemed like a long time.

Her eyes filled with tears. "Are you going to fire me?"

My half smile dropped. "Of course not! Josie, you don't have to worry about your job here at the shop just because you're dating my ex."

"Really? You're so nice!" She threw her arms around me and squeezed tight. I returned her hug with somewhat less enthusiasm. Then I thought of how charming Harris had been when we were dating, how romantic and attentive. And how all that had seemed to drain away the second the rice finished raining down on us outside the chapel. I thought of that, and I hugged her back as hard as I could.

"You just be careful, you hear? Harris isn't the most faithful guy."

She stepped back and beamed at me. "Oh, he's different now. He's *changed*. He really has."

I nodded, unable to speak. *I hope so, honey. For your sake.*

A MOTHER brought in her six-year-old daughter to see the Enchanted Garden. They were in town only for the day, but a friend of theirs had urged them to visit.

My favorite kind of referral.

I happily gave them the tour, pointing out the miniature succulent garden, the tiny bridges, a diminutive cottage, and the winged fairy figurines arranged in the rock cress and creeping thyme. By that time, the group of blue butterflies Nabby regularly attracted had grown to two dozen. They'd taken up residence in the magenta Buddleia—commonly known as butterfly bush for good reason. Nabby had crept into its shade to sleep. As we approached, he deigned to open his eyes long enough to stretch into a more comfortable position.

Enjoying the child's open-mouthed, head-back wonder as she gazed up at the electric blue wings, I asked, "Did you know a bunch of butterflies like that is called a kaleidoscope?"

Silently, she shook her head.

"Stunning," the mother said, her eyes glued to the insects as firmly as her daughter's were. "A kaleidoscope, you say?"

"All that color swirling together when they fly—it makes sense," I said. "Feel free to grab a drink and some cookies. Sweetie," I said to the girl, "there's lemonade in the little fridge under the coffee urn inside if you want some. Spend as much time out here as you'd like."

"Thank you," the mother murmured, a smile now tugging at her lips. "We'll do that."

I asked Josie to check on them and left her labeling bottles of vanilla-scented milk bath. Dash and I went out to Corona Street.

"Hey, Ellie! How's business been?" Zach Porter asked.

He was hanging a colorful box kite on the wall outside Flyrite Kites.

I smiled. "Pretty good. Yours?"

"It's picking up. There's a kite festival over in Silver Wells next week, so that helps." He lifted his hand in farewell and went inside his shop.

Reflecting that festivals were the lifeblood of tourist towns in the summer months, I walked across to the public lot, where I generally parked so as not to take up a space in front of any of the downtown businesses. After hoisting Dash into the passenger seat of my battered old Wrangler, I used the running board to boost myself in, started up the engine, and began driving toward First Bank over on Gilmore Street.

The butterfly visitation normally would have made me smile for the rest of the afternoon, but not today. "Distracted" didn't even begin to describe how I felt. Mostly I was torn between anger at Harris and a worried sense of protectiveness toward Josie. However, there was also the vague, sticky shadow of the same humiliation I'd felt at Harris' betrayal during our marriage. Apparently, that was going to take a bit more time to fade away entirely.

Of course, he wasn't betraying me now.

Maybe I should *start thinking about dating.* Dating. *Ugh.* The thought of shopping for a boyfriend on the Internet made me shudder.

I found myself turning into the parking lot of the stables on the north edge of town, bank deposit still in hand, with no recollection of how I got there. I put the Jeep in park. Dash put his front paws on the door and panted out the open window.

The distinctly musky smell of horses floated in the air along with dust particles that glittered in the sunshine. In the outdoor arena, Gessie King called instructions to a girl riding a buckskin quarter horse. Finally the animal broke into a canter, and a wide grin spread across the teenager's face. Her hair waved out behind her as she bent the horse around a corner.

"Can I pet your dog?"

Startled, I turned to find a broad-faced man who smelled of tobacco and earth looking in through the open passenger window.

"Sure, Pete," I said. "He loves attention."

His lips turned up in a wide smile, and he whirled around to show me the back of his T-shirt. It read KING OF THE BONGOS.

"*Bongo* Pete," he said, turning back around and reaching in to pet Dash. Lacking a tail, the corgi wiggled his entire behind in delight.

"Okay, thanks," the man said, and abruptly turned away and lumbered toward the rear of the barn.

I glanced down at the dog. "You have a fan."

Dash gave a soft woof and continued to gaze after the man.

Bongo Pete was a strange one, but sweet as they came. Gessie let him camp on the far side of the stables, and he did odd jobs for her as needed.

When he was out of sight, Dash turned back to me.

"I've decided the bank can wait," I said.

He panted his approval.

I toyed with the idea of going to see Thea. After all, I did need that compost. However, it had been months since

I'd taken even part of a day off, so instead I drove east into the foothills and found a stream still running fast from the spring snowmelt in the Sierra Nevadas. Dash and I spent the rest of the afternoon there, him dozing on his back in the sunshine and me staring into the sparkling reflections, inhaling the trout-laced scent of water until it washed away the past and my worries, and I felt clean and clear again.

CHAPTER 3

THE CLOSED sign was up in the front window of Scents & Nonsense, and Josie had left by the time Dash and I returned from our impromptu miniretreat a few minutes after six. The Greenstockings would be arriving around six fifteen, so I just had time to review the day's receipts—nothing to write home about, but it looked as though the customers I'd left enjoying the garden had purchased a selection of naturally scented play clay and a box of orange-and-clove drawer sachets. I added the Monday receipts to the deposit from the weekend. Since I'd failed to complete any of my errands for the day, I'd have to run by the bank tomorrow.

I filled Nabokov's bowl and fluffed his kitty bed. He came with the building, the real estate agent had told me. No one knew how old he was, but as he flowed through the door, touched his nose to Dash's in greeting, and wended his way to his food dish, he moved like a young jungle animal. Astrid had declared him to be in perfect health, and that was good enough for me.

He and Dash got along well, though Nabby barely tolerated other animals. Still, I couldn't convince him to sleep in the house with us. He was a shop cat, through and through.

Astrid arrived first for the Greenstocking meeting, elbowing her way through the garden gate with a platter of lemon bars in one hand and Tally's lead in the other.

"Oh, heavens," I said. "Let me help you." I hurried to take the sweet treats from her and led the way to the patio. She let Tally off the leash, and the big dog ambled over to join Dash under the ancient apple tree.

On my way through town, I'd picked up an order of bacon jalapeño poppers from the Sapphire Supper Club as my contribution to the meeting snacks. They sat under foil on the bistro table, and I set the lemon bars beside them. Astrid helped me arrange the mismatched rockers in a semicircle around the table, and we were lining up paper plates and napkins when the latch to the gate rattled.

"Looks like the mantrap has arrived," Astrid muttered under her breath.

"Stop that," I admonished with a little laugh as Cynthia Beck picked her way down the path in her open-toed pumps and a cloud of Chanel No. 5.

It was true that at thirty-six she had already been married twice and was not in the least bit shy when she was interested in a man. Tall, blond, super feminine and the most hard-driving business woman I knew, Cynthia was my polar opposite in almost all respects. Since she owned Foxy Locksies Hair Studio down the street, she was inevitably highlighted, manicured, polished, and buffed to perfection, and she was one of the few women in Poppyville who wore business suits. Today's was seashell pink over a white blouse.

"Ladies!" she called, and lifted the bottle of chardonnay in her hand. "I bring libations!"

"You are most welcome then," I assured her with a grin.

"I'll find some glasses," Astrid said, and went down to my house.

Cynthia had started the Greenstockings a few years before, determined that women should band together to help one another in the same way men did. When she'd invited me to join a few months back, I'd been flattered, but a little nervous. I'd still been learning about running my own business at that point. It had been great, though, and I'd learned a lot.

Gessie King came in as Cynthia was uncorking the wine. She still wore riding chaps but had changed out her mucky knee boots for well worn but clean paddock boots. She smelled of horse and alfalfa. Her iron gray curls clung close to her scalp, and her open-necked shirt revealed an elk's tooth on a leather thong around her throat. She was carrying a bowl of her famous guacamole.

"Yes!" Astrid exclaimed, returning with the glasses. "I swear, if I weren't a member, I'd still crash these meetings for your guacamole."

Gessie grinned and added the bowl of dip to the table along with a bag of corn chips. "Flatterer."

"Seriously. You should market that stuff."

The horsewoman just shook her head. "Good to see you, Ellie. Cynthia, you're looking well."

"Wine?" Cynthia asked with a smile.

"God, yes." Gessie plopped into one of the rockers with a sigh. "I exercised four horses and washed them down this afternoon, on top of my regular lessons. I'm tuckered."

Thea Nelson arrived next. We'd been in the same grade in school and had been casual friends ever since. However, we'd grown quite close during the creation of the Enchanted Garden. Rangy and slow-moving, Thea was a brilliant horticulturist and landscape artist who was willing to take the time to do things right. She was also willing to talk with me for hours about anything and everything plant related. She was a good listener, too. More than once, she and Astrid and I had spent pleasant evenings together while I mined them for advice on starting my business, dealing with Harris, and working with contractors.

"Girls," Thea said by way of greeting, and plopped a bag of peanut M&M's on the table. She didn't like to cook, and she didn't care who knew it.

We settled in with snacks and drinks. Gessie donned her reading glasses, and Cynthia brought out her electronic notebook.

"Anyone have any news to share before we get started?" Cynthia asked, looking around at us.

"I have a group of thirty-five coming in for a full hayride at the end of the week," Gessie said. "That means dinner and dancing and live music. It should be a hoot."

"Excellent!" Cynthia proclaimed.

Thea spoke up. "I got a message from Sophia Thelane. She wants me to do another landscaping project at their place."

"Nice," I said. The fashion model was rarely seen in

town, but had put a lot of money in Thea's bank account over the years.

Cynthia murmured her agreement, then said, "Let's get down to business. Two weeks ago we talked about following up with the Hotel California about reopening the museum in the basement."

She looked up. "I spoke with the owners, who, as we know, unfortunately don't even live in Poppyville. They were unconvinced that reopening the museum would be lucrative for them. I told them that anything that would appeal to tourists would be lucrative to the whole town, and tourists love information about the gold rush days."

"From the look on your face, they didn't buy it," Astrid said.

"No, they did not." Cynthia brightened. "But I'm not done yet."

I sat back, half listening to Cynthia work her way through the Greenstockings biweekly agenda, and sipped wine, reflecting on how lucky I was to know these women.

The meeting wrapped up after about forty-five minutes, and everyone left for their respective evening plans.

"You want to stay for some real food?" I asked Astrid, first to arrive but also last to leave.

"Can't," she said with a grin. "I've got a date."

"With that mountain biker guy?"

She nodded happily. "He's so buff."

"How are his conversational skills?"

She grinned. "I'll let you know if I ever find out."

After she'd gone, I double-checked the doors and walked the few steps to my home. After a light dinner of chicken salad and blueberries, I retired to the back porch with a glass of hard cider and my laptop. I placed orders for bulk supplies of sea salt, goat's milk powder, and eight ounces each of sandalwood and ginger essential oils.

Then I put the technology aside in favor of the burgeoning sunset, settling deeper into the porch swing with a light blanket across my lap and Dash keeping watch by my feet. Fuchsia and purple bruised the clouds above, and as they faded to the monochromatic slate blue of dusk, a six-point buck stepped out from a stand of trees three hundred feet away. He stood there alone, sans his usual harem of does, staring at me as if I were something for a deer to stare at. I met the velvet brown gaze for the longest time, it seemed.

Elliana sighed the wind through the trees. *Elliana,* the breeze-ruffled grass called.

Not really, of course. Because that would be silly, thinking the wind was calling my name. But even after I'd gone inside a little after nine, I couldn't shake the feeling that it had.

I retrieved Gamma's garden journal from one of the shelves tucked under the staircase. It was larger than what most people would think of a journal as being, thick, with well-worn pages beginning to fray at the corners. I sank onto the love seat and slowly flipped through the book, drinking in the comfort it always provided. She'd made notations in blocks and swirls and geometric shapes, tucked in bits of poems and flower lore, obscure recipes, suggestions for cultivation, and preferred habitats. Here was a drawing of a tiny golden-crowned kinglet, there the starburst of a thistle, and throughout it all, insects and butterflies. I paused at a whole page dripping with precise renderings of ladybugs.

Elliana, do you see them gathering on the fence as the thunderheads rear up above? Soon there will be thousands.

We have been blessed with sheltering a loveliness of lady-bugs from the storm.

Her voice faded from memory, and I ran my finger lightly over the words she'd written around the margins of another page:

Hyacinth for jealousy.
Ivy for fidelity.
Larkspur for fickleness.
Nasturtium for victory in battle.

The language of flowers, around for thousands of years and spanning every continent, but reinvigorated in Victorian times. Gamma had been an expert and had passed her love of this unique horticultural dialect on to me. With a sigh, I closed the worn and dirt-stained volume.

Despite the pleasant afternoon and evening, I felt slightly jittery and distracted. My thoughts kept returning to Josie's revelation that she was dating Harris. I didn't pine for him, that was certain, but I couldn't help wondering if things might still become awkward at the shop. And more important, I couldn't help wondering if my ex would break her heart. Josie was good people, and a very independent woman. I didn't think of her as particularly naive, either.

I didn't take sleeping pills, but I had the ingredients for a relaxing tea. In my narrow kitchen, I mixed dried valerian root with chamomile flowers and peppermint leaf I'd grown and dried the previous summer. I drank the brew as I stood over the kitchen sink, rinsed out the cup, and followed Dash up the carpeted staircase that wound to my sleeping loft.

Forty minutes later, I was still wide awake. I sat up. On the bed beside me, Dash came to his feet, eagerly watching to see what I had in mind.

"How about a walk?"

He woofed and jumped to the floor. I dressed in jeans, trail runners, and a warm hoody. I grabbed a flashlight, and a few minutes later we stepped off the back porch and headed for the path that led along the edge of Raven Creek and the nearby park. The moon was nearing full, and I found I could see perfectly well without added light. Dash kept to my left heel, as well trained as any show dog. Once in the park, we fast-walked a loop on the quarter-mile fitness trail and headed back.

"If this doesn't work I see a long night of reading ahead," I said to my dog when we were almost home. Just what I needed: another bout of the insomnia that had plagued me for months after I'd moved out on my own.

A rustle in the bushes behind us made me stop and turn. Dash woofed deep in his throat, and his long, pointed ears turned to catch every sound in the darkness. All was silent. I flicked on the flashlight, but saw only a cluster of low willows at the side of the trail. Dash stared into the night, and I saw the ridge of hair down the center of his back was on end.

My thoughts shot to the word I thought I'd seen on the river rock in the garden that morning: *Beware*.

Heart banging against my ribs, I turned and ran the rest of the way home.

Once Dash and I were back inside, though, I felt silly. *It was just some animal settling in for the night, you nervous Nellie.*

That gave me comfort as I put on my pajamas. Despite my earlier worries of not being able to sleep, I drifted off within minutes.

S OMETHING tugged me back to consciousness. For a few confused moments, I stared up at the angled skylight above my bed, registering the square of ripe blue that indicated the sun had been up for a while. Fresh air blew in from the open window to my right.

Elliana . . . Elliana . . .

The realization dawned slowly. I hadn't been awakened by wind or light, but by my olfactory nerves. My nostrils flared as I sat up, testing the air. Beside the bed, Dash came to his feet, and I saw his nose twitching, too. I swung my feet to the floor and hurried to the staircase. The corgi made his stout way down the outside of the spiral steps as I took the tighter inside route.

It was the same aroma I'd smelled the day before in the garden. The one I couldn't identify. Now it was stronger, pulling me, intoxicating in the way catnip must be to felines. Still in my pajamas, I opened the door and walked out into the morning, barefoot and goose bumped, my head swinging right and left like a hound on a trail as I tried to identify the source. It seemed to come from everywhere. Maybe over there—

And suddenly it was gone.

Just like that. Gone. As if the strange, heady scent had never existed in the first place. I stopped, one foot poised in front of the other. That was impossible.

Right?

Had my sense of smell turned on me? Or maybe I was losing my mind. Or both. *People with brain tumors smell things that aren't there,* I thought, scrambling for an explanation, however morbid it might be.

Dash growled low in his throat. Surprised, I looked down to see him standing with all four feet firmly planted and his muscles bunched like springs. He barked then, high and urgent, and took off like a shot for the partially open garden gate. My gaze followed him as I stood, still stunned, in the middle of the garden. He veered around an overturned rocking chair and stopped next to the gate. Something was there, on the ground, holding it open a few inches.

Something that shouldn't have been there.

I squinted.

A *boot*.

Dash looked over his shoulder and barked again.

CHAPTER 4

✣

BARE feet forgotten, I flew down the path. When I reached the gate, I pushed it open and fell to my hands and knees, all worries about smells or brain tumors forgotten.

Josie Overland lay crumpled on the ground at the end of the boardwalk that ran in front of Scents & Nonsense, shadowed by my fence. I recognized her work uniform from the Roux Grill: jeans and black T-shirt, the orange flames of the restaurant's logo visible under her arm. Her shiny brown hair fanned out, unbound, obscuring her face from view. She was on her side, one jeans-clad leg bent up toward her chest while the other stuck out straight, her foot wedged in the open gate. Her bare arms were wrapped around her torso as if she were trying to keep herself warm.

"Josie?" I reached a tentative hand toward that thick veil of hair, intending to push it aside. "Josie, honey?"

My voice was calm and soothing, which struck me as odd since my hand was shaking so badly I couldn't seem to grip a single lock of hair. When I touched it, the faint smell of cheap aftershave, mingled with garlic and green-apple conditioner, rose into the air.

Finally, my trembling fingers managed to reveal her face.

Josie's eyes were closed. She looked peaceful, as if she'd merely fallen asleep. Asleep—except she didn't seem to be breathing. I moved my hand to her shoulder and gave a little shake. Her skin felt cold beneath my palm. Clammy, even in the dry warm air.

Dash looked at me with worried eyes and nosed Josie's other cowboy boot.

Slowly, almost against my will, I placed my fingertips on her neck like I'd seen people do so many times on television. There was no pulse. But what if I wasn't doing it right?

It didn't matter. I knew she was dead. Blackness encroached on my peripheral vision, and my head swam. *Breathe*.

I forced oxygen into my lungs with a big whooping inhalation, and the darkness receded a fraction. It took a few more deep breaths before I felt able to stand. Pushing myself to my feet, I turned and stumbled back to where I'd left my door hanging open in my half-asleep scentual daze only minutes earlier.

My cell phone was charging on the kitchen counter. I waited through three rings before the 911 operator picked up.

"I found a woman collapsed out front," I panted. "I think . . . I think she might be dead." I took another wavering breath. "Please send help." The last sentence came out an octave higher.

There was a moment of shocked silence on the other end of the line before the dispatcher slipped into professional gear. "Are you all right, ma'am?"

"Yes," I said, impatient now. "I'm fine. But she's not breathing. At least I don't think so."

"What's the address?" she asked. I heard rapid typing in the background.

"Oh. Right." I reeled off my address. "It's Scents and Nonsense, at the end of Corona."

The typing stopped. "*Ellie?* Is that you?"

"Who's this?"

"It's Nan Walton."

I pictured the big-boned woman who always ordered the prime rib when she came into the Roux Grill. She knew the bartenders there quite well. "Nan, it's Josie Overland out front."

"Holy . . . okay, help is on the way," she said, typing again at a furious pace.

That was all I needed to know. I ended the call, grabbed my keys and phone, and ran back to Josie. Checked her pulse again, in case I'd missed something the first time.

Please let me be wrong.

But I wasn't. If anything, her skin felt even colder. Looking up, I saw how hard it would be for anyone on the street to see her. I swallowed down the lump forming in my throat.

I propped the gate all the way open with a rock and hurried to the back door of the shop. Unlocking the slider,

Dash and I went through to the boardwalk and walked a few doors down to watch for the ambulance. Most shops wouldn't open until nine or ten, but old Mr. Freti was sweeping in front of the hardware store down the street. A few people turned their heads as they drove by, and as I leaned against a vertical support for the covered boardwalk, a jogger pounded by me. He gave me a friendly nod, then did a double take before veering around the corner. At first, I thought he'd seen Josie tucked into the shadows, but, glancing down, I saw my feet were not only bare but now quite dirty. Also, I still wore my purple cotton pajamas.

Which were covered with pink dancing poodles. I'd bought them on clearance in the girl's department at Target.

Great.

The time on the huge round clock mounted above the library down the street showed eight thirty-eight. I had certainly slept longer than usual. My mind raced as I watched the minute hand tick by one, two, three minutes.

How long had Josie been there? Had she come straight from work? Her shift would have ended around midnight. Had she been trying to get help?

What had happened to her?

Then I saw the lime green Ford Fiesta parked down the street in front of the Raven Creek Park. Josie's car. She'd driven here. In the middle of the night? This morning? Why? Poppyville rolled up its sidewalks early. The Roux Grill and Sapphire Supper Club kept the latest hours, and both closed at midnight on weeknights.

Flashing lights colored the other end of Corona Street,

moving toward me with a roar of engines but no sirens. I hurried closer to where I'd found the body.

A police cruiser pulled into the disabled parking spot in front of the shop, and a uniformed woman I vaguely recognized emerged. "Did you report an emergency?"

"I did. She's over there." I waved toward the gate.

In seconds there seemed to be people everywhere; police and firemen and medical personnel and others whose roles I couldn't begin to guess. Two men immediately ran to Josie, and one reached for her neck, just as I had. He looked at his partner and shook his head.

Then I saw a few drops of blood on the ground beneath her.

"Excuse me," a man in a jumpsuit said as he brushed by me and went into the back garden.

"Come on, Dash."

We went back through the shop to the garden in order to stay out of everyone's way—and to keep an eye on things. I moved to the north fence and fingered the silky petal of a Don Juan rose that twined up the cedar post. The warming sun teased out its deep floral tone, yet I felt cold to the bone.

The back door of Scents & Nonsense opened, and Astrid stood on the threshold with a plate of oatmeal cookies in her hand. "Ellie?" Her hand flew to her chest in relief. "I saw all the police and thought something terrible had happened to you."

"I'm fine," I said.

But she was still talking. "They have a big tarp up, and the door was open, so I just came inside." Her words tumbled over one another.

She stepped down to the patio as I moved away from the fence. "Are you . . . *Oh, my God!*" Mouth agape, she stared through the open gate at Josie, who was now being photographed from different angles behind a makeshift tarp curtain.

"Ma'am! I'm sorry—who are you? I'm going to need you to move." A young officer gripped her elbow to hustle her back inside.

She tried to pull away. "Ellie, what happened? Are you okay?"

"I'm fine," I said again. "I'll call you as soon as I can."

Within moments, others had invaded Scents & Nonsense. It felt like a violation, but there wasn't anything I could do about it. Astrid was shown out to the boardwalk in front of the store and waved good-bye, mouthing "talk to you later." I watched it all through the back window, unwilling to leave the garden.

Or Josie.

My cell buzzed in my hand. The display said *Thea Nelson*.

"Are you the one who found her?" a woman asked.

I thumbed IGNORE on the phone and turned to look at her. Unlike most of the people working around me, the newcomer was a stranger to me. She was petite, not much taller than I was, and slender. Shiny black hair brushed the shoulders of the navy blazer she wore over a crisp white blouse. Her dark eyes drank in the scene and me with it. Observing. Concluding.

Judging.

Heart hammering, I said, "Um, yes. Is Josie, um, I mean . . . ?" I felt tears threaten and swallowed, hard.

Her eyes softened. "I'm afraid she is, indeed, deceased."

"Was she . . . ? I mean, did someone . . . ?" Apparently, I had lost the capacity to form full sentences.

"She has at least two stab wounds," the woman confirmed. "I take it you knew her?"

Josie had been *stabbed*? How could I not have seen that? The idea that she was dead—actually gone, and at the hand of another person—seemed unreal. I took a deep breath and tried to marshal my thoughts. "Yes. Her name is Josie Overland. She worked for me. Sometimes, I mean. She worked for my ex-husband, too."

Her eyes flashed at that. "You're Elliana Allbright. Someone told me that you opened this perfume shop after splitting with your ex."

She's been in Poppyville long enough to access the small-town grapevine. . . .

The woman looked around. "How's that working out?"

"Pretty well," I said. "At least until . . ." I gestured helplessly toward Josie and swallowed hard.

"I'm Detective Lupe Garcia. Is there someplace we can talk?"

Gesturing vaguely at my attire, I tried a smile. "Can I change my clothes first?"

A man behind her turned at my words. I recognized him immediately and nodded to him. "Hi, Max."

Max Lang. Detective Lang, actually. A longtime member of the Poppyville police force—and Harris' best friend.

Great.

He looked me up and down, gray eyes unblinking beneath his neat straw-colored hair. He was hefty, but tall enough to pull it off, giving the impression of a military background I happened to know he didn't have. "Ellie, why are you wearing—" He started to indicate my pajamas, then seemed to think better of it. "Where exactly are you living these days?"

"There." I pointed toward my house at the back of the lot.

Detective Garcia's eyes widened slightly. Her gaze took in the rough cedar-shingle siding, the door crafted of planks from a demolished barn, and the symmetrical four-paned windows on either side. Bloodred geraniums trailed from the window boxes among orange and yellow nasturtiums.

"Harris told me you were living off grid, but you live in a potting shed?" Detective Lang sounded downright insulted by the idea. "You can't be serious."

"It's not a potting shed," I said. "It's a house. A very small house, granted, but still a house."

He frowned. "It's not a house unless it has a bathroom. You can't just camp—"

"It has a three-quarter bath, full plumbing, and power," I assured him, doing my best to keep the irritation out of my voice. "Not exactly off the grid."

"It's a tiny house," Garcia breathed, and I knew she didn't mean it was simply small.

I smiled at her. "It's my home." I pointed at the storefront. "And Scents and Nonsense is my business." I blushed as I realized how silly that sentence sounded, as if I was a character in a Dr. Seuss book.

"To each his own, I guess," Lang said. "You've met my colleague." It wasn't a question, but I nodded anyway. "So when did you discover the victim?"

I stared at him. The victim? Josie had served him plenty of drinks when he was off duty, enough that they'd been on a first-name basis.

"Right after I got up this morning," I said. "I called nine-one-one right away. The library clock said eight thirty-eight."

"I see," he said. Detective Garcia had taken out a small notebook and was making notes while her partner quizzed me.

"And where were you last night, Ms. Allbright?" he asked, growing even more formal.

"The Greenstockings—that's the women's business group I belong to—met here in the garden at around six fifteen. They were here for an hour."

"And after they left?" he prompted.

I silently pointed at my house—my house where actual, grown-up clothes waited for me to change into them. I wondered if Lang enjoyed having me at a disadvantage. I squared my shoulders in false confidence.

"You were inside all night?" he asked. "Before you discovered the victim?"

"I walked the dog a little after ten. Before that, I was on the back porch for a while, watching the sunset. I went to sleep about ten thirty."

"And can anyone vouch for you?" His eyebrow twitched with sarcasm.

"Well, if you put it that way . . ."

"I am putting it that way."

I felt my lips thin. "Then, no."

Detective Garcia's eyes cut toward her partner, then to me, then back to her notebook. I snapped off a rose hip and rolled it between my thumb and forefinger like a horticultural worry stone. Around us, the activity seemed to be waning. It felt awkward to be having this discussion huddled in the corner of the garden.

Lang didn't seem to notice. "Did you hear or see anything suspicious?" he asked.

"No." My throat closed over the word. *Had I slept through her murder?*

"Did the victim visit you last evening?"

"No." I tried to regroup. "The last time I saw Josie was early yesterday afternoon. I left her tending the shop while I ran errands." *After she told me she was dating Harris. And I didn't actually run a single errand.* "She was gone by the time I got back. Had probably already started her shift at the Roux Grill."

Garcia broke in. "I like that place. Best steak tips I've ever eaten. It's your ex-husband's restaurant now, right? You mentioned that Ms. Overland worked for him, too?"

"She sure did," Lang answered for me. Something about the way he said it told me that he knew Harris had been dating "the victim."

Garcia spared him a quick look, but her face remained impassive. "It must have been an amicable divorce."

Lang snorted.

I chose to ignore that. "Josie works . . . worked Mondays and Tuesdays at Scents and Nonsense, as well as the occasional hour here and there when I needed extra help. She'd tended bar at the Roux Grill for a couple of years. She was good at it, too—cheerful, efficient, handled the occasional obnoxious customer with a deft hand. She also cleaned houses, and sometimes she'd sell one of her photographs.

You know how hard it is to make a living in Poppyville year round." Without warning, I felt tears threaten.

No. No crying. Not now.

I straightened my shoulders again. "How can I help you find who did that to her?"

Max Lang gave me a wry look. "I think we can handle it. Besides, you're a suspect."

I felt the blood drain from my face. "A . . . ? But why would I . . . ?"

He smiled at me. It wasn't a very nice smile. "She was killed on your property, and you don't seem to have a very good explanation for that."

"But she was on the boardwalk," I said. "Which is technically part of my property, but still a public area."

"Then why was her foot caught in your gate?" he asked with slightly raised eyebrows. I bit my lip.

Garcia looked up from her notebook. "Can you think of anyone who might have wanted to harm Ms. Overland?"

"I . . . I can't think of anyone," I stammered. "I didn't really know her all that well, though."

Lang's gaze sharpened.

"We didn't socialize," I clarified.

"All right, then. We'll be in touch if we have more questions," Garcia said.

Lang started to say something, but when his partner touched his arm he stopped, looked down at her, and nodded. "Right. We'll be in touch," he repeated.

They turned to go. The muscles in my neck began to unclench, but then Detective Lang stopped. "Oh, and Ellie? Don't leave Poppyville for the next few days."

"Why would I leave?" I infused the words with all the innocence I felt and then some.

"Just don't, okay?"

"Okay." I hated how timid I sounded.

He strode away. Detective Garcia reached into the pocket of her blazer and retrieved a business card. She handed it to me. "Call me if you think of anything else."

Glancing down at the number, I wondered—if Lang was the bad cop, was Garcia the good one? I was disconcerted to realize I couldn't tell. Usually, I was pretty good at reading people.

I nodded. "I will."

She leaned toward me and said in a low voice, "Well, I think they're cute."

I blinked. "What?"

"Your pajamas." A smile flitted across her face, and she turned to follow Lang.

CHAPTER 5

I T took hours for everyone to finish up. When they finally left, yellow police tape looped around a section of the boardwalk in front of the store. I had no idea what they were trying to preserve, since so many people had been all over the area. Back in the Enchanted Garden, the air smelled like lavender because someone had trampled the plant into the earth. Here and there, stems of cone flowers and Oriental poppies angled toward the ground, the victims of brusque professionals at work. Someone had stepped right in the middle of the sea glass pathway I'd just built and had knocked over an arrangement of miniature wicker chairs and tiny toadstools.

At least I'd had a chance to shower and dress in shorts and a T-shirt. Dash had stayed out of the way as I'd commanded, but the low whine in the back of his throat didn't stop until I'd put him inside the house. I'd kept the shop closed, ignoring the looky-loos peering in the front windows. I thought about lost business for a split second before reminding myself to keep some darn perspective. A bit less revenue was nothing compared to murder.

I'd tried to call Astrid, but she was working a full shift at the veterinarian's office. Surgeries were often scheduled on Tuesdays, so no matter how upset—and curious—she was, she might not be able to get back to me for a while. Then I'd spent an hour tidying the damage to the garden, which served as a kind of therapy. Now the afternoon loomed ahead of me. However, there were still all those errands I'd neglected the previous afternoon. I went into the office to get my keys, wallet, and the bank bag, then retrieved Dash from the house and took him out to the Wrangler.

As I sat in the drive-through at the bank, I pondered the questions the detectives had asked me. *Who could have wanted to hurt Josie?* She was sweet and had seemed open and happy. Could she have stumbled into something illegal without realizing it? Was there another side to Josie I didn't know about? And did Max Lang really think I was a murder suspect? My stomach twisted as I remembered the look on his face when he'd said it.

I told myself to calm down. The police hadn't even had a chance to investigate. Maybe Lang was just goading me. Had to be, because the very idea of me as a murderer was ridiculous.

The plastic tube containing my deposit receipt popped into view, and the bank teller wished me a nice day over the speaker. Reaching through my window to retrieve it,

I shook my head at myself. And the warning not to leave town? That was probably just a routine thing they told everyone who found a body.

Right?

Dash happily munched on one of his favorite cookies fresh out of the bag after we left Doggone Gourmet, and I headed over to Terra Green Nursery.

Guiding the Wrangler around to the back, I parked next to the piles of bagged compost. I had a compost bin, of course, but the current batch was still percolating into rich, dark nourishment. I was considering my options when a door slammed behind me, and I turned to see Thea standing by her mint green step-side pickup. As I watched, she reached into the back of the pickup and lifted out a plastic pot containing a sad-looking hydrangea.

"Hey, Ellie!" she called. "What can I do you for?"

"Just need a bag of mushroom compost for the new herb bed," I said.

"Good choice. And I have something else for you." She hoisted the pot in her hand.

"That poor plant?" I asked as she approached.

She looked down at the withering leaves. "If you save it, you can have it—and heaven knows you can save pretty much anything. This little guy needs a good dose of water and a bit of acid-based fertilizer to bring it around."

"Coffee grounds," I said. "My grandmother always told me to use them if you wanted your hydrangeas to have blue blooms."

"She was right." She squinted skyward, her irises reflecting the color above. "Of course it's the aluminum in the soil that makes them blue, but acid helps the plant to absorb it." She looked back down at me. "I think I like the blue flowers better than pink. You?"

"I guess I do, now that you mention it."

"Ellie? You sound kind of funny." She ducked her head closer, probing me with her gaze. "Are you okay?"

I opened my mouth, then closed it again. What to say? Was there a protocol for informing someone that you found one of your employees, who also happened to be your ex's girlfriend, murdered on your doorstep?

Probably not something Miss Manners covered.

Her expression sharpened. "What happened?"

I opened my mouth to respond, words of explanation ready if not exactly organized. But to my horror, all that came out was a soft whimper.

"Holy cow, Ellie!" She bent and put the hydrangea down on the ground so she could give me a hug.

Well, that sent me right over the edge. A sob erupted from my throat, and tears squeezed out of my eyes.

Thea patted me on the back. "There, there."

"Now what's all this?" came a deep voice from behind me.

Startled out of crying, I whirled around to find a man standing there.

I recognized him instantly. He'd aged a bit since I'd seen him last—what? Twelve years ago? But if anything, he'd gotten better looking. The light blue chambray shirt couldn't hide the wide shoulders or the way his torso tapered down to his hips. He wore jeans and scuffed brown work boots. Sun-kissed strands streaked his chestnut hair, and lashes a model would kill for framed eyes the same clear blue as his sister's.

Ritter Nelson. Three years older than me, which in high school had been kind of a big deal. It sure hadn't stopped me from crushing on my friend Thea's big brother, though.

All this registered in the split second it took my face to turn bright red. I reached up and wiped my eyes, stammering out, "Ritter . . . hi . . . I . . . I . . ." I took a deep breath and sniffed. "Hi."

"Well, hi, yourself, Elliana." He stepped around me to stand by Thea, who absently patted him on the arm the same way she'd patted my back. "It's nice to see you again. But tears? That's no good."

"Nice to see you again, too," I said, an octave too high. Mortified, I stared at him, afraid to say another word.

"Ellie!" Thea said. "Are you going to tell us what's the matter? Or—" She looked at her brother then back at me. "Is it, you know, *girl* stuff?"

By then I was pretty sure every drop of blood in my body had migrated to my overheated, tearstained face. I shook my head vigorously. "No. No, not at all. Of course not."

Get a grip, Ellie!

"It's Josie," I blurted.

Took a deep breath and tried again. "She's been murdered. I found her this morning."

Their lips parted in surprise. *"Murdered?"* Thea repeated in a quiet, stunned tone.

I nodded. "Stabbed."

"You're *kidding.* That's just *awful.* When did it happen?

Who did it? Why didn't you call me?" She sounded truly outraged.

"It just happened this morning. Or at least that's when I found her," I said.

"Who's Josie?" Ritter asked.

"Of course," I said. "You wouldn't know."

"She's a bartender at the Roux Grill," Thea said. "And she works part-time for Ellie at Scents and Nonsense."

"Scents and—" he said.

His sister cut him off. "Never mind that right now." Then to me. "You found her? Good Lord. No wonder you're upset, darlin'."

Ritter moved away from his sister and reached in through the window of the Wrangler to stroke Dash's ears with his fingertips. My corgi nosed his hand, begging for more.

I took a deep breath. "I'm okay. Sorry about the—" I waved my hand as if trying to dispel what happened. "You, know. Crying."

"Jeez, Elliana. I'd cry, too," Ritter said.

I highly doubted that, but it made me feel kind of fuzzy that he'd said it.

"So tell us what happened," Thea urged, leading me over to a bench snugged into the shade of the barn-red retail shop. Ritter ambled over to lean against the wall.

I filled them both in on the details, leaving out the bit where I was wearing my little-girl pajamas the whole time and that Lang had said I was a suspect.

"Good Lord," Thea said again when I was done. Then, "I wonder who could have done such a thing here in Poppyville?"

I looked down at the ground, still highly aware of

Ritter standing so close. "I know. We have such a tame little town."

Ritter said, "There's no such thing, I've found. Spent the last six months working out of three different hardly there towns in the wilds of Alaska, and by the time I left every one of them, it was clear each had something going on under the surface."

"Oh, hush, you," Thea said. "This isn't some rough-and-ready place full of mountain men and wolves. It's the same Poppyville we moved to in elementary school."

A phone trilled on the other side of the wall. Thea started to get up.

Ritter waved her back. "I'll get it. Might as well start in right away." As he walked toward the open Dutch door, he called over his shoulder. "See you later, Elliana."

As soon as he'd gone, I leaned over and hissed, "When did he get back into town?"

She looked surprised. "Yesterday. You know his team has been studying environmental threats to the Alaskan tundra? Well, he's between grants right now and came back to hang out with his little sis—and put his degree to work in a real business for a while." Botany ran in the Nelson family.

"Why didn't you tell us that at the Greenstockings meeting?"

"Because I didn't think it was a big . . . oh. Wait." She grinned. "I forgot you have a thing for Ritter."

"I do not!" Never mind the way my stomach had done a somersault when I'd turned around to find him standing *right there*.

Her grin got bigger. "Uh-huh. So you want me to set you guys up?"

"Of course not!"

Maybe. The thought made my toes tingle at the same time it sent fear arrowing through my solar plexus.

My phone buzzed in my pocket. I took it out and saw Astrid had called twice, but I'd managed to miss her both times. Now she'd resorted to a text.

> The police came to Dr. Ericsson's office—Josie was murdered!? Oh, honey—please call me. Am worried about you.

I grimaced. "I think I'd better get going. Astrid happened into the whole scene this morning, but the police made her leave. Now she's off work."

Thea stood. "Let me get you that hydrangea. If you don't mind?"

"No, I'm happy to do what I can," I said.

She retrieved it, and I loaded it into the back of the Wrangler.

"You take care of yourself, Ellie," she said and I climbed into the passenger seat. "And call if you need to talk."

"Thanks," I said.

Behind her, I saw Ritter emerge from the gift store. He sketched a vague wave in my direction before turning away and heading for the greenhouse.

Thea glanced over her shoulder, and I forced myself to look away from his retreating figure—and those well-fitting jeans.

Her lips twitched, and she said, "He's probably not going to be in town all that long, you know. The new grant money should come through in a few weeks."

I smiled and waved my hand, all devil-may-care. "It's nice that you get to see him for that long, then. I'd better take off." I started the vehicle and put it in gear.

As I turned out of Terra Green, I saw Thea in my rearview mirror, standing with her hands on her hips and watching me go. That was when I realized that I'd completely forgotten to buy the compost I'd come for in the first place.

I PULLED over and called Astrid, and we agreed to meet at Scents & Nonsense. On the way back, I mulled over running into Ritter again after so many years. It was crazy how seeing him had made me feel. After all, I'd been sixteen when he'd left for college, though he'd come back to Poppyville for holidays during the years he'd worked through a four-year botany degree and then moved on to getting his master's in environmental science. Every time he'd come back to town, he'd piqued my interest, but by then I'd had my own very full life and had left high school infatuations behind.

So what was different now? Why couldn't I get the image of his sidelong glance or the sound of his voice out of my mind? How had I forgotten that he'd always called me Elliana, instead of Ellie like everyone else?

I remembered how he'd smelled of wool and cedar, and nearly ran a stop sign. Dash woofed his disapproval as the Wrangler lurched to a standstill.

Stop it. Think about something else.

Which, of course, led me back to my horrible discovery that morning, which, honestly, I'd been trying to avoid thinking about. Accelerating again, I considered why—and how—Josie could have been killed.

She'd worked at the Roux Grill thirty hours or so a week, mostly bartending but also waiting tables or even busing when things got busy. Harris and I had often argued over whether we should hire full-time or part-time staff, but he was unwilling to pay benefits. Hiring part-time help, especially during high tourist season, was a common practice in places like Poppyville, where the cost of goods was high and employee turnover higher. Some restaurants brought in students from other countries to work the busy times in the summer, paying them a pittance for the privilege of spending time in the United States and working their tails off. At least Harris had agreed that we should hire locals.

As I'd told the detectives, Josie had worked another twelve hours at my shop, split between Mondays and Tuesdays. She'd also cleaned houses for a few regular clients who had opted to live in low-key Poppyville rather than a larger city, but still had big houses and the bank accounts to match. I wasn't sure who her current clients were.

Once, when we'd been chatting in the Roux Grill, Josie had told me her real dream was to make a living as a professional photographer. I'd encouraged her to hang a few pieces in the restaurant, and if they were any indication of her overall talent, she might have really made a go of it.

Now she'd never have the chance.

"Who would do such a thing?" I asked Dash as I pulled into a parking space.

He cocked his head at me and made a noise low in his throat.

I sighed and rubbed my eyes with my fingertips.

* * *

I FOUND Astrid staring out the back window at the garden and nibbling on one of the otherwise untouched oatmeal cookies she'd brought that morning. Nabby, who had made himself scarce at the first sign of flashing lights earlier, now stretched languidly across his poufy bed. The red plush of the fabric accented the gray of his fur. A heavy purr rumbled from his chest, and he *mrow*ed when he saw me.

Astrid had turned when she heard the door open. Her eyes widened, and she quickly crossed to give me a big hug. She smelled of sugar and sandalwood, and I instantly felt better. After a few seconds, she held me at arm's length and examined my face.

"Are you all right?"

My chin bobbed.

"Truly?"

"Truly."

The crease in her forehead eased a bit. "The police asked a bunch of questions, but didn't tell me much about what happened to Josie."

"She was stabbed."

Her throat worked. "Oh, good heavens. That's awful. Do they know who did it?"

"Not unless they figured it out in the last few hours. I'm apparently a suspect, however."

Astrid looked surprised, then frowned. "So that's why they were asking me all those questions about you and Harris."

I blinked. "Detective Lang said I was automatically a suspect because she was killed on my property. I imagine they asked about Harris and me simply because Josie worked for both of us." At least, I hoped so.

The phone in the office rang. The noise made me jump, and I realized I was as jittery as an aspen in the wind.

"You want me to get that?" Astrid asked.

I shook my head. "I changed the message to let people know the shop is closed today."

The ringing stopped, followed by the trilling of my cell phone in my pocket. I fished it out, inexplicably hoping it was Ritter.

Of course, it wasn't.

My finger hovered over the IGNORE button, but with a sigh I shifted it to ANSWER. Suppressing a sigh, I said, "Harris."

Astrid frowned and crossed her arms over her chest.

"Josie's gone," my ex-husband choked out.

"I know." What to say to him? I felt sick about Josie, but also disconcerted that hearing Harris' voice brought back how it had felt when I'd learned the truth about their relationship, an unpleasant mixture of distaste and humiliation. "I'm sorry."

"The cops said she died there, at your house."

"In front of the shop," I said. "I . . . I discovered her this morning."

Harris sniffled. I tried to connect the sound with the man I knew. Had I ever seen him cry? Maybe he really had loved her. I felt my heart soften.

"She told me you two were dating," I said. "Are you okay?"

"Of course not!"

I tried again, slowly. "I'm sorry for your loss, Harris. This is pretty shocking, I know."

Boy, do I know.

Astrid's frown deepened as she listened.

"Shocking? Ellie, that's a bit of an understatement, don't you think?"

I couldn't help but feel bad for the guy. "Oh, Harris—"

"What am I going to do?" he wailed, shocking me into silence. "She was my love, my life. I don't know how I can go on now. Why did this have to happen to me?"

Ah, there it was.

Trust him to make Josie's death about him.

With an effort, I kept my voice even. "It'll be all right." Would it? How could it be? "You'll get through this. Really, you will. Do you have any idea who"—my voice broke; I swallowed in an attempt to moisten my dry mouth—"who might have killed her?"

"The police came by. Talked to the staff and especially to me."

"Detectives Lang and Garcia?" I asked.

"Is that her name? Mostly I talked with Max. She kept interrupting with a bunch of questions."

I suppressed a sigh. "They're doing their jobs. They questioned Astrid at work, too."

He snorted, and Astrid rolled her eyes. They had always disliked each other.

"I talked with them this morning," I said. "I'm sure they'll find whoever did this to Josie." I believed it. I had to. Thanks to his friendship with Harris, Detective Lang might not care for me personally, but I had to hope he knew how to detect. Lupe Garcia had certainly struck me as a capable, experienced professional.

"Oh, I bet they did talk to you, Ellie," Harris said. "But don't think that's the end of it. I told them, you know."

Brow wrinkling, I asked, "Told them what?"

"Erm." His version of backpedaling.

My stomach tightened. "Harris." My voice held warning.

"Well, they were asking a lot of questions about how you and Josie got along. You being my ex-wife and all. And her being my girlfriend."

"You know I liked her, for heaven's sake. What did you tell them?"

"There's no call to be mean, Ellie. Especially at a time like this. After all—"

"What did you tell them?"

"Nothing much. But last night Josie said that she'd finally come clean with you about our feelings for each other. She said you stomped out of Scents and Nonsense right after that."

"I had errands to run!" And I was pretty sure Josie hadn't said any such thing.

"Sure. Whatever. But I know you must have been jealous. It's the way women are—especially you."

"That's not true!"

"Look at how upset you got about Wanda."

"That was different," I grated out. "We were actually married when you and Wanda—"

"Yeah, okay," he said. "But I mentioned your jealous streak to the cops when they were here. They seemed *very* interested."

"Heaven help me, Harris—" I stopped myself and

grabbed a bottle of rose essential oil off the shelf. I inhaled deeply. It helped a little. "It's bad enough that she's dead," I said. "Thanks a lot for telling the cops I did it."

"Well, I didn't say that. Not in so many words."

I stopped myself from saying more. When was I going to learn? Arguing with him like this was futile.

"I have to go," I said.

"Ellie, what am I going to do?" Harris repeated, his voice starting to rise.

"Well, for one thing, stop telling people I killed your girlfriend." I hung up.

CHAPTER 6

ASTRID's fists were on her hips, and her expression was livid. "Harris can't go around spreading lies about you, Ellie. Your ex is classically passive-aggressive."

I sighed. She was right, of course. He was an expert manipulator. He'd even turned around the fact that I'd walked in on him boffing Wanda, somehow making it my problem.

Thinking about that day brought anger I'd thought I'd let go of to the surface again. Today had been a long terrible day already, and the last thing I needed was Harris fueling Detective Lang's suspicions against me.

I looked at my watch. "It's almost five o'clock. And I don't know about you, but after today, I'm ready for a drink."

"Well, then, let's go to the Sapphire. We'll hit happy hour, and I'll even buy you some of those bacon jalapeño bites you like so much."

I shook my head. "Nope. We're going to the Roux. Josie was close to Maggie—the head bartender? And I want to stop by and see how she's doing. And while we're there, maybe I'll just have a little talk with Harris."

One of Astrid's eyebrows slowly lifted. "Oh, yeah?"

"Yeah."

A grin lit her face, but quickly dropped away. "Do you think he could have had anything to do with Josie . . . you know?"

I blanched. "You don't think Harris killed . . . ? No. He is, as you have so often put it, a jerk. But he's not a murderer."

"Maybe. But neither are you. And now the police think you had a reason to kill her. That's on him. I'm with you, Ellie. You have to let him know what he did is *not* okay." She marched toward the door and opened it. Pausing on the threshold, she looked at me over her shoulder.

"I'm coming," I said. "Let me put Dash inside the house and grab my wallet."

As Astrid and I walked down Corona Street, our footfalls on the wooden boardwalk reflected the sounds from more than a century and a half earlier, when Poppyville had erupted near the foothills of the Sierra Nevada Mountains to support the herds of gold miners. The closer we got to the Roux Grill, the more my stomach roiled.

Two years older than me, Astrid had become my great friend in college, where I'd studied horticulture. She'd been there when I arrived, and still there when I left, a perpetual student and late-blooming flower child who changed her major from anthropology to women's studies before transferring to veterinary medicine. We'd stayed in touch, and on a visit to see me in Poppyville, she'd fallen in love with the place. I still remembered the phone conversation when she told me she was moving to my hometown.

I'd known from the day I met her that Astrid Moneypenny would rush to my defense in any situation or support me in any endeavor—which was exactly what she was doing now.

Poppyville's Corona Street was only six blocks long. Scents & Nonsense was on one end, and the Roux Grill was very near the other. We sauntered past Flyrite Kites, the Kneadful Things Bakery, and the quaint Poppyville Library where Maria Canto had an unnerving ability to know what people needed to read as well as the ability to track down the answer to any obscure question a patron might ask.

There was Tessa's Tea Room and Cynthia's Foxy Locksies Hair Studio and the Juke Diner, all interspersed with shops selling T-shirts, tchotchkes, and gold-panning kits. The sporting goods store shared a wall with Rexall Drugs, and Rosen's New York Deli was on the other side. Flaubert's Department Store had been a staple of Poppyville since the 1950s, and they still used an old pneumatic tube, much like the one at the bank's drive-through, to get checks approved in the upstairs office overlooking the main floor.

One block was devoted to the courthouse, police headquarters, and the city jail. There was an antique mall, and a craft brewery that the tourists especially loved. Farther down, beyond the Roux Grill, the old stables where I'd stopped with Dash just the day before had been renovated, and Gessie King ran a trail rides and taught dressage on the side.

We passed the Hotel California, originally Poppyville's saloon and brothel. Most people thought Poppyville was named for the state flower, but in truth it was named for the local madam, whose girls catered to the miners in the late 1800s. Her name was Pauline Thierry, but everyone called her Miss Poppy. She'd displayed a deft hand in guiding the development of what was then called Springtown, and after her passing, the town fathers had changed the name to Poppyville. One of those town fathers had been my maternal great-great-great-grandfather. I was one of few born-and-bred Poppyvillians.

I loved this town from stem to stern, and even after the divorce, when more than one person had suggested a fresh start somewhere else, I couldn't imagine ever leaving. The place was in my blood.

As we walked by Deely's Garage, I asked Astrid about her date the night before.

"Meh. You're right. He's not big on conversation."

"Mmm. Sorry." Then I asked as casually as I could manage, "So, guess who's back in town?"

Astrid glanced over at me. "Who?"

"Thea's big brother."

"I didn't even know she had a brother," she said.

"Yup. Ritter. He's been in Alaska. Some kind of environmental plant study in the tundra."

"Plants, huh. That sounds right up your alley."

"I guess." I kept my voice noncommittal.

It didn't work.

"Why, Ellie Allbright. You're interested in him."

"Nah, I just . . ."

"Tell me about him," she urged as we neared our destination.

"I already have, at least what I know. I haven't seen him for years. He's back in Poppyville, helping Thea out at Terra Green while he waits for some grant money to come through."

A skeptical expression settled on her face. "I'm sure there's more you can tell me," she said. "But I can wait."

We'd reached the Roux Grill and stopped. The cedar siding was stained a warm reddish brown, and a hitching post ran alongside the covered boardwalk. The dozen tables arranged out in front and along the wraparound porch on the side were empty except for two couples taking advantage of happy hour. Big half-barrel planters stood at each corner, filled with sad pink petunias that looked as though they needed a dose of fish fertilizer to perk them up. When I'd been in charge of their care, the barrels had overflowed with a variety of vibrant blooms and sprays of fountain grass.

I put my hand on the wooden railing, trying for casual but actually feeling a little wobbly. "A martini would be nice."

"Ellie," Astrid said. "When was the last time you were in the Roux?"

I took a deep breath. "It's been awhile."

"When?"

"When I found Harris and Wanda Simmons doing it in the walk-in freezer." I felt my nostrils flare. "I left and never came back."

She stared at me. "Seriously? You managed to avoid coming in here all this time?"

"It's only been a year," I said.

"But this was your life. These were your friends."

"I like my new life just fine," I said. "And it's not like this town is so big I never see any of them." I lifted my chin. "But if we're going to do this, let's do it now."

Astrid put her hand on the railing and grinned. "The walk-in freezer." She shook her head. "I'd almost forgotten that part."

I snorted out a giggle. It really was pretty funny.

Especially since I'd learned later that the lovebirds had waited half an hour to venture out. Probably afraid I'd be waiting for them with a cast iron frying pan or a butcher knife. According to a gossipy physician's assistant at the Poppyville Clinic, Harris had suffered from a bit of frost-bite. She hadn't revealed the details regarding which part of his anatomy had been affected.

I had my hopes, though.

Clenching my jaw, I pushed the door open, and we went inside.

The smells of braising beef, vinegary barbecue sauce, fresh bread, and garlic filled my sinuses. I envisioned the baking sheets filled with rows of bite-sized dinner rolls back in the kitchen. Soon they would be dropped into bowls of warm butter in which garlic had been steeping for hours. Those bowls of garlic rolls were a Roux Grill signature that waitstaff brought to every customer's table along with menus and a practiced recitation of the nightly specials.

One thing about my ex: He was a great cook and had excellent instincts for running a restaurant. However, those pungent, savory rolls had been my contribution. Harris had fought the idea, saying we should just offer the standard bread and butter. Cheaper, he said. Better business. But I'd convinced him to offer them for a couple of nights, and that was all it took for the garlicky nuggets to become insanely popular. Smelling them now, I almost swooned with a feeling akin to homesickness.

The hostess station was empty except for a sign inviting people to seat themselves. A gleaming mahogany bar ran the length of the wall to the right, the mirror behind it reflecting brightly lit liquor bottles like jewels. Booths ran along the left wall, and in between tables ranged back to the stone fireplace at the rear of the dining room. Two doors in the back corners led to the kitchen.

A low murmur of conversation came from the smattering of customers, who, like the folks outside, were taking advantage of the low-priced well drinks from four to six. Linda, a waitress who had been with the Roux since it opened, came out of the kitchen carrying a platter of appetizers. She saw me, smiled, and nodded a greeting. I gave her a brief wave in return. Behind the bar, Maggie Clement sliced limes with lightning speed.

I absently looked over the patrons as I thought about what to say to Maggie—and to Harris. Suddenly, my attention snagged on one couple in particular. My breath hitched in my chest.

"You know, I should come in here more often . . . Ellie?" Astrid interrupted herself. "What's the matter?"

Her gaze followed mine to the booth where Cynthia Beck, wearing more bling than I would ever own and a low-cut blouse I would never own, sat across from Ritter Nelson. He'd put on a sports coat over his chambray shirt, and the overhead light glinted off the lighter strands in his wavy hair. Her elbows were on the table, and her chin rested on her laced fingers as she stared at her date as if she wanted to eat him.

"Uh-oh," Astrid said. "Do not, just do *not*, tell me that gorgeous hunk of man flesh is Thea's brother."

Jaw clenched, I nodded. "He's only been in town a day or so."

"Well, honey, you'd better do something soon if you want to land that one, because Cynthia works fast. As you can see."

Unaware she was being watched, Cynthia bit her vermilion—and artificially plump—lower lip between her teeth and reached out to stroke Ritter's arm with a manicured nail.

"Oh, good heavens," I said.

He looked surprised for a moment, but continued with whatever he was saying. She nodded enthusiastically. I couldn't help wondering what they were talking about.

Not that it mattered. No way could I compete with Cynthia on a good day, and I was seriously out of practice on the dating front.

I sighed.

To my right, Maggie Clement looked up from her citrus prep. "Ellie! Oh, my God! Ellie, you come here right now!" She was well padded and pushing sixty, a woman who mothered everyone she came into contact with. Now she enveloped me in a hug and a cloud of White Shoulders perfume before pushing me back to arm's length. "Honey, you look so much better than the last time I saw you!"

"Um, thanks." I racked my brain as to when that might have been. Probably when I'd been putting in the garden behind Scents & Nonsense, so I would have been covered with dirt and sweat.

She shook her head, and her bleached blond hair swung back and forth. "This whole thing with Josie is so terrible. I just can't believe it."

I nodded, finding it hard to speak. But this was why I was here, not Ritter. I patted her shoulder, feeling awkward. "How are you holding up?"

Maggie made a face. "You know those stages of grief? Well, I'm in the anger one right now. I feel like I could break someone in two—if it was the right someone. Have you heard anything else about what happened? Do they have a suspect?"

Astrid and I exchanged a glance. "Not that I know of," I said, glad to know Maggie was okay. For now, at least.

She turned and hugged Astrid, too. "And you haven't been in here for almost as long as Ellie here. How's the pet-sitting biz?" She tsked without waiting for an answer. "Oh, that poor girl. I just can't believe anyone would kill her." Then she seemed to remember where she was. "What can I get you?"

"Buffalo Trace," Astrid answered without hesitation. "Neat."

"Coming right up! Ellie?"

"Um," I said. "How about—"

"Ellie?"

I turned to find Harris weaving through the tables. He didn't look terribly happy to see me.

He stopped in front of me. Even now I had to admit Harris Madigan was a handsome man. Dark hair flipped down over his forehead, his tanned complexion complemented eyes the color of pine straw, and his Elvis Presley lips curved over a solid square chin. Unfortunately, those lips often curved down in a frown rather than up in a smile.

"What are you doing here?" he asked.

"Checking in on Maggie. And, er, you seemed pretty upset on the phone—" I began.

"How dare you tell the cops Ellie killed Josie Overland?" Astrid demanded.

Maggie's fingers crept to her mouth, and her eyes widened. The group of women in the nearby booth turned their heads to look at us. Ritter's head came up, and Cynthia twisted in her seat.

"Astrid," I hissed. I hadn't brought her along so she could confront him for me.

Harris' face flushed a dangerous crimson, and his eyes narrowed. "Ellie? Now we can't even have a conversation without you blowing it all out of proportion to your friends?"

My heart was pounding. God, I hated conflict, and I especially hated conflict with Harris because it seemed as though I could never win.

Not this time.

"Maybe we could talk in your office?" I asked.

He gave a curt nod and stalked toward the back of the restaurant.

We followed—and every eye in the place followed us. As we went by the bar, Astrid reached over and picked up the bourbon Maggie had poured for her and offered it to me. I shook my head. Astrid slugged the shot back with a grimace and thumped the empty glass on the bar.

As I passed by, Ritter quirked an eyebrow and gave me a smile and a subtle nod. Ignoring Cynthia's scowl, I felt my lips flutter up in a tentative smile in return.

The smells of garlic and butter increased once we were through the kitchen door, along with roasting chicken and the heady aromas of dried rosemary, thyme, and sage that a man I didn't know was crushing with a mortar and pestle. He was all freckles and ginger hair, gangly arms and knobby joints, which gave him an air of youth. When he grinned down at me, that pang of almost homesickness for the restaurant shot through me again, followed immediately by knee-wobbling relief that I didn't have to work twelve-hour days in this place anymore.

The office was much as I remembered it: too-big desk facing the door, antique brass lamp in need of a good buffing, and a low file cabinet with piles of paper waiting to find a home inside. The blind over the window was gray with dust. He'd added a new guest chair, and the computer monitor had been upgraded. Somehow, he'd managed to almost kill the lonely philodendron that hung in the corner. It smelled like dust and . . . I caught a smell that was familiar, but I couldn't quite . . .

No, wait. It was the cheap aftershave I'd smelled on

Josie when I'd discovered her body. Well, that made sense, I guessed. After all, she and Harris were close. I was just glad he hadn't started using that stuff when we'd been together. It would have driven me away faster than Wanda Simmons had.

"Who do you think you are, coming in here and embarrassing me in front of my staff and my customers?" Harris asked as he closed the door. Those pretty lips curled in a grimace as he waited for me to answer.

Beside me, Astrid rose to her full height. "Listen, you can't bully—"

"I asked Ellie!" He glowered down at me.

"Stop it, Harris," I said, keeping my tone firm. I had to stand up to him sometime. "You did a bang-up job of humiliating me last year. The whole town knew what you did, but apparently now you're the one who needs to let go of the past. I'm over our failed marriage, and I'm over you."

He let out a long, wounded sigh. "Oh, Ellie. So that's it? You're trying to get back at me?"

"Not at all. I'm telling you to stop spreading lies about me. I know you don't seriously think I killed Josie."

He shrugged.

"But you know what? Out of pure pettiness, you've complicated the murder investigation," I said, my voice rising. "You said Josie was the love of your life. What if the police waste time investigating me, and, as a result, don't find the real killer before he gets away?"

Harris blinked.

Astrid put her hand on my shoulder and squeezed her encouragement.

A sudden crash in the kitchen drew all our attention. Swearing under his breath, Harris jerked the door open and ran out to see what the commotion was. I went to stand in the doorway.

The redhead who had been grinding the herbs stood next to an overturned pan of steaming macaroni and cheese. Gooey sauce flowed slowly from beneath it like yellow lava. He cringed as Harris approached, pointing his finger and streaming curses. I felt sorry for the poor guy; I'd done much the same thing with a vat of gravy once, and had heard about it for a week. And back then I'd supposedly worked with Harris, not for him.

"Come on," Astrid said from behind me.

"What?" I craned my neck to look up at her.

"You've said your piece. You think more will help?"

"Probably not." I wasn't convinced anything I'd said would make a difference. For all I knew, I'd only made Harris angry enough to spread more lies and get me into even more trouble.

Skirting the edge of the kitchen, we made our way to the dining room door and slipped out. I didn't think Harris even noticed, involved in his vitriolic tirade at his employee, but the redheaded cook caught my eye as we left.

He looked utterly miserable, and I felt like a heel for taking off and leaving him there. Part of the reason my ex was reacting so badly to his simple mistake was because of me. Then the cook's eyes flashed, and he turned back to Harris, who was still hurling insults like a monkey hurling food in its cage. Something in the set of the man's shoulders set my mind at ease. He was a tough cookie. He'd be fine.

Ritter and Cynthia were gone, their half-finished drinks holding down a couple of ten-dollar bills. The remaining customers, along with a table of newcomers, watched Astrid and me as we made our way back through the dining room. A few murmured comments in our wake, but I couldn't make out the words.

"What on earth happened back there?" Maggie asked.

"Just an everyday kitchen mishap," I said. "Though you might run out of mac and cheese a bit early tonight."

She frowned, then her face cleared, and she shook her head. "Dropped it?"

I nodded. "Just one pan."

"That Karl. He is a clumsy one."

"Will Harris fire him?" Astrid asked, placing money on the bar for her drink and waving away Maggie's offer of change.

"Nah. At least he hasn't so far, and it isn't the first time. I think that man of yours just likes to yell sometimes."

"Not mine, Maggie. Not for a long time."

"Good for you, honey. Boy, he and Josie sure got into it last night . . ." she trailed off.

"They fought?" I prompted.

Maggie whispered. "By the time we closed, they weren't even speaking to each other."

"Come on, Ellie." Astrid tugged on my arm.

But I leaned closer to the bartender. "When did she leave?"

Maggie shrugged. "The usual time. Around midnight."

"And what were she and Harris arguing about?" I asked, wondering if it was because she'd told me they were dating.

The door to the kitchen banged open, and Harris filled the door. Suddenly I didn't care what their fight had been about. I was ready to leave.

Astrid pulled at my arm again, and this time I didn't resist. "Gotta go," I said. "See you later, Maggie."

CHAPTER 7

On the boardwalk outside, foot traffic was increasing as the dinner hour approached. "I never got my martini," I said ruefully.

"I have an idea," Astrid said. She was grinning.

"What?" I asked, instantly suspicious.

"I have a key to Josie's apartment. Let's go over there."

"Are you insane?" I asked.

"Listen, from what you've told me, the police consider you a serious suspect, Ellie. Harris only made it worse with his lies. I don't get the feeling he's going to retract what he said, either. So it might just come down to you finding out what happened to that poor girl yourself."

"You *are* insane," I said. But that didn't mean she was wrong.

"There's a fish," she said.

"A . . . what are you talking about?"

"Josie had a fish," Astrid said. "I know because she hired me to feed him when she had to be gone for a few days—which is why I have her key. Pretty little betta fish, all by his lonesome in his little acrylic tank, with no one to feed him now. He could starve to death."

I made a face. "That's dirty pool."

She raised her eyebrows. "I just have to pop by my place to pick up the key. And we don't have to look around if you don't want to. Just grab the fish and run."

I opened my mouth to protest again, then stopped. I looked at my watch. "Well, I guess it can't hurt to take a look. And there is that poor fish."

"Now?" Astrid asked with a smile.

I hesitated for moment before nodding. "Yeah, okay."

We hurried back down Corona. I had to double step to keep up with my taller friend.

"God. I hope her apartment isn't some love nest for those two," I said.

Astrid made a noise of derision. "Please. It was a perfectly nice little apartment when I was there before." Her eyes cut to me, but she didn't break stride. "Or is Harris into something weird?"

I snorted a laugh. "Hardly."

"Well, they probably spent all their time in your old house, anyway," she said.

We'd reached the corner of Corona and Gilpin, and she turned right. "I'll grab the key and ride over on my bike."

She owned an old Peugeot, but drove it only when she had to haul her animal clients—or other people—around.

Otherwise she was always on her bicycle. I, on the other hand, was more of a walker.

"Okay. See you in a few," I said.

She strode away, and I continued toward Scents & Nonsense.

I eyed the yellow crime-scene tape out on the boardwalk and on my gate, then let myself into the shop and locked the door behind me. As I stepped out the back door, I thought about the ranch-style home Harris and I had lived in. I'd liked it well enough, but it hadn't been hard to give up as part of the divorce settlement. Pseudo-suburban living hadn't really been my style, I reflected as I made my way down the path to my current abode.

My steps faltered as my situation really hit home. If I didn't fix this, I could go to prison. I stopped and looked around the garden I loved so much and at my dream business, closed for the day. I'd be darned if I was going to give up all that I'd worked so hard for over the last year.

I grabbed my car keys and a light jacket, then let Dash out to enjoy the garden. He followed behind me as I returned to the back patio. It would be nice when I could use the garden gate again.

"Now, will you just look at that!" I stopped and reached for the bowl of the fused-glass birdbath at the edge of the patio. Someone had knocked it askew, and it teetered precariously on its stand, on the verge of falling and shattering into a bazillion pieces. Carefully, I snugged it firmly back into place. "I'll have to remember to refill it when I get back."

I checked once more to make sure the birdbath was

stable and noticed a thread-thin bright green tendril breaking through the moss at its base. *Probably bindweed,* I thought. *Better pull it out before it can spread.*

"I won't be long," I told Dash. He gazed up at me with liquid brown eyes. "I promise."

He grinned easygoing agreement, then went to his bed on the back patio, turned around three times, and lay down with his chin on his paws to await my return.

Astrid was waiting out front, checking the messages on her phone. When I came outside, she stuck the phone in the pocket of her skirt, and we quickly walked to the Wrangler.

Once she'd climbed into the seat, she held up a key hanging from a purple beaded fob. She turned her hand so I could see the name stitched onto it.

JOSIE

Then she put it on her lap and folded her hands over it. "Do you know where she lived?" my friend asked. "Or do you need directions?"

"I took her home a couple of times when her car was in the shop," I said.

Her car. When I'd returned from the Roux Grill, the Fiesta hadn't been parked down the street anymore. As I pulled away from the curb, I imagined it sitting in the police impound lot out by the fairgrounds and wondered who would end up with it. Most people her age didn't have wills if they didn't have children, and try as I might, I couldn't remember Josie talking about her parents or any siblings.

* * *

I PARKED the Wrangler in the lot of a convenience store, and Astrid and I hoofed it down the block. Josie had lived in an eight-plex on the west side of Poppyville, four up and four down. Hers was an upstairs end unit. Astrid and I looked at each other.

"Maybe this isn't such a good idea," she said.

I glared at her. "This was *your* idea."

At least to start with.

She shrugged.

Now that we were here, I was curious about what we might find in Josie's home. Though I'd dropped her off, I'd never been inside. I could only hope we might find something to help clear my Harris-smudged name.

"Come on," I said, and strode up the steps as if we were expected.

Astrid hurried after, then stood behind me as I worked the key into the door lock and gave it a twist. Quickly, we slipped inside.

Standing with our backs to the closed door, we surveyed the living room. Though small, it was quite a bit larger than mine, boasting a sofa and recliner, with a nondescript floor lamp between them. The carpet was sculpted, neutral beige, and the walls were painted a slightly lighter shade of the same color. To the left, a nook held a small table and four chairs, and the open kitchen farther down on the left offered additional seating at the short counter that divided it from the living room.

The walls were covered with enlarged photographs, most of which depicted nature or animals. We took a few tentative steps into the room. The air smelled of toast. The strains of seventies rock and roll sifted through the thin wall from the adjoining apartment.

"What are we looking for?" Astrid asked.

I shot her a look. "This was your brain wave."

But she just shook her head, her gaze sweeping the room, back and forth, eyes glistening. "God. I can't believe she's never coming back."

The feelings of loss and disbelief had been circling through my psyche all day, and in that short amount of time I'd grown used to, if not comfortable with, the idea that I'd found Josie's body that morning. Astrid had seen her for only a brief moment, though, and I realized Josie's death had been largely theoretical to my friend until right then.

I put my hand on her shoulder. "Maybe we can help find her killer."

She sniffed and patted my hand with her own. "Right." She took a deep breath. "Okay. Clues. Look for clues."

"That's helpful," I said, rolling my eyes. "Don't touch anything. The last thing we need is for the police to find our fingerprints in here."

"Good point," she said, walking to the short hallway that led to the bathroom and bedroom. "I'll look in here." Using her elbow, she pushed aside the beaded curtain and went into the other room. The strings of beads clicked and rustled behind her.

I left her to the bedroom, suddenly unwilling to stumble into some blatant evidence of Harris sleeping there.

Not that I cared where he slept. It was just . . . unsettling.

I walked around, inspecting the pictures on the walls. There was a stunning close-up of a mariposa lily, the red spots at the base of each of the three petals like spots of blood on white linen. Another photo showed collections of new cattails and alien-looking pussy paws. I was impressed by how Josie had captured the dignity of yerba santa—blessed herb—a gummy purple-topped weed that grew nearly seven feet tall. Gamma had called it nature's Band-Aid.

Next to it were photos of a field full of blue lupine, goldenrod, and clarkia. Another field was overrun with drifts of daisies. My breath caught, and I began to touch my finger to the frame before remembering and jerking it back. Gamma's voice rang in my mind:

Daisies for innocence. Chestnuts for justice. Chrysanthemums for truth.

I swallowed, and moved on.

The next picture revealed a steep mountain trail I was pretty sure wound up to Kestrel Peak. Yes: I recognized Falcon Rock, its base worn away by water long rerouted by geologic time to the underground spring that now ran beneath Poppyville. The wide, swooping extensions at the top of the formation did resemble a bird if you stared at it long enough—or if you possessed the talent for photographic composition that Josie obviously had. The stone bird marked the trail halfway to the summit, and, given the flowers in bloom around it, Josie had taken the pictures in the spring.

Only two photos were portraits: one of Josie herself and one of a man wearing a dark suit and a stern expression. He looked a bit older than Josie, but there was something about the shape of the eyes that told me she'd had at least one sibling.

I stepped back and looked at the array as a whole. There was a picture missing. The blank space off to one side in the arrangement had the hanger still protruding from the wall.

Maybe she sold whatever was there and didn't have a chance to replace it.

I spied a shoebox of loose photo printouts sitting on the coffee table. Settling on the edge of the sofa, I carefully dumped them out, using my fingertips on the cardboard and then slipping my jacket over my hand in order to spread them out.

Most had been taken inside the Roux Grill. These weren't arty in the least, but a record of Josie's friends and coworkers. Most were group photos with the subjects grinning into the camera, arms slung around one another in camaraderie.

I recognized many of the waitstaff I had worked with for so many years. There was Maggie, of course, standing behind the bar while Linda and Raleigh mugged on the stools in front. Another showed two waitresses and two waiters in the same logo T-shirt and jeans combo Josie had been wearing when I found her. One of the waitresses had been hired since I'd left, though I knew Rhonda, a rabbity-looking woman who'd occasionally accompanied her mother into Scents & Nonsense. As I recalled, she had a particular fondness for Astrid's amaretto cookies.

Then there was a picture of the new waitress and the redheaded cook who had dropped the vat of macaroni and cheese. The cook looked considerably happier than when I'd seen him last, his arm pulling the waitress to him. There were no customers in the background, so my bet was the photo session had been after hours.

I moved some of the pictures around, revealing one of Harris alone in the office. He was looking up from his desk with an expression of surprise on his face. Josie had caught him unaware and without any of his many masks. I stared at the picture, seeing a flicker of the man I'd once fallen so hard for.

Next was one of Harris and Josie, laughing. It looked like a candid shot, and I wondered who had taken the photo. They looked shockingly happy.

Did Harris and I ever look like that?

I couldn't remember. I shoved the photos back into the box and stood.

Shelves filled most of the back wall of the living room, and, in the middle of the unit, a drop-down desk was open. The surface was clear. I moved closer, peering at the spines of books tucked between items Josie had culled from nature: a pile of smooth pebbles, gnarled chunks of driftwood, a rock studded with pyrite and mica, and dozens of swirly snail shells piled into a glass bowl. The titles were mostly nonfiction, with lots of natural history and photography books.

On another shelf, a small acrylic tank with a blue lid held the supposed reason for our visit. The betta fish's elaborate, blue-and-red fins waved languidly as it nosed the glass. I grabbed the jar of food granules and pinched some between thumb and forefinger to sprinkle into the water before remembering my own admonition not to touch anything. I put the cap back on and tucked the fish food in my pocket.

Cubbyholes behind the desk held various office supplies. Leaning forward, I inspected the contents. Nothing stood out—until I realized there were no bills or paperwork. Then I saw the faint rectangular outline of dust on the surface of the desk—a shape very much like that of a laptop computer.

Straightening, I took in the room details with new eyes. Items had been shifted, and the sofa cushions were slightly out of kilter. Going into the kitchen, I saw two drawers had been left open a few inches.

"Astrid?" I called. "What do you see in there?"

Her head popped through the vertical curtain. "Not much. But something's off. Her bed is pristine, but the closet door is open and there are a couple of things on the floor. She wasn't much of a clothes hog, but the girl had a real thing for boots. There are eight pairs in there. Nothing looks to be missing, but her dresser drawers are messier than I'd expect from someone who folds their socks so neatly, and one was hanging open. You know what I think?"

I pressed my lips together and nodded. "Either someone was looking for something, or the police have been through her stuff already."

She pointed her finger at me. "Bingo."

My cell buzzed in my pocket, and I pulled it out to look at the display. The number looked familiar, and when I realized why, I felt the blood drain from my face.

"Ellie?" Astrid closed the distance between us and peered over my shoulder.

The phone buzzed again as I fished in my wallet and pulled out the card Lupe Garcia had given me that morning. Sure enough, that was the number on my phone's screen.

Panic arrowed through my solar plexus. "It's Detective Garcia." I met Astrid's eyes. "Do you think she knows we're here?"

"Nah. How could she?" But she sounded unsure.

The phone stopped ringing. Slowly, I slid it back into my pocket. I thought of my Jeep parked at the convenience store down the street. Was Garcia calling because we'd essentially broken into a murder victim's apartment?

"The police would have found any clues here already." Astrid's disappointment was obvious, and I realized that in spite of her earlier nervousness, she had been kind of enjoying herself.

"Guess we'd better go," I said, turning toward the door and putting my hand in the pocket of my jacket. My fingers wrapped around the canister of fish food. "Darn it," I said, pulling it out and looking across the room at the betta fish on the shelf. "I almost forgot the fish."

It eyed me through a plastic plant frond. I could simply wipe off the food container and put it back on the shelf and hope Harris or someone else would take care of the little guy. But, of course, that wasn't what I was going to do. I marched over, unplugged the acrylic tank, and picked it up.

I lifted the betta fish up to eye level. "Hi, there. How about you come and live with me for a while?" I looked at Astrid. "Unless you want to take it?"

She shook her head. "I have enough critters to deal with. He's a pretty little guy. Keep him in the shop."

"Nabby will love that," I said wryly, checking the room

one more time. The faint toast smell still hung in the air, from at least the day before. I wondered if Josie liked jam on her toast.

Taking a deep breath, I nodded at the door. "Let's blow this joint."

Astrid turned the knob and stepped out to the small deck with me on her heels.

"Hey! What were you doing in there?"

I jumped and almost dropped Josie's fish. Astrid whirled at the harsh voice, glaring at the man it belonged to.

CHAPTER 8

❧

WHAT'S it to you?" Astrid demanded, fists on her hips and her chin jutted out in defiance. My friend might have been a bit hippy dippy, but she could really stand up for herself or others.

The man stood on the wooden decking in front of an apartment entrance to the left of Josie's. The door hung open, treating us to a miasma of burnt sausage, dirty socks, and stale cigar smoke. His blue Dockers and once-white T-shirt were stained with grease, and he blinked his myopic anger through thick glasses with aviator frames that would have looked pretty cool in the 1970s.

"I'm the manager here," he grated. "Tom Steinhart. And you have no right to be in that chick's place." He licked his lips in a thoroughly unappetizing way.

Chick? I lifted the tank. "We came by to pick up

Leonard here." As I said the words, I wanted to kick myself. What if he knew the fish's real name? For that matter, did it even have a name?

"Hmmph. Haven't seen you here before. And the cops said no one was supposed to go inside. Tenant's dead." His tone was flat.

At least now we knew it was the police and not someone else who had tossed Josie's belongings.

I nodded gravely. "We know. That's why we came to pick up the fish."

His response was a disconcerting leer. "Did the cops tell you to take her stuff?"

I glanced over at Astrid. She shrugged, but I could tell Tom Steinhart was rubbing her the wrong way. My alarm bells were going off as well. Something about him smelled off—rotten—and it wasn't coming from his apartment.

"We didn't ask them for permission to rescue our friend's pet," I said firmly. "It was just the right thing to do."

"Was that you in there earlier?" he asked.

I squinted. "There was someone else in Josie's apartment besides the authorities?"

He lifted one shoulder and let it drop. "Thought I heard someone in there before the cops showed up. Didn't give it a thought. Figured it was the chick who lived there."

"Did you tell the police that you heard someone in the murdered woman's apartment?" Astrid asked. Her mild tone sounded forced to me, but he didn't seem to notice.

"I don't want anything to do with the cops." He ogled me through his thick lenses. "Murder. Sheesh. Not that I'm that surprised."

Stunned, I rested the fish tank on the deck railing,

keeping my hands on both sides to steady it. "Why aren't you surprised?" I asked. Astrid's eyes had narrowed.

He shrugged. "She was a little snot—that's for sure. Wouldn't give me the time of day. Even complained to the owners about me one time."

"Why would she do that?" Astrid asked sharply. My own distaste for the man ratcheted up another level.

He turned to her, looked her up and down much as he had me, and sniffed. "No reason."

"There had to be a reason," she said.

"Astrid—"

"I imagine the police would like to know about Josie's complaint," she said.

Tom Steinhart paled.

"Was something unsatisfactory about the apartment?" I asked.

His lips pooched out, and then he sucked them back in, a gesture that struck me as weirdly obscene though I couldn't have said exactly why.

"I gotta go." He turned to go back into his apartment. Before closing the door, he said over his shoulder. "Better not see you two around here again."

"Sheesh!" Astrid breathed when we were halfway back to the car. "What a toad."

"That's not a very nice thing to say," I said.

She looked at me.

I grinned. "About toads, I mean. They're very beneficial in the garden."

Astrid rolled her eyes, but echoed my smile.

"You never ran into Mr. Steinhart when you fed Josie's fish, I take it."

"Thankfully, no." She shuddered.

I stopped on the sidewalk. "Here. Take this for a sec." I handed her the betta fish and pulled out my phone. There was one new voice mail. Bracing myself, I held the phone to my ear and waited. Astrid watched me with interest.

"Ms. Allbright, this is Detective Garcia. I wanted to let you know that we will be releasing the crime scene next to your place of business tomorrow. It's been determined that the murder victim—" She paused, and when she spoke again her professional brusqueness had been replaced with a softer tone. "Josie Overland wasn't attacked on your property, though she did ultimately die there. We found evidence that she was assaulted in Raven Creek Park. I'll come by in the morning to make it official. Good-bye."

Returning my phone to my pocket, I began walking again. "Josie was killed in the park," I said slowly.

My mind was racing, though. She obviously hadn't died right away, or she wouldn't have made it to the boardwalk. Unless someone had moved her? Surely the police would have found evidence of that, though. I wondered if they could tell when she'd been attacked. All I knew was that it had to have been after she left the Roux Grill at midnight.

"In the park? Then why . . ." Astrid trailed off.

"She must have made her way to my place to try to get help." And I'd been sleeping like a baby by that time.

ARE you sure you don't want to come stay with me tonight? The sofa pulls out," Astrid said. We were standing in front of Scents & Nonsense as the sun lowered in the western sky. Several hundred yards away, a Poppyville police cruiser was parked at the junction of Corona Street and Raven Road, very near where I'd seen Josie's car. It didn't look like anyone was inside.

"Nah. I'll be fine," I said.

"Aren't you worried?"

"About what?" I asked.

She spluttered. "*Murder*, Ellie. You could be in danger."

I blinked. The idea that whoever had killed Josie might want to do me harm as well had honestly never occurred to me. After all, other than my cranky ex-husband, I didn't have any enemies. That I knew of, at least. Now, a frisson of fear tickled the edges of my nerves. I pushed it away. I'd moved past feeling afraid and unsure during the last year, and I wasn't going to start in again now.

"This is my home," I said. "And no one's going to drive me out of it."

She looked to the sky as if for suggestions on how to deal with me, then met my eyes. "If she was killed in the park, how do you know it wasn't some vagrant who happened onto Josie by accident? And if so, who's to say he isn't still around? That he won't do it again? I just hate to think of you here by yourself."

I pointed to the police car. "If it was someone passing through, I bet the cops have chased him off by now." And an attack by a random transient didn't begin to explain why Josie would have been on this side of town so late.

She took a deep breath. "Keep Dash by your side."

"Of course."

Astrid suddenly smiled and waggled her eyebrows.

"Or you could call Ritter to come over for the night. To protect you. I bet he'd be happy to oblige."

I felt myself redden. "That's ridiculous."

She laughed. "Lordy, Elliana. You are going to have to make some kind of a move as soon as possible if you want to knock Cynthia Man Trap off his radar. In twenty-four hours she's already started staking a claim."

"Could you please stop talking about my mild interest in Ritter in clichés? And no, I'm not going to 'make a move' by inviting him over to protect me for the night. What's wrong with you?"

The humor left her face. "Oh, gosh. Ellie, I'm sorry. I was just kidding around. You really like him, don't you?" she asked with a gentle smile.

I opened my mouth, then shut it again.

She raised her eyebrows, waiting.

"Like I said—mild interest."

"Mm hmm. With those baby blues? Oh, sorry—cliché. But I saw how he looked at you in the Roux."

I looked down and smiled. Then I met her eyes. "I used to like him. A lot, actually. But I was a kid then. I don't even know him now. That's what worries me."

Her forehead wrinkled. "I don't get it."

"I liked Harris, too. A lot. At first, I mean."

Understanding dawned on her face. "Oh, for Pete's sake. You can't possibly be afraid Thea's brother is anything like Harris."

"No . . ." I drew the word out. "I just don't trust my own judgment when it comes to men."

She turned to go, but gave me a knowing look over her

shoulder. "Uh-huh. A little attention from Ritter Nelson, and I think you're going to get over that in a hurry."

Astrid's warning about safety came back to me as I stepped into the shop and put the fish tank on the counter. I plugged it in and continued out to the back patio of the Enchanted Garden. Dash greeted me with a wiggling behind, grinning up at me until I bent and gave him a good scratch behind the ears. When I straightened, he promptly rolled over onto his back and looked at me upside down.

"You goofball," I said, smiling.

He sneezed.

I looked out at the garden, breathing in the calm it always provided. This was my sanctuary, but death had come so close to tainting it forever. Even if Harris hadn't tried to implicate me in Josie's murder, the fact that she'd worked for me and died in front of my shop was enough to make me want to know who killed her.

And why.

My eyes scanned the banks of flowers. Tendrils of jasmine twisted around the base of a shepherd's crook. A hollowed gourd hung from the crook. It swayed in the slight breeze, and a brightly colored finch clung to the opening, pecking at the thistle seed inside. Morning glories wound up copper trellises, the day's blooms furled in the gloaming. Night-blooming Nicotiana shook off the fading light and began filling the garden with sweetness.

The flapping of the police tape by the gate drew my attention. Anger began to build out of the numbness I'd been steeping in all day. Not fear, despite Astrid's worries. Anger—like Maggie's.

Just yesterday morning I'd realized that after a long year of change and deliberately forging a new life, I was finally settled and happier than ever before. I had found the best parts of me again. Josie, too, had seemed happy. Sure, she'd been dumb to get involved with Harris, but I'd done the same thing at one time. Josie's innocence had been a strength, not a weakness.

Now someone had stolen not only her strength, but her very life.

Anger flared again, and I found myself searching the shadows for any sign of threat. A plaintive meow sounded from behind me. I let out my breath, turned, and slid open the screen door. Nabby shot past my ankle, pausing to look toward the gate. His tail fluffed, and he hissed once before threading his way through the plants to his favorite spot on the low terraced wall where he liked to survey his domain.

I went inside and put the canister of fish food on the counter by the tank. The betta fish circled a couple of times, then stopped, eyeing me with piscine skepticism.

"You'll like it here," I told him. I wished I knew his name—or if it was even a "him." How could you tell? But Astrid had use the male pronoun, and I figured she'd know if anyone did. "How about if I just keep calling you Leonard?"

The fish didn't disagree.

I went back out to the garden, closing the door behind me. Nabby had disappeared, but I wasn't concerned. Despite the easy access to the wilds beyond the fences and hedges of the garden, he was loath to venture outside the immediate environs of the shop.

Dash stayed at my left heel every step of the way to my little house. I let him out to the meadow to do his business and made myself a peanut butter and tomato jam sandwich. I took it, along with a bottle of hard cider, out to the back porch, intending to watch the sunset again. But everything was different now. The sandwich stuck in my throat. I took a long pull on the cider to try to wash it down.

What if Astrid was right, and a transient had killed Josie in the river park? That seemed awfully convenient, especially since, to the best of my knowledge, there was no homeless population on this end of town. There were those few men and women whom Gessie allowed to pitch tents at the back of her stable property, away from the tourist clientele she took out on trail rides. But Bongo Pete, the woman who called herself Queenie, and a couple of others were well-known in town and certainly not violent.

It could have been someone passing through, I thought, giving the last bite of sandwich to Dash and finishing off the cider. But that still raised the question of why Josie had been in the river park after midnight. Maggie had confirmed that Josie had worked her usual shift at the Roux Grill. She'd also mentioned a bitter fight between Harris and Josie. Bet he hadn't mentioned *that* to Detective Max Lang. What had they been fighting about? Maggie hadn't had a chance to fill me in before Astrid dragged me away.

Could it possibly have been something serious enough for Harris to stab his girlfriend over? I just couldn't wrap my head around the idea. Harris was a lot of things, but to my knowledge he'd never once been violent.

Beside me, Dash busied himself with licking peanut butter off the roof of his mouth.

The temperature had dropped with the sun, and I jammed my hands into the pockets of my jacket.

"Time to let Nabby back in," I said.

Dash kept licking.

CHAPTER 9

NABBY was waiting by the back door of the shop. I
let him in and checked his food bowl. Examining
the betta tank, I determined that short of knocking the
whole thing off the counter, Nabby couldn't get to Leonard if he felt the need for a fishy midnight snack.

"Be nice to the little guy," I said to the cat. "Looks like
he's ours now."

I locked the door behind Dash and me, and turned
toward a hot shower and a soft bed. My corgi had won
his battle with the peanut butter, and slopped a long drink
from his bowl by the rocking chairs. I waited for him to
finish, my senses on super alert. As we walked on the
moonlit path, I mentally sifted through the night sounds
and floral essences, watching for any indication of threat.
A tiny flash of brightness made me turn my head. There
it was again, just a flicker, close to the ground.

What on earth? Fireflies in California? Unlikely.

Slowly, I approached the birdbath I'd righted earlier. The green and red and blue glass of the bowl glowed faintly. A soft rustling rose around me, the whisper of wordless secrets, a sigh of invitation. The ground beneath the birdbath twinkled. As I grew near, the sparks flew into the air.

Apparently not impossible, I thought, watching the glowing insects disperse into the top of the oak tree and beyond.

But nothing I'd ever seen before. Fireflies loved humidity. Poppyville had its underground springs, but humid, it wasn't.

"The moss below the birdbath is usually damp," I said to Dash. "Maybe that drew them. But from where?"

He tipped his foxy head to the side.

My cell phone rang. I reached into my pocket and thumbed it off without looking, while I watched the tiny flickering lightning bugs scatter farther and farther apart.

Until they disappeared altogether.

In the darkness, a mysterious scent rose from the ground like tule fog, cool against my skin, caressing my cheek. I swayed on my feet, drinking its heady sweetness, inhaling so deeply I felt dizziness wash over me.

My eyes popped open, and I stumbled, barely managing to catch myself. I hadn't even realized I'd closed them. And then the strange perfume faded. But not entirely this time. A vestige of it clung to me, soaked in through my pores to reside in my very core.

I made my way to the porch and reached for my keys. It

felt as if I was moving in slow motion. Then my cell chirped, alerting me to a text message, and the feeling faded.

Inside, I flipped on the light and checked my phone. Both the call and the text had been from my brother, Colby.

Tried to call just now, but no answer. You out on the town?

I called him back. He answered on the second ring.

"Hey, sis!"

"Hey, yourself. Where are you calling from this time?" Colby lived in a Westfalia van and wandered the U.S.— and sometimes Canada—with his array of horseshoeing implements, knife sharpeners, and handyman tools to support him. It was the ultimate rebellion against a brief career as an investment banker, which had not suited him in the least. I adored Colby, and in the last four years since he'd taken up the freewheeling, itinerant lifestyle, he'd never sounded happier. I missed him like crazy, though.

"I'm in Crested Butte," he said. "You on a date?"

"Why is everyone so interested in my love life all of a sudden?"

"Sorry!" A pause. "What do you mean, *everyone*?"

"Never mind. Where's Crested Butte?" I imagined him in his camper van, a home tinier even than my own. He'd be wearing stained jeans, a plaid shirt, and a gimme cap from some random feed store, and had probably grown a beard by now.

"Colorado," he said. "You wouldn't believe how pretty it is. You should come visit."

"I'd love to, believe me. But you know I can't leave the shop."

"You sound grumpy, Ellie."

"Well, it's been one heck of a crazy day." I sighed before I could stop myself.

I settled in on my sofa and thumbed on the jazz station with the stereo remote. Dash padded to his food dish, and the sound of crunching joined the low music.

"Does it have anything to do with finding Josie Overland dead this morning?"

I sat up. "What? How on earth did you know about that?"

"Got a call from the cops, clear out here in the Rocky Mountains."

My forehead wrinkled. "They called you about Josie?"

"They called me about *you.*"

Dang it.

"About you and Harris, specifically. How you got along, if you ever talked about wanting to get back together with him, were you the jealous type. Stuff like that."

"What did you tell them?" I sat up straighter, feeling the blood rising in my face.

"I said that I thought you'd established a new life after the divorce. That you were happier without Harris than with him. That I wasn't aware of a jealous bone in your body."

"Thanks," I said. "That's all true."

"I know. But why were they asking me questions like that?"

"Apparently they—or at least Detective Lang—think I'm a prime suspect in Josie's murder. Since she technically died on my property, and it looked as if she was trying to get in my front gate when she collapsed. Then Harris went and told them I was upset about Josie dating him."

There was a long silence, then, "That's not good. Not good at all."

"Tell me about it," I said. "But it turns out Josie was actually attacked in the park, not on my property. I'm hoping that means I'm off the hook."

"Good." My brother's voice held heartfelt relief. "That you're off the hook, I mean. Well, I'm going to let you get some shut-eye. I'll check in with you in a day or so."

He wished me a good night's sleep, and we said good-bye.

The conversation with my brother calmed me, but it still took three cups of valerian root tea before I managed to drift off. My thoughts ping-ponged among Josie's murder, Ritter Nelson, and the scent that had recently begun to haunt the Enchanted Garden. Could it be a night-scented flower in a neighbor's garden that Gamma hadn't taught me about? Could it have somehow drawn the fireflies to it as it had appealed to me?

"I need to check her journal," I murmured to Dash, before turning over and sinking into unconsciousness.

I WOKE at dawn, slowly surfacing from the depths of slumber. The soft duvet enveloped me in a cocoon of comfort. Tendrils of a dream clung to my growing consciousness. My grandmother, kneeling in her garden, patting the dirt around a transplanted seedling, and talking softly to someone behind her that I couldn't see, and then to me.

You mustn't forget, Elliana. You have a gift. You need to . . .

I stretched and opened my eyes to the new light nudging in through the skylight, feeling the last vestiges of the dream evaporate. Early birds chirped loudly outside—the nasal call of chickadees, the liquid notes of a meadowlark, the piercing screech of a blue jay trying to imitate the red-tailed hawks that nested near the river. Dash sprawled on the bed beside me, upside down and oblivious.

A deep breath then, and with it came the flood of memory.

Josie had been murdered.

Adrenaline shot through my veins, a flight or fight response triggered by . . . what?

After all, Detective Garcia had said they were releasing the area in front of my shop, so I could open Scents & Nonsense and go back to doing what I loved best. Other than Harris being a dolt and trying to pin his girlfriend's death on me, they had no evidence against me—because there wasn't any.

All I had to do was ride this whole thing out. Time had healed things before. It would now, too. Right?

As long as whoever had killed Josie was caught and convicted. Really, that was what it came down to more than anything.

Justice for Josie, and freedom for me.

"Come on, Dash. Let's get to work."

He rolled over, instantly awake. Downstairs, he tucked into his kibble while I gnawed unenthusiastically on an apple and swigged my first cup of coffee. Twenty minutes later, I'd showered and dressed in a flowing knee-length skirt the color of flax flowers and a sleeveless ivory blouse, and Dash and I made the short trip to the day job.

At the spigot, I filled the water can and carried it to the fused-glass birdbath. After topping it off, I looked down. A swath of violet light painted the ground below: sun shining through the colored glass of the bowl. The lush carpet of verdant moss at the base of the pedestal sparkled with moisture, a result of Thea's carefully thought out drip irrigation.

Then I saw the tiny sprout that had been pushing through the soil the previous day was now seven inches tall, and its winding, corkscrew stem supported blue-green leaves that looked as if they'd been dipped in wax. Seven fat buds roosted on top, their dark sepals still furled around the promised blooms.

Definitely not bindweed.

Slowly, I reached down and touched one with my fingertip. *What the heck is that?* I'd never seen anything like it, had never heard of such a plant in any of my horticulture classes. Anything that grew that fast had to be invasive. Still, my curiosity wouldn't let me pull it out until I knew what it was—and what those flowers looked—and smelled—like.

I returned the watering can and quickly rinsed my hands. Throwing a glance at the unusual plant, I called Dash and strode across the patio to the door. I deliberately turned away from the police tape still looped around the garden gate.

Soon it will be over. Or at least that stupid yellow plastic will be gone.

Astrid was letting herself in the front door as we came in the back. Today she wore flowy Thai fisherman pants in brown cotton and a black T-shirt. Her burnished copper hair was in a loose braid over one shoulder, and she carried a covered plate that broadcast ginger and molasses to my nose.

"Hey!" she greeted me.

I smiled. "Hey. What's on the menu?"

"Ginger softies. I didn't know if you'd even want cookies today, but I'm so much in the habit of starting my day whipping them up that I went ahead."

"Thanks. I'm planning to open up later today, and I'm sure that plate will be empty in no time." As she walked by I snagged one and took a bite. "Yum! These are delicious! Way better than the apple I had for breakfast."

She grinned. "I combined two recipes to make them, and I have to say I'm pretty pleased." She walked over to where Nabby hunkered on the counter next to Leonard's bowl and set the cookies down. "Well, lookie here. I don't think I've ever seen Nabokov up here. He's usually more of a window cat."

"Me neither," I said. "But now there's extra entertainment on offer."

She leaned down to the cat, who raised his chin for a scritch. "At least you didn't eat him. Good boy, Nabby."

He blinked at her, looking bored, and sat up to his full

height. Astrid reached for the tank, rotating it on the counter for a better view of the betta fish.

Nabby growled.

Her mouth fell open, and I felt my own jaw slacken.

"Nabokov!" I said.

"He's guarding the fish," Astrid said in wonder. "Well, I never."

I laughed. "I think you're right. Nabby, do you like your new pet?"

He squinted at me, and a purr rumbled from his chest. *Mrow.*

"How about if I put him down here on the end." I lifted the bowl, watching Nabby. He followed me to the end of the counter, away from the register, and settled in next to the newly relocated fish tank.

"Weirdo," I muttered to the cat and moved across to the coffeemaker.

Movement outside caught my eye, and I went to the front window. Detective Garcia, wearing another white shirt, only with a brown blazer this time, was unfastening one end of the tape from the back fence. Hope bloomed in my chest. Surely this was a step in the right direction.

Then Detective Lang moved into the frame.

Garcia's phone message hadn't said anything about her partner coming over this morning. The hope withered a little as he pointed to the ground where I'd found Josie, then toward the park. Garcia said something, and he shook his head. He jerked his chin toward the shop. She replied and pointed straight at me, standing there in the window. I hadn't realized that she'd seen me.

Lang's head rose, and his eyes met mine. He marched over and pushed open the unlocked door and stood in the entrance. "Ms. Allbright. You're up early." Sarcasm laced his tone.

"I usually am."

"Then how is it you didn't report Josie Overland's body until nearly nine o'clock yesterday morning?"

"It was closer to eight thirty, actually. I told you I overslept."

His lips thinned into a skeptical line. "Are you sure you weren't trying to come up with a good story?"

I snorted. I couldn't help it. "Detective Lang, don't you think I could come up with something better than waking up and stumbling onto my dead employee outside my gate?"

Behind him, a ghost of a smile crossed Garcia's lips as she turned away and began rolling the tape into a messy ball.

He rolled his eyes and pushed into Scents & Nonsense.

"Detective," Astrid stepped toward him. "Can I offer you a cookie?"

But he was staring over her shoulder at the counter. At Leonard the betta fish. He shouldered Astrid aside, took a few steps, then whirled back to me.

"You stole the victim's fish?"

"No! Of course not." I scrambled for what to say. I couldn't deny that we'd been to Josie's. The creepy apartment manager would be happy to tell the cops he'd seen us there if they asked. "We . . . I just wanted to make sure Leonard was okay. Take care of him, since Josie—" I felt my throat tighten and swallowed against it. "Since she can't anymore."

Detective Lang regarded me for a long moment. His partner had come to stand in the doorway and watched us all, her gaze speculative.

"Where did you get the key?" Lang asked.

CHAPTER 10

A STRID had a key," I said.

The expression on his face made my stomach cramp. I racked my brain for a scent that would ease the sensation and came up empty. Was there a flower essence to assuage intimidation?

"Because here's a funny coincidence, Ellie," Lang said. "I talked to Harris last night, and he told me his key to Josie Overland's apartment went missing." His eyes grew wide, and his mouth formed an O of exaggerated surprise. "And guess what else? He also said you visited him at the restaurant yesterday for the first time in months. Right before he noticed the key was gone! I find that timing pretty interesting, don't you?"

"But . . . but . . ." I stammered.

Garcia's expression had sharpened, though her tone remained mild. "I hadn't realized you'd spoken with Mr.

Madigan last evening, Detective Lang. You'll have to fill me in."

He shrugged. "Meh. We just had a beer."

She stared at him for few beats, her face a mask of neutrality.

Then I remembered something Tom Steinhart had said. "When we were there, the manager of Josie's apartment building said someone else had been in her apartment— before you, even."

"Gee, he didn't mention that to us."

"He didn't strike me as someone with a particular affection for the police," Astrid said. "I bet he has a sheet."

Lang lifted an eyebrow at that. "A 'sheet'? Ms. Moneypenny, I think you might want to cut back on the television crime dramas."

Garcia didn't comment, instead turning to me. "You say you already had a key to Ms. Overland's home?"

I gave a little nod.

Astrid stepped forward. "I had the key. Josie gave it to me a while back."

Lang shook his head.

"You were good friends with the victim, then, Ms. Moneypenny?" Garcia asked. "Because that wasn't the impression I got from our conversation at your workplace yesterday."

"She gave it to me so I could feed Leonard while she was out of town," Astrid said. "It's what I do."

The detectives appeared confused. She walked over to where she'd dumped her backpack behind the counter and retrieved a business card. Handing it to them, she said, "Moneypenny Pet Care. Specializing in difficult or chronically ill animals."

They looked at each other and then back at Astrid.

"I'm a petrepreneur," she said.

Garcia laughed. "A pet . . . I see. So you knew about the fish and told your friend here."

Astrid grinned and held her palms up in a gesture of innocence. "Exactly."

Relief whooshed through me. "So it's okay if I keep Leonard here?" I asked. "Or is there someone in Josie's family who might want him?"

Lang went over to the fish to take a look. "Yeah. You can keep it for now."

Garcia said, "The only family we've been able to track down is Ms. Overland's older brother. I doubt he'd want the fish, but we'll let him know it's here."

I blinked. "Where does he live?"

"Silver Wells. He's a lawyer there."

"You talked to him on the phone?" I asked.

"Of course," Lang replied in a gruff tone. "We had to notify next of kin."

"Well, did he have any ideas about who Josie's enemies might have been?"

Lang glared at me.

"Vance Overland and his sister were estranged," Garcia said, more forthcoming than her partner. "He refused to speak about her after we informed him she'd been killed." She looked sad, and I felt a pang of something coming from her.

Melancholy. Nostalgia and melancholy. She misses her family.

Lang reached out and tapped the glass of the fish tank with his fingernail. Nabby's paw flashed out, and the detective jerked his hand back. "Ouch! Why you—" He swiped at Nabby, who scooted out of reach. "Is that thing licensed?" he demanded, pointing at the cat who was now glaring at him from his perch by the window.

"Of course," Astrid said before I could respond. She held out her palm to the detective. "Let me see."

He extended his hand. She took it and leaned closer to examine the injury, while I scurried into the office to retrieve the first-aid kit. In less than two minutes, Astrid had cleaned and bandaged the tiny scratch as if it were a war wound.

"Thanks," Detective Lang said grudgingly.

While Astrid had been playing nurse, Detective Garcia had been strolling among the displays, picking up items here and there, and then setting them down again. I'd been keeping casual track of her from the corner of my eye, a skill that anyone who works in retail for any amount of time automatically develops. Now I saw her pause with something in her hand. A stillness settled around her, and the nostalgia I'd tuned into earlier increased. I turned my full attention to her. Astrid's gaze followed mine.

"What's this scent?" Detective Garcia asked. Her voice was hushed.

"Excuse me," I said to Lang, and joined her.

As soon as I was within a few feet of Lupe Garcia, the sharpness of her bittersweet emotion surprised me. Not because nostalgia was an unusual reaction from customers in the shop—it was perhaps the most common feeling that people broadcast. After all, it was no secret that smell was the most primitive of the senses, and also the one most linked to memory.

Whatever she held in her hand had sparked a very strong memory for Detective Garcia. I tilted my head to see what it was.

"That's a sachet," I said. It was a simple muslin bag filled with spices. "To scent closets and drawers. The strongest smell in that one is cinnamon. It contains pieces of the bark from true cinnamon trees, unlike most cinnamon that you use in the kitchen, which is actually from the bark of the cassia tree."

"I've sure never smelled cinnamon like this in my kitchen," she breathed, holding the sachet to her face.

"Let's see." I leaned over, and she held the bundle out to me. Inhaling deeply, I nodded. "There are also cocoa beans in that bundle, as well as cracked cardamom."

A grin split her face. "That's it! Cardamom. That's what's been missing." My puzzlement must have shown, because she went on. "I've been trying to recreate the drink my great aunt used to make when I was a child in Albuquerque. *Champurrado.* It was a thick hot drink, with plenty of cinnamon like most Mexican hot chocolate. But there was a secret ingredient, and I could never quite get it right. This is very close."

"Hang on," I said, and hurried back to my storeroom.

Astrid stepped out of the way as Lang boomed, "Are you about done over there, Garcia? Maybe you could shop on your own time."

"I'll only be a moment, Max," she answered, her words measured. "And I'll make you some of the hot chocolate I'm talking about. You'll like it."

He harrumphed.

I returned with a chunk of cocoa butter in a small

plastic bag. Its ecru creaminess filled the air with a strong scent of chocolate, head-swimmingly pungent and redolent of decadence.

"Yum," Astrid murmured under her breath as I passed. "You are *so* getting chocolate cookies tomorrow."

"That's it!" Garcia said when I handed it to her and she'd taken a deep sniff of the cocoa with the scented sachet. "What is this?"

I felt the nostalgia sharpen, but the sad, melancholic element dissolved, leaving behind a lovely strong memory.

"Nondeodorized cocoa butter," I said. "It's not food grade, but it is from the same source as really good chocolate. I use it in some of my lotion bars, but it's nice on your skin by itself, too. Plus, it makes you smell like a chocolate kiss." I smiled. "Of course, it's also available with the scent removed."

"Now who would want that?" she asked. "I'd like to buy this. How much?"

I waved my hand. "It's yours."

She frowned, and her friendly expression vanished. "It doesn't work that way. I can't take a gift from a murder suspect."

I heard Astrid's sudden intake of breath behind me.

"Hang on a minute," I protested. "You said Josie was killed in the park." I waved my hand vaguely in that direction. "And you released my property just now. You can't still consider me a murder suspect just because my ex-husband carries a grudge. If you want to know who actually had a fight with her the night she died, it was him."

"Nice try," Lang said in a dry tone. "Harris doesn't have a motive, and you do."

"But—" Astrid broke in.

Lang stopped her with an upraised hand. "And did I mention a witness saw you in the park that night, Ms. All-bright?"

"*What?* That's impossible!"

But when I saw Detective Lang's smug face I realized he'd been saving this bombshell to spring on me. He looked like he was savoring every second, too.

I glanced at Garcia. She'd donned an impenetrable poker face, and was watching me with the same assessment I'd seen in her eyes when I'd first met her over Josie's body.

"If anyone says they saw Ellie attack Josie, they're lying!" Astrid said.

"Not attack," Lang admitted. "Just that she was there in the park."

"Who's your witness?" I asked in a quiet voice.

Lang said, "Pete Grimly."

My confusion must have shown on my face, because Garcia clarified. "You might know him as Bongo Pete."

"Oh." I let out my breath in a little laugh and felt my shoulders relax. "That guy Gessie King lets camp behind her stables?" I remembered how he'd come to pet Dash when I'd parked in Gessie's lot the afternoon before Josie's murder. Bongo Pete was a big guy, gentle as a lamb. Like the rest of our small homeless enclave, the citizens of Poppyville looked out for him, made sure he was well fed and safe, but everyone knew he wasn't quite all there.

"You had me worried," I said.

"He says he saw you walking your dog along the fit-ness trail that night." Lang looked pointedly at Dash, who was gazing obliviously out the door at the birds breakfasting at their feeder. "Is that true?"

"Ellie—" Astrid started.

But I was already talking, "Well, yeah—I took Dash for a walk before bed. I told you that. But that was a little after ten. Josie didn't get off work until midnight. I was fast asleep by the time she was killed."

"Not according to Pete. He says it was well after midnight," Lang said.

"Detective, seriously," Astrid broke in. "Bongo Pete doesn't know what time it is any given moment."

"He did see me earlier that day, but *way* earlier," I said. "He's a nice guy, and I wish him no ill, but he doesn't even know what *day* it is most of the time."

"He's willing to testify," Lang said, not breaking eye contact with me. "Come on, Lupe. We've got a bit more work to do before we can wrap this up. Oh, Ms. Allbright?"

"What?" I practically growled.

"I don't suppose you'd like to tell us where you hid the murder weapon."

"Very funny," I said, not liking how my voice wavered.

"Mmm. I'll see you outside, Detective." And he went out to the boardwalk.

I looked at Garcia, unable to keep the dismay off my face.

She had the grace to meet my eyes. "I'll ask you one more time," she said. "Do you know of anyone who might have wanted to hurt Josie Overland?"

I blinked. "Not yet."

"Does that mean you plan on finding out?"

I didn't answer.

"Because I can't *officially* recommend that," she said in a mild tone. "Now, what do I owe you for these items?"

"Oh, for heaven's sake." Frustration leaked out around my words. "The price is on the sachet. I don't know what to charge you for the cocoa butter, because it's a raw ingredient, which I don't usually sell. How about you double the price of the sachet, and we'll call it good?" I was overcharging her, but I didn't care.

Her chin dipped in a single decisive gesture. "That works." She reached into her pocket, extracted a few bills folded together, and handed me one. "I don't need any change."

Lang looked back at us from outside. I could almost sense his urge to tap his foot.

"Fine." I gave the money to Astrid, who went behind the counter and opened the register drawer.

"Thanks," Detective Garcia said, and joined her partner out on the boardwalk.

I turned to Astrid, who regarded me from behind the counter with one eyebrow raised. "Now what?" she asked.

My shoulders slumped. "Do you think Lang's trying to railroad me? All because of Harris?"

She leaned her hip against the counter. "Or to show how fast he can solve a murder. To impress the chief of police. Or to impress his new partner. I heard Lupe Garcia transferred from Las Vegas. He might feel like he has to prove something about his small-town department."

"More like he has to prove something about his small something else," I muttered under my breath.

Astrid heard me and grinned. Then she sobered. "Seriously, Ellie. What are you going to do?"

Reaching for the rose oil, I took a whiff and sighed. "I'm going back to the Roux later." Seeing her expression, I said, "I want to talk to Maggie again. Yesterday I didn't get a chance to find out what the fight between Harris and Josie was about. It's probably nothing, but you never know. Maybe I can talk to some of the other waitstaff, too." Not to mention that walking back into the restaurant the day before, while unsettling, had also made me feel as though I'd taken yet another aspect of my life back. Returning today might keep that momentum going.

"Yeah," she said slowly. But I could tell she was unconvinced.

I climbed onto one of the counter stools and swiveled to face my friend. "I need to find out more about Josie. I mean, *someone* hated her enough to kill her." I sighed. "It's a shame about her brother. If my sister was murdered, even if we weren't close, I'd be there in the thick of things."

"You *aren't* close to your sister," my friend said.

"Half sister," I said. "But that proves my point. If anything happened to her I'd at least show up in Los Angeles to see if I could help."

"Would Colby?" she asked.

"Sure," I said.

Astrid shrugged. "I don't know. Men are different." She pushed back and reached for her backpack on the floor. "Besides, Silver Wells is only forty minutes away. It's not like Josie's brother can't make the trip to Poppyville if the police need him for any reason."

"Somebody is going to have to clean out Josie's apartment," I said. "Maybe I'll go see him. Offer my condolences and see if there isn't some way I could help with that."

"Um, I don't think Detective Lang would like you 'help-ing' to dispose of Josie's things," Astrid said with a dry expression. "Not until you're cleared as a suspect at least."

Rubbing my hand over my face, I said, "Yeah, you're right. But I'd still like to talk to her brother, maybe learn something about her background. I knew so little about her." Out of nowhere, tears threatened. I blinked them away. "That's kind of awful, when you think about it. She worked for me at the Roux Grill and then here, and I didn't know too much about her."

"You can't be expected to know everything about everyone," Astrid said.

She was trying to help, I knew. But I still felt guilty. Hopping down from the stool, I reached behind the counter and retrieved a pad of paper and a pen to make a list.

"So one thing is to talk to her brother, Vance Overland." I looked up. "I wonder why they didn't get along?" I jotted a note on the pad. "Who else could have had it in for Josie?"

"Harris."

I grimaced and tapped the pen against my chin. "I thought of that. Still, I don't think he has it in him to stab anyone. He'd yell and swear, but if he ever *really* wanted someone dead and screwed up the courage to do it—which is pretty unlikely—he'd poison them. Stabbing is . . . too messy."

Slowly, Astrid nodded. "I see what you mean."

"Josie moved here a few years ago from Silver Wells. I was thinking about how sometimes the past can catch up with a person. For all we know, her murderer might not even be from here. That's one reason I want to talk to her brother."

Astrid looked skeptical.

"Yeah. Unlikely, huh. But who in town had it in for her? Her coworkers at the Roux Grill?"

"How about her creepy apartment manager?" Astrid made a face as though she'd just squished a spider.

Pointing my finger at my friend, I nodded. "Good point. Tom Steinhart definitely disliked her." I added him to my list. "What about her cleaning clients?" I looked up. "She was so busy that I think she only had three or four at any given time."

"Ooh," Astrid breathed. "But who knows what kinds of untoward secrets a housekeeper might stumble into?"

CHAPTER 11

I FELT a frisson of excitement at her words. I might just be able to pull off finding Josie's killer. And even if I couldn't, I could at least expand the suspect pool beyond yours truly. My shoulders slumped. "But I don't know who they were." Then I brightened. "I bet Maggie can tell me."

"Well, I know of one house Josie cleaned," Astrid said, swinging the backpack over her shoulder. "Gene and John Trace."

"John's involved with the community theater, isn't he?" I asked. "And as I recall, last year Gene helped Maria Canto with the fund-raiser to update the children's section in the library." From what else I knew, they were a couple of former Internet moguls from Silicon Valley who had retired to Poppyville about four years before.

"That's them," she said. "They live out on the south side of town, in that Frank Lloyd Wright–style place overlooking the river. But they're off the hook as murder suspects, because they've been gone a week. They won't be back from San Francisco until this afternoon."

"How do you know that?" I asked.

"I take care of their German shepherd when the guys are gone. I pick her up and board her at Dr. Ericsson's, then take her out for a run or two every day."

"Didn't you have to jog a German shepherd the other morning?" I asked. The morning before Josie died.

She nodded. "Yes, that's her. Alexandra. She's a sweetie—older, has arthritis."

"They sound pretty wealthy. I bet they could have hired someone to kill Josie," I mused.

Astrid rolled her eyes. "Right. Because that happens all the time in real life. Besides, those guys are so nice. Philanthropists and advocates for the homeless. I can't imagine Gene and John had any reason to dislike Josie, forget killing her."

"You know, I've always been curious about that house," I said with a smile.

"It's beautiful—if you like Prairie School architecture."

"I'd love to see inside," I hinted again. "Are you taking the dog to them, or do they pick her up?"

One side of her mouth pulled back as she caught my drift. "I'm taking Alexandra back to them this evening. You want to come with?"

I grinned. "That would be great." They might not be suspects, but perhaps they could tell me something useful about Josie.

"Okay, I'll let you know," she said with a smile in return.

Then it dropped as she glanced toward the door and changed the subject. "So what's the deal with Bongo Pete? Did you do something to make him angry?"

"Of course not. In fact I saw him the day before. He wanted to pet Dash—who loved it, of course. When Bongo Pete left he wasn't any different from usual."

"He's just mistaken, then," she said. "I'm sure anything he says won't stand up in court, anyway." She walked toward the door.

Astrid paused and shaded her eyes to peer out at the street. She turned to me and waggled her eyebrows. "Looks like you have company."

"Who?" I asked, looking at my watch. It was nine o'clock on the dot.

"It's Thea. And she's not alone." Astrid held the door open for the Nelsons. "The shop isn't open yet, but Ellie's here."

"Hey, Astrid," Thea said, stepping inside. "I'd like you to meet my brother, Ritter. He's helping me out at the nursery—at least for a while."

"Ellie mentioned you were back in town," Astrid said, stepping forward to shake his hand.

I felt myself blush.

"I'm Astrid Moneypenny."

"Astrid," he said. "Saw you with Elliana at the Roux Grill yesterday. Nice to meet you."

"The Roux?" Thea asked.

"Welcome to Poppyville," Astrid said, saving me from answering. I wondered whether Thea knew Cynthia Beck had already snagged drinks with her brother.

And who knows what else . . .

"I've got to go, but I'm sure we'll run into each other again. See you later, Elligator," Astrid said.

After she'd gone, Thea turned to me. "I was showing Ritter what's changed in Poppyville since he's been gone, and we brought along that mushroom compost you were looking for yesterday. Ritter, go get it."

"Yes, ma'am," he said with good humor. "Elliana, where would you like it?"

"Oh! Out back. Through the gate there at the end of the boardwalk." I walked over to point it out. As I stood next to him, the top of my head didn't even come up to his chin. He still smelled of cedar, but now it was tempered with the scent of running water, subtle and enticing.

I looked up at him. "Or just leave it out here. I can take it back to the garden."

He looked surprised. "I won't hear of it."

"She's stronger than she looks," Thea said.

Ritter smiled at me. "No doubt."

I felt a tingle.

His grin widened, and for a moment I wondered if my face had betrayed my thoughts. Then he turned away and strode out to Thea's step-side pickup.

"Let's grab some coffee and meet him out there," I said to her.

Thea raised her eyebrows at me. "I thought you said the gate was cordoned off. Is it okay to go out there now?"

"It turns out Josie was actually attacked in the park. The police released the boardwalk just before you got here," I said. "I'll open up the shop a bit later. And you know I can't resist showing off the garden. I'd like Ritter to see your handiwork."

She harrumphed. "Mostly your handiwork, Ellie, and you know it."

I shrugged. "I couldn't have created the Enchanted Garden without you. Besides, I have something I want to ask you about."

We went through the shop and grabbed three mugs of coffee and some of Astrid's ginger softies. I slid open the door, and we stepped out to the patio. Ritter had dumped the bag of compost by the hose spigot. He distractedly took the steaming mug from his sister, his head swinging back and forth as he studied the plantings, the fence line, and the flagstones.

I was pleased that there was little evidence that careless feet had tromped through the garden. I'd trimmed the lavender into a neat mound, removed the broken rose canes and snapped cone flowers, and smoothed the crushed hazelnut shells I used as mulch. I'd even had time to repair the green sea glass path that lead to the purple fairy door.

"So you found Josie out front?" Thea asked.

"Yes," I said quietly. "Her foot was caught in the gate there."

Ritter looked over at me. "That must have been scary."

"It was. And it sure doesn't help that"—I licked my lips—"the police still consider me their best suspect." I'd left out that tidbit the previous afternoon when I'd filled in the Nelsons on Josie's murder.

Now Ritter eyed me. "You? Why?"

I ticked the reasons off on my fingers. "Because she died here. Because I found her. And because she was dating my ex-husband."

He tipped his head to the side, his gaze assessing. "And you still have a thing for your ex."

"No!" I cleared my throat. "Sorry. No, I don't. But that didn't stop him from telling the police that I was crazy jealous, and that made them assume I wanted Josie dead."

Thea said, "Wait a minute. I thought the police figured out Josie was attacked in the park, not here."

"That's right. But you know what?" I held up my pinkie finger. "The fourth reason they think I killed her is because Bongo Pete says he saw me walking Dash after midnight—in Raven Creek Park."

Ritter sat down on another rocker, his brow wrinkle deepening. "Bongo Pete?"

"Homeless guy who does odd jobs for Gessie," Thea explained. "But . . . were you even there, Ellie?"

"See? Anyone in town would have asked the same question, given the source of the information." I sighed, and my voice lowered. "But yeah, I was there. I couldn't sleep, so Dash and I went out for a bit of fresh air a bit after ten."

"What were you thinking?" She sounded scandalized. "Walking by yourself at night like that—and in a secluded area, too."

I shrugged. "I was thinking that this is Poppyville, and taking a quick walk after dark would be fine. Dash was with me. And you know what? It *was* fine." I turned toward where I'd found Josie. "Well, except for . . . you know. And I did hear a rustle, behind me in the trees, on my way back."

Thea closed her eyes and pressed her lips together.

Ritter muttered, "Jeez," under his breath.

"But Bongo Pete was wrong about when he saw me. If he saw me at all," I said.

"The man definitely has a unique relationship with time—and reality," Thea said, and then to Ritter. "Pete is a good guy, nice, but he has some problems."

"When I was walking in the park that night," I said, "Josie was still at work at the Roux Grill. But I can't prove that." I took a deep breath. "I feel terrible that she's dead. Someone needs to pay for that—but not me. If Detective Lang is going to focus entirely on making the case against me, then I need to come up with a better answer for the next time Detective Garcia asks if I know of anyone who might have wanted to hurt Josie."

Thea leaned forward. "Is that what you wanted to ask me about?"

Actually, I'd wanted to ask her about the strange vine that had appeared near the birdbath. I turned toward it and opened my mouth to ask if she recognized it, but instead found myself asking, "Would you go to Silver Wells with me to talk with Josie's brother?"

CHAPTER 12

THEA and Ritter both looked surprised. He leaned his elbows on his knees and gazed up at me from under his brow. "Why do you want to talk to him?"

"I was hoping he might be able to tell me something about Josie that would help find her killer. And I thought having someone else along might be a good idea."

Thea raised an eyebrow.

"Detective Garcia said that Josie and her brother didn't get along. I don't know the guy, and have no idea what he might do or say." I glanced at Ritter. "For all I know, Vance Overland could be crazy or violent. And he might have really hated Josie."

"Enough to kill her?" Ritter asked, getting right to the meat of what I'd been trying to say.

I lifted one shoulder and let it drop again.

"Ellie, I don't know if going to see her brother is such

a good idea," Thea said, looking thoughtful. "What if Max Lang finds out?"

"What if he does? He's not interested in finding any evidence that doesn't point to me, and he seems to be the one leading the investigation." Never mind that Lang had also come right out and told me not to leave town.

"I don't know . . ."

"I'm going to Silver Wells whether you come with me or not," I heard myself say, surprised at the determination in my voice.

"You can't just call him?" Thea tried again.

"I'll go with you, Elliana," Ritter said. "If you think it might be dangerous, maybe it would be better to have a guy with you." He raised his palm. "Not that you can't take care of yourself, or that you and my sister here wouldn't be a formidable team. I'm just sayin'."

Relief flooded Thea's face. "Ritter, no one is taking offense. And honestly, it would be hard for me to get away from the nursery for a chunk of time right now—we're busy as blazes. Still, I don't want Ellie to go alone. I'd feel a lot better if you went with her."

Ritter rocked forward. "What do you say, Elliana. Will I do as a fill-in for my sister?"

Boy, will you!

But I simply smiled and said, "That'd be great. Thanks for the offer."

He tipped an imaginary hat. "My pleasure, ma'am. Just let me know when you want to go to Silver Wells. I'll drive if Thea will let me borrow her truck."

Thea grinned. "Sure, big brother. If you remember how to drive in the big city after being in the field for so long."

He stood. "I think I can manage."

She rose, too, giving me a little wink that made me wonder if she was really as busy at Terra Green as she'd claimed, or if this was a ploy for me to spend some time with Ritter.

Either way, it was okay with me.

Ritter looked at me and said, "What do you say? This afternoon?"

"Oh, gosh," I said, figuring timetables in my head. Lang had intimated that they had to tie up only a few loose ends before arresting me. "Sooner is better, but I should check with Astrid to see if she can watch the shop." If I absolutely had to, though, I'd keep Scents & Nonsense closed for the rest of the day. Clearing my name was more important at the moment.

The thought that I had to make that choice made me angry at Max Lang all over again.

"Forget that. I'll call her, but let's go ahead and make a plan," I said. "How does one thirty sound?"

"Perfect," Ritter said.

I saw them to the front door and locked it behind them. Given the circumstances, I wondered if it was wrong to feel such anticipation about going on this little venture with Ritter. Returning to the garden, I saw that the plant beneath the birdbath appeared to have grown a couple of inches just since that morning. And now there was a hint of purplish petals beginning to push one of the buds open.

Maybe I'd get a chance to ask Ritter about it later that day, I thought as I went in to get my wallet from the kitchen counter. After all, he was a botanist, and probably knew as much, or more, about plants as Thea did.

I knew I wouldn't ask, though. For some reason, that plant didn't want to be talked about.

Stuffing my wallet in my pocket, I returned to the shop, dialing Astrid's cell as I walked back through the Enchanted Garden. When she didn't answer, I left a message. Since she'd left work at the veterinary clinic early the day before, my bet was she wouldn't have time to watch the shop while I went to Silver Wells with Ritter. Still, it couldn't hurt to ask.

I'm going to have to find another helper. Maybe someone who can come in more often than twice a week.

I was in the office checking to see if there were any phone messages on the landline, when the sound of someone trying the front door brought Dash to his feet like a pointer. I tried to ignore it, but couldn't. I rose and left the office to explain that the shop would be closed for a while longer.

Inga Fowler stood with her nose nearly touching the glass door, one hand cupped around her eyes to shield them from the morning glare, while the other firmly clasped the hand of a three-year-old boy. A little girl, maybe a year older than her brother, stood on her other side. Inga took a step back, frowning when she saw the hastily scribbled sign I'd placed in the window:

CLOSED DUE TO EMERGENCY

Then she saw me approaching and waved. I unlocked the door and gestured her inside. As usual, Inga looked as if she'd fallen right off a catalog page: black yoga pants with a high-end logo on the hip, a tight tank in lime green that showed off her stick-thin arms, and she'd harnessed her long straight blond hair with a leather scrunchie at the base of her neck. Nervous energy came off her in waves.

She tugged her son forward, while the little girl trailed behind. They were also perfectly dressed and tidy. "I got your message that you had my perfume ready and thought I'd pick it up on the way to the gym." Inga pointed to the placard taped to the glass. "Then I saw that. Is everything all right?"

Glancing down at the kids I said, "Hey guys. You want to check out the fairy gardens out back?"

"Yes, please!" the little girl said.

Inga looked surprised. "We have only a few minutes . . ." Then she saw my face, and realized I didn't want to talk in front of the kids. "Molly, you can go on out for a little while. Take your brother with you."

"There are some cookies by the coffee urn," I said.

"Just one," Inga called to Molly with a tight smile before turning to me. "I try to limit their sugar."

Her daughter stopped by the plate and scooped up a couple of ginger softies. She glanced at her mother, handed one to her little brother, then led him outside. I heard her say, "Lookit this! I bet a whole family of fairies live in that tree. Oh! Hello, cat!" Her voice faded as she moved farther into the Enchanted Garden.

Inga and I went as far as the back door, so she could keep an eye on them. They were stooped over now, looking at one of the tiny pathways that disappeared into a cluster of purple sage. She turned to me with a questioning look. "Is it bad?"

I took a deep breath. "You know Josie Overland, don't you?"

A quick intake of breath, a flash of anxiety in her eyes. She nodded. "Of course. She cleans for me every two weeks."

"Oh, gosh. I didn't know that," I said. *With Astrid's Internet moguls that makes two housecleaning clients of Josie's.* "You heard what happened to her, then."

The skin on her face tightened with alarm, and her trademark anxiousness flashed again. "No. We've been in Sacramento for the last week. Just got back into town last night."

And two for two out of town at the time of the murder. I suppressed a sigh.

Inga was always high-strung, but today it was worse than usual. She called the concoction I made for her "perfume," and it did smell delightful, but in truth it was an aromatherapy remedy I'd developed to help her battle the nervous worry she was so prone to. I didn't know what caused it—perhaps the stress of feeling as if she had to be so perfect all the time. Her husband, Brock Fowler, was wealthy from several different sources, and rumor had it he had some big political aspirations. I also didn't know whether Inga took any prescription medication to soothe her anxiety, but I did know that the blend of lavender, sweet marjoram, ylang-ylang, and rosewood helped to calm her.

I didn't like having to tell her Josie was dead when she was in such a state of disquiet; I was already empathically picking up on her energy to the point where I felt jittery. Nevertheless, I plunged ahead as gently as I could.

"Honey, I'm afraid she's gone."

"What do you mean, 'gone'?" Her voice rose. Molly looked back at her mother from the far side of the garden.

"She was killed two nights ago," I said.

Inga's anxiety ratcheted way up, and I felt my own heartbeat quicken.

I put my hand on her arm. "Let me get you your perfume, and then I'll tell you all about it." I practically ran into the office to retrieve it. Quickly, I unscrewed the cap and took a deep whiff of it myself. Instantly, the jumpiness I'd absorbed dissipated.

Hurrying back out to where she waited, I thrust the bottle into her hand. I wanted to slather it under her nose. There was no need, however. She immediately spun the cap off and dabbed a bit behind her ears before breathing the vapor directly. Her eyes closed, and I watched her reassert control. After a moment, they snapped back open. "So what was it? Some kind of accident?"

I filled her in on the details.

"That's horrible," she finally whispered. Her gaze went to her children. "In Poppyville? But Brock and I moved here to get away from the big city with all its crime. We wanted to raise our kids where it was safe."

"I know how you feel. But this is an anomaly—you know? The police will catch whoever did it, and things will go back to normal. It's a safe place—I'm sure of it." I couldn't help defending the town I loved so much.

Inga looked skeptical. "Where did it happen?"

"In the park."

"If it happened in the park, then why are you closed?" she asked.

"I hope to open Scents and Nonsense again this afternoon," I nonanswered.

Distracted, Inga didn't pursue it. She gave me her credit card and called for her children as I got the charge approved. As they came inside, I was happy to see their noses were a bit pink and their hair messy. Molly had a smear of mud on her tennis shoe, just like a normal little kid. Her mother didn't seem to notice, still preoccupied by the bad news I'd just given her.

When they left, driving west toward the gym, I locked the front door again and let Dash out to the garden. Walking down to my house, I passed the strange waxy-leaved plant by the birdbath. In the past fifteen minutes, a single bud on the interloper had unfurled into a deep plum-colored bloom: seven-petaled with a pale blue center and bright orange pollen-covered stamens that reached toward the sun. I'd never seen anything like it in any of my horticultural studies or any of my books.

My books. But now that I could see what the flowers looked like, I seemed to remember something like that in Gamma's nature journal.

Just because I'd decided to end my self-imposed banishment from the restaurant didn't mean I wanted to deal with my ex again right away. I checked my watch. It was ten minutes to eleven. Harris left for the bank at eleven thirty every day, and then he stopped by the post office before coming back to the Roux to help with the lunch rush. My guess was his routine hadn't changed just because I wasn't in the picture anymore.

So, I could spare a few minutes to try to identify the mystery plant.

"Come on, Dash. Let's take a quick look."

I retrieved the journal from under the staircase and brought it out to where the new flower had taken root. Bumblebees droned nearby as I flipped through the pages, scanning drawings and descriptions in Gamma's flowery script. A recipe for cowslip cordial caught my eye.

To Procure Sleep and Rest.
Cowslips aka Fairy Cups.
Means Winning Grace.

Whatever "winning grace" meant, procuring sleep and rest seemed like a pretty good idea. I made a mental note and kept searching.

There! In the center of the book, I saw the plant that was growing under the birdbath. I smiled broadly and whispered. "I knew you'd know what it is, Gamma."

The wind chimes tinkled, and I looked up. There was no breeze. They tinkled again.

Frowning, I returned my attention to the drawing. It was faded, certainly, but visible. She'd rendered it in colored pencil, yet somehow managed to capture the waxy texture of the leaves along with the whimsical corkscrew of the stem like something out of a children's picture book. Her version showed seven blooms at the top of the plant, just as the buds on the one in front of me promised. Each had seven petals, plum-colored and silkylooking, decorated with sky blue spots down near the stem and arrayed around brilliant orange stamens fluffy with pollen.

A notation well below the faded drawing had an

arrow pointing toward the depiction of the flower. It took me a while to make out all the letters. They spelled "mnemosyne."

My forehead squinched. The name was familiar, but I couldn't place it.

And there was writing in a spiral around the flower as well. I squinted to make it out, turning the journal slowly in my hands to follow the circular writing, which turned out to be a kind of verse.

> *Hidden memory,*
> *Unbound*
> *Only when ready,*
> *When needed.*
> *And however heady,*
> *Best heeded.*

And below that, a block of less cryptic information.

> *Aids in the access of memory. Rare convolvulus. Cannot be cultivated; seeds germinate only in the perfect medium of time and readiness.*

The perfect medium of time and readiness? Okay, that bit wasn't less cryptic. I kept reading.

> *Fast growing and extremely short-lived. Single harvest. Distill flowers only. Use with caution; powerful and sometimes dangerous in essential form. Always dilute with carrier oil.*

As I read each word, I grew more excited. This was something new. Something I'd never encountered before, heard of before, and . . . my breath caught as I read the last line.

Anticipated by potent unique fragrance, intoxicating to those of us with the gift.

The scent that had teased and plagued me for the last two days suddenly enveloped me. It was coming from the plant! I looked back at the journal.

Mnemosyne. Squeezing my eyes shut and inhaling deeply, I reached back to a Greek mythology class I'd taken in college years before. Mnemosyne was a goddess. Like Narcissus, also the name of a plant, apparently. What had she been the goddess of? I opened my eyes, and shook my head. I couldn't remember. I whipped out my phone and did a quick search. The name did not bring up any reference to a flower, even when I added "convolvulus" to the keywords. However, I did discover that Mnemosyne was the Greek goddess of memory.

Which made perfect sense, given Gamma's notes.

But what had her reference to a gift been about? Was she just talking about having a sense of smell that was so fine-tuned that I could use it to sense emotion? Or something else? A feather of memory tickled at the periphery of my mind. When I reached for it, though, it wisped away like vapor.

I looked down at Dash, who had rolled onto his back beneath the plant and stared up at the sky with half-closed eyes, totally blissed out. For a split second, I actually thought about joining him, but I pushed the feeling away.

"Mnemosyne," I muttered, and took one last look at the picture before closing the journal. The scent of the plant was just as strong, and I still reveled in it, but now it didn't affect me as intensely as it had the first few times I'd smelled it. Perhaps simply knowing where it came from helped take the edge off. Again, a swirl of memories teased from some back room in my mind as I inhaled the heady fragrance, but try as I might that door wasn't ready to open yet.

I must distill the essence of this flower. Soon, but not yet.

I didn't know what I'd find, but I felt sure the mnemosyne had germinated in the Enchanted Garden for good reason. I felt obligated to preserve it. Gamma would have expected me to.

The senescence—the natural life span—of anything that grew so quickly would likely be quite short. However, I also wanted to be able to use as many of the full blooms as possible. Using my copper steam distiller, I would be able to extract at least a few precious drops of essential oil, as well as the concentrated liquid hydrosol.

If this emits such a heady perfume now, I wonder what it will be like concentrated a hundred times?

I was counting the buds that had yet to bloom when Dash bounded to his feet, barked, and took off after a squirrel. It ran up the apple tree, and he stopped at the bottom. Not for the first time, I marveled that he never dug in the dirt and seemed to understand how delicate the miniature tableaus were. Even on the hunt, as he was now, he skirted the tiny gazebo next to the trunk.

"Come on, tough guy," I said, and headed to the house at the back of the lot. He lost interest in the squirrel, which was chattering his displeasure at both of us.

On the front step, I opened Gamma's journal to take one last look at the mnemosyne flower. As I gazed at the purple blossoms on the page, a light wind blew through the oak leaves, and I could have sworn it carried the faintest of giggles.

CHAPTER 13

✣

Leaving Nabokov dozing in the garden, Dash and I retraced the path down Corona Street to the Roux Grill.

The foot traffic was brisk, but not nearly as crowded as it sometimes became when Poppyville hosted a festival or event. I loved to see the varied mix of people our little town attracted. Bermuda shorts–clad retirees mixed with entire families on vacation and moony-eyed couples on romantic getaways.

In between wishing people good morning and sidestepping the occasional stroller, I pondered what I knew—and didn't know—about Josie Overland. There seemed to be a lot more of the latter. What had her life been like growing up? Had her mother died when she was as young as I'd been when mine had passed? What was her father like? If she had only a brother now, some tragedy must have marked her life.

At least I had my half siblings and my dad. He and my stepmom had moved to Pompano Beach, Florida, years before. After my mother was gone, he'd mourned her for over four years before remarrying. My stepmom was a dynamo, volunteering for so many good causes it was like a full-time job. I was closest to Colby, and even though I didn't see him very often, we were good about keeping in regular touch by phone. Still, he was due for a visit, soon, and the next time I talked to him I was going to remind him of that.

My half sister, Darcy, was ten years younger than me and a serious type-A go-getter who sold high-end real estate in Los Angeles. She was a huge success, and I wished her the best. She was a bit skeptical of the mundane—and not terribly lucrative—career choices Colby and I had made.

I might have been a fifth-generation Poppyvillian, but it was on my mother's side. None of my living family shared that history, or my deep love of the town and its environs. But Mama and Gamma had. I mused for a few minutes on the journal, on the mnemosyne flower, and on Gamma's cryptic verse.

Hidden memory,
Unbound
Only when ready,
When needed.
And however heady,
Best heeded.

What had she meant by that? To me it sounded as if the appearance of the plant was some kind of sign. I didn't know if that was crazy or if it made perfect sense, but the idea was intriguing.

The perfect medium of time and readiness.

It was true that the soil of my life felt rich and ready after the last year. I never would have thought that would engender an actual plant, though. I'd been thinking more in terms of eventual romance.

And that made me think of Ritter—who was seeing Cynthia Beck, but was also taking me to Silver Wells that afternoon. Not that it was a date, but still. Astrid would approve.

And thinking of going to Silver Wells brought me full circle back to who could have killed Josie.

Could it have been someone at the Roux Grill? I couldn't believe it—at least not any of the people that I'd worked with. But there were new people there now. The redheaded cook for one. The sharp-looking waitress in Josie's photographs for another. I'd ask Maggie more about them if I got the chance. She was as bad—or good—of a gossip as one could hope to find in a small town.

Then there was Josie's brother. I could only hope he might know who held a grudge against his sister. Or maybe he'd made the trip over from Silver Wells and attacked her himself. I hated to think such a thing, but it sure hadn't sounded like either of the detectives had spent much time talking with him. I crossed my fingers that I'd have better luck in person.

Dash jogging by my side, I strode by the ice-cream shop, inhaled the yeasty goodness of fresh bread outside Kneadful Things, and waved to Maria, who was deadheading geraniums in front of the library. She saw me and waved back with a smile. She was one of my regular customers. At least I wasn't persona non grata in Poppyville . . . yet.

As I neared the restaurant, I recalled Inga's fearful reaction to the news of the murder. Of course, I didn't want to be arrested for something I hadn't done, and the idea that Detective Lang's shortsighted investigation might also let the real killer go free in my little town made my blood boil.

A group of tourists ambled by holding dripping chili dogs from the Pie in the Sky Snack Shop. The boardwalk was full of people enjoying the sunshine. I sighed. All I really wanted to do was tend to my garden and run Scents & Nonsense.

At the Roux Grill, I led Dash around to the tie-up area for dogs. He lapped up some of the complimentary water from the communal dish and settled into the shade with a friendly labradoodle.

I braced myself for the second time in two days, and stiff-armed the door open.

Inside, the atmosphere felt lighter than it had when Astrid and I had visited the previous afternoon. Maggie waved to me from behind the bar. "Harris isn't here, hon. He's at the bank."

I felt my shoulders relax at her words. *Nice to be right about something.*

The place was busy even though it was the middle of

the week. In addition to the meaty dinner entrees, the Roux was known for its amazing brunch menu. Harris had developed it, and the head chef, Raleigh Stone, implemented it to perfection. Right now, Raleigh would be buzzing around the kitchen, keeping things moving smoothly and quickly. He was not only an experienced chef, but a superb manager.

On the weekends there was a Bloody Mary bar by the fireplace, stocked with flavored vodkas and all manner of mixers and spices, vegetables, pickles, olives, slabs of crispy bacon, and skewers of jalapeño peppers and savory cheese. During the week, Maggie made customers' drinks to order, but the full menu was still available. It consisted mostly of diner breakfast fare with an upscale flair.

Waxy potatoes from a local farm were diced and tossed with onions, peppers, sweet potatoes, and fresh herbs, then roasted until brown and chewy with caramelization. Another farmer supplied fresh eggs daily, their deep orange yolks and rich flavor the result of hens living on pasture. Those gems went into fluffy omelets and four types of Eggs Benedict: lox and cream cheese with capers and béarnaise; caprese with tomatoes and fresh mozzarella dosed with nutty pesto; roasted green chilies and chorizo with homemade salsa; and the standard Canadian bacon and lemony hollandaise.

I loved the fluffy buttermilk biscuits under a blanket of gravy spiked with chunks of spicy Italian sausage. The cinnamon-roll French toast was to die for, too, but my all-time favorite was the croque monsieur—a grilled ham and cheese sandwich typically smothered in béchamel sauce, but at the Roux Grill it was served drowning in a rich poblano cream that made my mouth water just thinking about it.

Despite everything I loved about my new life, I had to admit I didn't eat nearly as well now. I needed to do something about that.

A tall man vacated a seat at the end of the bar, and I slid onto it. "That's okay," I said to Maggie. "I'm not here to see Harris."

"Who are you here to see, then, Ellie?" Maggie put her elbows on the bar and propped her chin on her hands. Her light hair was frizzy, and her round face shone with a light glow of perspiration. She looked overheated in her black T-shirt with the flame logo on it. "You want something to drink?"

"You," I said. "And I'll take a ginger ale. How's business been?"

She frowned and reached for a glass from under the bar. "Good. It's always good."

I tilted my head. "So why do you have that look on your face?"

Her lips pressed together as she considered me. But Maggie wasn't one to keep things to herself. "Business is good, but Harris cut back hours. For everyone."

"That doesn't make sense. How can you handle the traffic?"

Her eyes flared, but her voice lowered. Not that the couple sitting next to me had any attention to spare from each other. "By working like dogs—and making less money than ever. We're so busy that our service isn't as good as usual, so tips are down, too."

"Josie never told me that. I'm sorry to hear it."

"He cut my hours *again* on Monday. Josie was furious. Sweet thing that she was, she went to bat for me with Harris."

"You did mention they got in a big fight Monday night." I took a swallow of ginger ale, savoring the sweet fizziness on my tongue.

Her head inclined. "That was it. She said she had other income, so she could walk away from this job anytime and still make ends meet. Not all of the staff have the same luxury, especially those with families. She, um . . ." Maggie paused, then seemed to make a decision. "Well, they were in the office with the door closed. But, you know"— she waved her hand—"a few of us were in the kitchen and overheard."

She meant they had all been eavesdropping, but I wasn't about to call her on it.

"Anyway, Josie said maybe you were right when you told her to be careful with Harris."

My lips parted in surprise. "Uh-oh." I ran my hand over my face. "I imagine Harris didn't take too kindly to hearing that from his girlfriend."

She barked a laugh, then clamped her hand over her mouth. "Oops." Her eyes cut left and right but no one was paying attention. "No," she said. "He didn't appreciate Josie bringing you up at all." She tsked. "Lordy, that man does love to yell."

No kidding. But it was hardly a motive for murder.

A sharp-featured woman with hair the color of peanut butter elbowed in next to me. With a start, I recognized one of the waitresses from Josie's photos. I shifted away from her, feeling as though my personal space had been invaded.

She didn't seem to notice.

"Bloody Mary, spicy, no celery, extra pickle. Mimosa— number three for the lush in the corner over there. And a glass of iced tea." She rattled off the order without bothering to even look at Maggie, instead checking her lipstick in the mirror behind the bar.

"You know where the tea is," Maggie said mildly.

"Can't you just get it with the rest of the drinks?" the waitress said.

"That's not how it works."

The woman sighed, then turned to see me watching her.

"Something wrong?" she asked.

"Not at all," I said.

She held my gaze for a few more seconds, then moved behind the bar to fill up a glass from the iced tea pitcher. Maggie had the rest of the drinks ready by then, and the waitress hefted the tray and carried it out to the dining room without a word.

I looked around the room again. The tables were almost full, but there were only two waitresses working them. "I know Rhonda, of course," I said to Maggie as I watched the mousy woman bus a table. "But who was that?" I gestured with my chin toward the rude woman with the bony elbows.

"That's Shyla," Maggie said. Something in her voice sharpened my focus on the waitress. She cast a furtive look down at one of Rhonda's tables as she passed. The party was getting ready to leave, and I got the distinct feeling she was scoping the tip. An elderly woman called to her, and she sauntered over, shrugged at whatever the customer said, and turned toward the kitchen. As she did so, I saw her roll her eyes.

"I'm not sure about that one," I said.

Maggie snorted her agreement. "She's dating the cook. The other day I couldn't find either of them, and stumbled on them necking in the alley."

"Oh, brother." I rolled my own eyes. "Wait—not Raleigh. He's still happily married, isn't he?"

She laughed. "He is. I'm talking about Karl."

"The cook I met yesterday," I said.

Putting a coaster under my drink, she nodded. "Karl Evers. He's pretty new. Been here six months or so. Clumsy, as you've seen, but still pretty good at his job. But he's a horrible flirt. Shyla doesn't like it one bit, either."

"Did he flirt with Josie?"

Maggie gave an exaggerated nod and bent toward me. "He sure did. More than any of the others." She tipped her head to the side. "One time he said something that made me think they might have dated before he started working here."

"Did Harris know that?"

She shrugged. "I don't know. But Shyla might have known. She absolutely despised Josie." She glanced over at the waitress, who was now gazing off into space and snapping her gum while a nearby table tried to get her attention. "And that girl can be mean, I tell you."

Hmm. "Where did Karl work before he came to Roux Grill?" I asked.

"Over at the Sapphire," Maggie said. "Before that, I don't know. He's a pretty good cook, though. Says he wants to go to culinary school and become a real chef someday. The guy's got ambition; I have to give him that."

"And a tendency to drop things."

She laughed. "That, too. But he's talented." She shifted position and changed the subject. "I don't suppose you need any help at Scents and Nonsense. I could sure use the money." Her face fell. "Not that I'm trying to take advantage . . . I mean, I know Josie worked for you . . . God, I feel like a jerk."

"No, no. Don't feel like that." I hesitated. Harris would just love it if I hired another employee from the Roux to work at my shop. Still, he was cutting everyone's hours, and I could really use the help. Plus, I already knew Maggie would be a great addition to the shop. I made the decision and put my hand on her wrist. "I'd love to have you work for me. I can pay you a bit more per hour than here, but there won't be any tips."

"I'll take it!"

We grinned at each other like idiots for a few seconds.

"When are you off here?" I asked, looking at my watch. Harris was going to be back in fifteen minutes, or so.

"This afternoon." She checked the clock over the fireplace. "At one. Starting today, I only work through lunch."

"Can you come by Scents and Nonsense when you're done here? I need to leave for the afternoon, and I'd love to keep the shop open."

She looked surprised. "Today? Really? Don't you want to train me?"

"I'm sure you'll pick up on it in no time. And if anyone has any questions you can't answer, just take their number, and I'll get back to them. For right now, I just want the doors open and someone to run the register."

"Well, I can do that," she said, eyes bright. "I'll come right over when I'm done here. And, Ellie? Thanks!"

I smiled. "Thank *you*. We can talk about some regular hours later."

She nodded as a large group entered the restaurant. Soon she was helping to pull tables together to seat a raucous family of twelve.

With everyone's attention on the new arrivals, I left my half-finished ginger ale and slipped down the bank of booths to the door to the kitchen. I wanted to say hello to Raleigh since I rarely ran into him outside of the Roux. Instead, I found a young Hispanic man I didn't know working the grill. I nodded and smiled at him, but he was busy keeping about eight orders going. As I watched, he flipped three pancakes, turned a row of bacon, and started an omelet.

The door to the walk-in freezer—the one of Wanda Simmons fame—was open, and I heard rustling inside. I was working up the gumption to see if Raleigh was back there—looking in that freezer wasn't high on my list of fun things to do—when the door of Harris' office opened, nearly giving me a heart attack.

But it was only Raleigh. When he saw me, his leathery face creased into a grin and his eyes lit up.

"Ellie!" His deep, South Carolina accent flowed around my name like honey.

We hugged, and then he stepped back to eye me up and down. It was a fatherly assessment, which resulted in a frown.

"You're too skinny."

He took a couple of steps to the grill and grabbed two pieces of Texas toast. He wedged a slab of Cheddar and a few rounds of Canadian bacon between them, along with a smear of Major Grey's mango chutney, and put the sandwich on the grill. He pressed a bacon iron on top for weight and turned back to me.

"Raleigh," I said with a laugh, "I came back to the kitchen to say hello, not for you to feed me."

"We can do both," he said.

So, while he mixed up another batch of sausage gravy, he gave me the CliffsNotes version of how his family— wife, four children, and six grandchildren—was faring. He handed me the hot, crunchy, sweet, salty, smoky sandwich when it was done, and I dove in as I listened.

It wasn't long before he began rubbing spices into a giant brisket destined for the smoker and I changed the subject to Josie.

"Do you know of any trouble she was having with anyone?" I asked, and took another bite.

He looked up at me from under his bushy eyebrows. "Not that I know of. That was one who kept to herself, though. Friendly, but not one to jabber. She had depths, but I doubt anyone here at work knew much about them." He looked thoughtful. "Except Maggie, maybe."

My lips parted in surprise. "Do you think she had secrets?"

His smile was rueful. "Ellie, we all have secrets. Don't you?"

I didn't say anything. There were things I didn't talk about. Did that make them secrets?

Probably so.

"See?"

"Hey, boss?" The grill cook's voice was tentative, but when Raleigh looked over he pointed at the customer orders that were piling up.

I waved at him. "I'm sorry. Didn't mean to interrupt—I know this is a busy time of day. Just wanted to say hi."

"Darlin', you come by anytime you want to. I'll make time for you."

"Thanks, Raleigh." I gave him a warm smile, popped the last bite of sandwich in my mouth, and slid off the stool I'd been sitting on.

A year ago the head chef and kitchen manager hadn't been working the line. If I'd realized how his duties had expanded—no doubt a result of Harris' cutbacks on hours—I never would have monopolized his time.

"Karl!" he bellowed, making me jump. "Where are you?"

The red-haired cook hurried out of the walk-in. "Here, boss. Oh!" he said when he saw me. And then a more rueful "Oh" when he saw the orders. "Sorry, boss." He reached for the slips and began gathering ingredients.

I turned to go, hoping to be able to ask Maggie one last question, when I saw the poor little philodendron hanging in the corner of Harris' office. Grabbing a water glass, I filled it at the industrial sink. Wrinkling my nose at the smell of his stupid aftershave, I went in to give the dry plant a drink. Upon examination, it wasn't dead. It needed some fertilizer and to move from the dark corner into the sunshine.

Not my place, though. Harris would throw a fit if I started moving stuff around in his office. I eyed the closed blinds and decided against opening them.

"Sorry, little guy," I said to the philodendron. "Good luck."

I swung the office door back open. Karl stood right outside as if waiting for me. His eyes twinkled. "I thought I saw you go in there."

"I was watering the plant," I said.

"Uh-huh," Karl said with a grin. "I get it. So did you find whatever you were looking for?"

I glared at him and turned toward the door to the dining area. "I wasn't looking for anything!"

He sniffed. I took a step.

"Sure you don't want to go out the back door?" he asked.

"Don't be ridiculous."

"Harris will be very interested to learn you were in his office."

"Well, you be sure and tell him the second he gets back, then," I said. It would have been nice if my voice hadn't warbled, though.

His lips turned down, creating parentheses around his mouth. "Don't worry. Your secret is safe with me."

I rolled my eyes. "See you later, Raleigh," I called.

He looked up from plating an order and waved.

If anything, it was busier out front. Maggie was mixing and shaking drinks like a madwoman, and didn't even see me leave.

I'll ask her about Josie's cleaning clients when she comes to work for me this afternoon.

The thought that I'd be able to open Scents & Nonsense that afternoon buoyed me as I untied Dash and we headed home.

CHAPTER 14

❧

Back at Scents & Nonsense, I finally opened the doors for the first time in a day and a half. Almost immediately a young couple came in the shop. The woman spent several minutes perusing the fragrant body oils while her boyfriend grabbed a ginger softie and went out to the Enchanted Garden. He settled into a seat by one of the bistro tables in the sun, seemingly content to eat his cookie and read something on his phone while she shopped. The woman finally chose a potent combination of juniper berry and basil with a soupçon of sandalwood mixed in as a base note. I inhaled the scents from across the room, smiling at her as she made her way to the register and paid for her purchase.

While she browsed, I'd looked up Vance Overland in Silver Wells on the Internet. He worked for a firm called Clary, Bittel and Sorgenson. Sounded pretty fancy schmancy. It occurred to me that Josie's brother might not be available that afternoon. If not, I wondered if I could convince Ritter to wait until after hours and try to catch him away from work. The thought made me itchy, though. I didn't have time to waste.

There were pictures of the three partners online, but none of Vance. However, remembering the photo of the man on Josie's wall, I thought I had a pretty good idea of what Josie's brother looked like. He might say they didn't get along, but Josie had his picture up in her apartment where she could see it every day. Vance must have been a lot angrier with his sister than she'd been with him.

As soon as my customers had gone, I crossed my fingers and punched in the number of the law firm on my business landline. I waited through three rings, and then a woman answered.

"Clary, Bittel and Sorgenson."

"Hi. I'd like to talk with Mr. . . . wait. No. I would like to make an appointment with Mr. Overland." I'd pay for his time, if I had to.

"Really?"

Her response confused me. "He does work there, doesn't he?"

"Sure. Yeah, okay. I'll make an appointment for you. When?"

"Um, this afternoon if he can squeeze me in."

She laughed. "Oh, I think he can manage that. What time?"

I did a few quick calculations in my head. Ritter would be here at one thirty, it would take us forty minutes to get to Silver Wells. . . . "Does he have anything open around three?"

There came her laugh again. I had no idea what was so funny. "Yes, I think we can do that, Ms. . . . ?"

"Allbright," I said.

"See you at three, then."

"Thank you."

"Buh bye."

I looked at the receiver for a few seconds before hanging up, still a little puzzled. I guess I'd find out what that was all about in a few hours.

There was just enough time before my new helper arrived to mix up a little scentual something to take with me on the afternoon's fact-finding mission. I wanted something to help Josie's brother in case he really was grieving, and I also wanted to encourage him to talk with us.

Maggie showed up at five minutes after one, raring to go. I corked the tiny bottle I'd just filled, and showed her where to stow her stuff in the office. Before giving her the rundown on Scents & Nonsense, I asked her about Josie's cleaning clients.

"I know about the Traces," I said. "And Inga Fowler."

She nodded. "There were only two others. You know the Tillman place?"

I gave her a wry look. "Everyone knows the Tillman place, or at least of it." She was referring to Rance Tillman, the actor. A few months before, I'd talked to him for a few minutes at the Scottish Irish Festival.

"Well, his wife, Sophia Thelane. You know, the model?"

I nodded.

"She hired Josie to help out their full-time housekeeper sometimes."

I whistled. "Boy, I bet their house is amazing."

Maggie smiled. "Josie said it was more of an estate than a house, but yeah—amazing."

And Thea had mentioned that Sophia wanted her to do a landscaping project for her. I wondered what the timeline on that was.

"Who else?" I asked.

"Missy Renault, the former Olympic ice-skater."

"Ah." Ms. Renault did not often deign to talk to the common folk like me. Two haircuts ago, she'd been in Foxy Locksies having her long black hair trimmed. When the stylist was done, it had looked fine to me, but Missy had thrown an enormous hissy fit. In the end, Cynthia hadn't charged her. I wondered if she was as particular about her house as she was about her hair.

I explained to Maggie how the register worked. It was similar enough to the one at the restaurant that she hardly needed any instruction. Then I gave her a quick tour of the different areas of the shop.

"Candles are all in this area. Bath items are all on this wall. Children's items are mostly in this corner. And there are miscellaneous goodies on all the display tables." I stopped in front of the locked display case. Bottles of all shapes and sizes stood in colorful, glittering rows on the shelves. "This is where I keep the perfumes that aren't custom-made. The bottles are so small it's easy to slip one in a pocket and some of those oils are pretty expensive, so I usually keep this locked. The key is in the register."

"Sounds good," Maggie said with her hands on her

hips as she surveyed her new place of employment. "I'll make myself familiar with everything in no time."

"I'm sure of it. There's coffee and cookies there by the back door, and customers are welcome to spend time out in the garden."

Her face lit up. "Oh, I've heard about that garden!"

I smiled. "You should check it out. Just keep the back door open so you can hear if customers come in while you're out there."

"Okeydoke."

I heard her breathe a contented sigh as I left to change my clothes.

This afternoon I wanted something a bit more businesslike than my usual attire. Dash watched from the foot of the bed as I rifled through the built-in armoire, finally decided on beige linen slacks and a light yellow button-down silk shirt.

"What do you think?" I asked him.

He grinned his approval.

"You have excellent taste." I slipped into leather flats and added a pair of simple earrings and a silver chain necklace.

We returned to Scents & Nonsense to find Maggie leaning on the counter, chatting with Ritter. He wore a dark blue shirt that called out his eyes, tidy jeans, and cowboy boots.

He looked up when Dash and I came in from the back patio, a smile flashing across his face. "You look nice, Elliana."

"Thanks," I said. "So do you. Don't want to show up at the lawyer's office looking too shabby."

"Are you sure the brother will talk to us?".

I could almost see Maggie's ears perk up. I hadn't mentioned where I would be going that afternoon. Now I explained. "We're going to Silver Wells to talk with Vance Overland. See if there's anything I can do to help with his sister's . . . arrangements."

"Oh, that's nice of you," she said. "Josie never talked about him much."

"Um," I said, debating how to say it and deciding on candor. "Could you keep this little trip to yourself for right now? I don't know if the police will approve."

She looked puzzled, but shrugged. "I'm the very picture of discretion."

I highly doubted that, but nodded anyway. What was the worst that could happen? Lang had told me not to leave town, but he hadn't left me a lot of choice, either. I'd be back before he knew it. Still, I was glad Ritter had offered to drive.

"You stick here with Maggie and take care of the shop," I said to Dash.

He gazed up at me with disappointed brown eyes, inducing an instant wave of guilt.

"Aw, Dash. Don't do that," I said with a groan.

"He can come with," Ritter said. "It's not too hot out, and he can stay in the truck with the windows down, can't he?"

"You sure you don't mind?" I asked.

"Come on, little guy," he said in answer, leading the corgi to the door and holding it open for both of us.

"I shouldn't be more than a couple of hours," I told Maggie.

"Don't worry about me. I've got your number, and I'll

call if anything urgent comes up. I'm happy to hold down the fort for as long as you need."

"You're a gem," I said, meaning it. I knew how lucky I was to have found someone to help out at Scents & Nonsense so quickly. I began running numbers in my head to see if I could bring Maggie in five afternoons a week in order to give me more time to concentrate on the delicate perfume side of my business.

Ritter lifted Dash into Thea's vintage Chevy truck, parked in front of Scents & Nonsense. He offered his hand to me next. I took it and stepped onto the wide running board, then settled in beside Dash and fastened my seat belt. The corgi had regained his usual cheer, and sat on the bench seat, eagerly looking out the windshield. The big engine purred like a leopard cub as Ritter pulled onto Corona—just as Detective Max Lang turned onto the street and drove toward us.

I ducked down, suddenly interested in the concoction I'd tucked into my purse on the floor. If Ritter noticed I was invisible to the detective as we passed, he didn't say anything. I could only hope Lang hadn't noted my dog sitting on the seat next to Thea's brother.

Straightening with the bottle in my hand, I held it up to the light streaming in the window. Even through the blue glass of the bottle, the oils looked dark.

"What's that?"

I glanced over at Ritter to see genuine interest on his face. "It's a combination of essential oils. I find that they sometimes help in certain . . . situations."

He still looked interested, but now a little puzzled.

I tried again. "You know I make perfumes, right? And

I'm an aromatherapist." It was the first time I'd actually called myself that out loud, and it felt good. Even though I didn't have any kind of certificate on the wall to prove my bona fides, I knew—and felt—more about scent than anyone I knew.

"So I made up a little preparation, just in case it might be helpful." I didn't mention that I had only guessed what might be most useful, and that normally I'd try to intuit that information upon meeting Josie's brother. That hadn't been possible in this situation, though.

"Are you going to tell me what's in it?" he asked in a teasing tone. "Or is that a proprietary secret?"

"You really want to know?"

He nodded.

"White poppy, for one. For consolation," I happily explained. "Then there's bittersweet for truth. And finally, a little heather." *For protection.* I figured that last couldn't hurt.

"Can I smell it?"

I uncorked the bottle and held it out to him. He took a sniff and passed it back. "Subtle. But nice."

I shrugged. "Maybe I go overboard with the whole aromatherapy thing."

He shook his head. "Never apologize for what you're passionate about." He turned toward the highway to Silver Wells, his long fingers curled around the big steering wheel. Strong hands. Tan and capable. As I watched, he reached up and ran one through his sun-highlighted hair, then looked over at me.

"What?" he asked.

Feeling myself blush, I looked away. I'd been thinking what it might be like to run my own hand through that thick mane. "Thanks for saying that. About my passion for scent." I looked back, but his eyes had returned to the road. "You know, I'd forgotten that about you."

His eyes cut my way for a second. "What?"

"You're a really good listener, and you don't judge." He'd been like that even with his little sister's obnoxious friend back in high school. "People respond to that."

"People like the brother of a murder victim?" he asked with a sideways grin. I was glad he wasn't taking me too seriously.

"Exactly."

"People like you?" Still grinning, but now his words held more weight.

"Maybe," I said, quickly looking out my window.

Dash settled back and looked between us. Ritter rolled down his window, and the cab filled with the smells of new-mown alfalfa hay from a nearby field, hummingbird sage, and chaparral currant. I closed my eyes, enjoying the air caressing my cheek.

S ILVER Wells was big enough to have a Trader Joe's on one side of town and a Walmart on the other. The law firm Vance Overland worked at was two blocks off the main drag. It was housed in a renovated Victorian painted a drab cream color, gingerbread and all. Ritter parked in the small lot next to it, and we got out.

Dash stood with his front paws on the door, and I reached

through the open window to rub his velvety ears. "Stay here, be good, and don't bark if any other dogs walk by. Okay?"

He barked his agreement, which made me wonder if he might be toying with me.

Ritter and I climbed the front steps of Clary, Bittel and Sorgenson, and he held the door open for me. I paused inside, blinking as my eyes adjusted to the dim light. A young woman lounged behind a metal desk, her blond tresses caught up in two ponytails on top of her head. Her T-shirt looked to be a size too small and advertised a band I'd never heard of. It went well with her jeans and the jeweled flip-flops on her feet—which were on the top of the desk.

Feeling positively overdressed, I approached.

"Help you?" she asked.

"I have an appointment with Vance Overland," I said. "We're a little early."

She pointed at me. "Right. You're the one. I'll get him." She swung her feet to the floor and stood. "Follow me. You can wait in here."

Trailing behind her, I breathed in her effluence of baby powder and butterscotch candies. She showed us into a conference room with a table and six folding chairs around it. The only other pieces of furniture were a file cabinet with folders overflowing from the half-shut drawers, and an industrial floor lamp to augment the sunlight streaming in the windows. The hint of Indian takeout from lunchtime still lingered faintly in the air.

Suddenly I understood the receptionist's attitude on the phone earlier. Everything about the place screamed "ambulance chasers."

"Have a seat. I'll grab Vance." She closed the door.

I looked at Ritter. "I don't think I'll be hiring any lawyers from this place."

A grimace crossed his face. "I'm with you on that." He pulled out a chair and sat down.

Putting my purse on the table, I extracted the blue vial and marched to the floor lamp. Three drops of the elixir went onto the bulb, and then I turned it on and returned to the table.

Bittersweet for truth. Here goes.

The lamp light was hardly noticeable in the bright room. I was sitting by the time the door opened and Vance Overland walked in.

Immediately I recognized him from the photo hanging in his sister's apartment. She'd been a brunette, and he had hair light enough to be called blond, but their eyes had been the same shape, and there was something familiar about the curve of his lips—though his certainly weren't curved up in a smile. Instead he frowned down at the file in his hand, flipping through a sheaf of papers.

"Excuse me, but I can't seem to find your name anywhere in the class action suit." His gaze flicked to Ritter, then to me. "You're Mrs. Allbright?"

"Elliana," I said. "And this is Ritter Nelson. We aren't part of any suit."

He blinked. "I don't understand. You asked for me, specifically, right?"

Ritter and I exchanged a look. "We're here about your sister."

His eyes narrowed. "Josie? She's dead."

Now I was the one who blinked. "Yes, I know. I . . . she used to work for me."

"Bully for her." His tone was bitter as he dropped into a chair across the table from us. "What do you want from me?"

"Well, I was wondering if you needed any help with her, um, affairs?"

Vance snorted. "Affairs? She had plenty of those—that's for sure."

Really? "I meant the funeral," I said. "And her things."

He waved his hand. The disturbance in the air alerted me that the oils were heating up on the lightbulb. "I don't want her crap. Let her boyfriend figure out the rest."

I leaned forward as Ritter asked, "Did you know her boyfriend?"

Josie's brother transferred his attention to him. "No. I haven't talked to her for over two years."

"Why is that?" I asked.

He glared at me, and I had the feeling we were about to be unceremoniously thrown out of the offices of Clary, Bittel and Sorgenson. Instead, he grated out, "Because she ruined my life."

CHAPTER 15

RITTER opened his mouth to speak, then closed it when Vance rose and walked to the window. He drew up the blind a few more inches, gazing out at the street. He spoke without turning around.

"I'm not supposed to be working in this, this *hole*." His jaw worked. "I'm supposed to be on a partner track at Anderson and Moffet on the other side of town and eventually move to their offices in Sacramento. But my dear sister ruined my chances of working there, ruined my reputation in this town, and ruined my life. Now"— his arm shot out and he turned toward us with a sweeping gesture—"now I work here, researching for a class action suit against a vitamin company. Big thrills. But at least the hours are insane, and the pay still manages to suck." Resentment flared behind his eyes with every word.

I breathed in the subtle perfume of bittersweet from the lightbulb and asked, in the most sympathetic voice I could muster, "What did she do?"

"Started blabbing about me to the wrong person one night in that dive club she worked at. The Calla Club." He turned to look out the window again. "I'd worked my behind off, all the way through law school, passed the bar, while she dropped out of community college to take pretty pictures and work in that disgusting place. It's not fair." He whirled back. "Do you know how tough the competition is for law grads to get good jobs anymore? Do you know how many of us there are?"

I shook my head.

"A *lot*. So Anderson and Moffet are very careful about who they hire. They even bring in investigators before making an offer. I was *so close* to working there."

"The Calla Club . . ." Ritter said. I caught his eye. He knew the place.

"Strip joint."

My jaw went slack. I sure hadn't expected that.

"She was always hanging out with losers," he went on. "I'm not surprised one of them killed her." The last words were choked. His head came up, and I saw tears in his eyes. And alarm. He hadn't meant to share all this with us.

Without another word, he stalked out, leaving the door open behind him.

Slowly, Ritter and I stood. We looked at each other and then at the door.

"I don't think he's coming back," Ritter said.

I nodded. "Let's go."

The receptionist barely looked up from her magazine when we left.

Out on the sidewalk, I took a deep breath to try to clear my mind. "That was weird," I said. "A strip club?"

"Elliana? How about you keep that little blue bottle of yours corked up tight on the way home," Ritter said.

I reached into to my purse and took it out. "Do you suppose . . . ?"

He put his hand on my shoulder, guiding me toward the truck. "I don't know. But that guy just spilled his guts to us, and he doesn't even know us." He opened the door. Dash jumped to the ground and hurried to a bush at the edge of the lot.

I climbed in, and Ritter closed the door. Then he boosted the corgi back in and got in himself.

"You know, aromatherapy blends don't usually have that dramatic an effect," I said slowly. "Unless someone is already primed. Scents aren't forceful—you know what I mean?"

He put the key in the ignition and sat back. Nodded.

"They're more like invitations, if that makes any sense. You know what I think?"

The engine rumbled to life and Ritter asked, "What?"

"Vance Overland is a lot more upset about his sister than he's willing to let on."

"Conflicted," Ritter said, putting the Chevy into gear.

"Exactly! Sorry that Josie's gone—but still really, really angry at her."

Ritter turned to me, foot on the brake. "Angry enough to kill her?"

I bit my lip. "I don't know. Maybe."

* * *

WE analyzed and picked apart our brief time with Vance Overland on the way back to Poppyville. It felt comfortable, as if I'd known Ritter forever. Which, in a way, I had. But not like this.

Josie had revealed something about her brother to someone investigating him for a potential employer, but it also sounded as though she hadn't realized she was causing damage. Also, Vance hadn't implied that whatever information she'd "blabbed" about him wasn't true. What had she revealed, though? We bandied around ideas encompassing everything from underage drinking to murder, but in the end we couldn't know without Vance himself telling us. Or the private investigator for Anderson and Moffet.

It had happened over two years before, though, just before Josie had moved to Poppyville. Even if Vance had actively wanted her dead, biding his time for that long seemed unlikely. Still, I wanted to pass on the information to Detective Garcia. Maybe she'd be willing to check on Vance Overland's shady background, and while she was at it, see if he could establish an alibi. In the meantime, I had at least expanded the field of possible suspects by one more.

"Have you ever been in the Calla Club?" I asked Ritter.

His cheeks reddened. "Just once. Bachelor party."

"I don't suppose you saw Josie there?"

"Can't say that I did. How old was she?"

"Twenty-nine," I said.

"I think she would have been way too young to work

in anyplace that served alcohol back when I was there."
He narrowed his eyes, thinking. "Do you think she was
actually a stripper?"

I held up my palms. "I wouldn't have thought it. She
always seemed so . . . not innocent. Just not worldly, you
know? Trusting and open. But that doesn't mean she
wasn't—and it doesn't mean I was right about her, either."
I imagined what staid, uptight Harris would say if he found
out his girlfriend had been a stripper. And then I thought
about what Raleigh had said about secrets and everyone
having them. "Maybe there was a lot more to Josie than the
citizens of Poppyville knew."

Ritter looked thoughtful. "Did she have a best friend
in town?"

"You know, I've wondered about that, but it seems as if
she socialized mostly with the people she worked with. And
if I count as one of them, she wasn't exactly forthcoming
about herself—or her past." My hand drifted over to Dash's
head. I began kneading the thick ruff around his neck, and
he closed his eyes with pleasure. "Is the Calla Club a dive
like Vance said?"

He laughed. "Definitely. In fact, it was so bad that
they've gone out of business."

"Aha! And you know this how?" I grinned.

"Heard it through the grapevine." He winked.

The trip had taken longer than I'd thought. It was
nearly closing time for the shop when Ritter pulled into
a parking space in front.

"Are you hungry?" he asked. "We could go grab a bite."

My heart tripped. After that over-the-top grilled
cheese Raleigh had whipped up for me, I wondered if I'd

ever need to eat again, but I would have made the effort to prolong our time together.

However, Astrid had texted to let me know we were on for a drive to the software moguls' house as soon as I closed Scents & Nonsense for the evening.

"I can't. I have plans with Astrid." I was pleased that he looked disappointed. "Maybe another time?" I got out of the truck. "Thanks for going to Silver Wells with me. It was . . . interesting."

He smiled through the window at me. "And yet it was fun, kind of. No?" He put the truck into gear. "See ya," he called, and drove away.

Dash waddled over and sat next to my foot. "Yes," I said to him. "It was kind of fun."

M AGGIE looked tired but happy when Ritter dropped me off at the store. She reported that sales had been decent that afternoon, some tourists but also a few locals who had stopped in to find out more about Josie's murder. I thanked her profusely and sent her home after asking if she could work the next afternoon, figuring that I might need the time to pursue my inquiries about who might have had a motive to kill Josie.

So far I sure hadn't had much luck. I was ready for a break.

Luckily, I had a few minutes of downtime. I made a cup of peppermint tea and took it out to a bench in the garden near the fence that abutted Flyrite Kites. I sat down sideways and put my feet up. Dash settled in to doze nearby.

Nabby saw an opportunity for some extended petting,

and, leaving his usual perch, jumped up on my lap. A few
head butts later, he curled up and lifted his chin for a
scratch. I happily complied, savoring the velvet of his fur,
the purr rumbling from his chest, and the fragrant steam
wafting from my cup.

I hadn't had much of a chance to work in the Enchanted
Garden over the last few days, but it didn't look the worse
for wear. Bachelor's buttons waved their cheerful blue heads
from beside the bench. Beyond, corkscrew rush twisted
skyward, interspersed with the pom-pom heads of purple
allium, starting to fade. I noted that the climbing rose cling-
ing to the fence needed a bit of deadheading, and the red-hot
poker plants needed thinning. Soon the iris rhizomes could
be separated, and . . .

I looked down at Nabby, who had rolled onto his side
so I could reach his soft tummy. I loved the work of gardening, but sometimes I forgot to simply enjoy the results
it produced.

So that's what I did until Astrid showed.

ASTRID pulled up in her Peugeot at six thirty. A big
German shepherd filled the entire backseat, her big
head hanging out the window, tongue lolling. I grabbed
my jacket and hurried outside, eager to see the Prairie
School architecture of the Trace's home—and to see if they
could shed any light on Josie's life in Poppyville.

My friend waited until I fastened my seat belt, then
took off like a shot toward Raven Road. Gripping the door
with one hand and the edge of the seat with my other, I
thanked my lucky stars I was not her frequent passenger.

Astrid drove like a horde of angry bees was chasing her car at all times, jamming her Birkenstock sandal down on the accelerator and brake with equal fervor. I grinned at her through gritted teeth and braced myself against the back of the seat. Behind me, the dog seemed unfazed.

We wound southeast out of town, turning right and then left and then right again until we were on a narrow asphalt road. I was pretty sure I hadn't been on it since looking for a place to make out with a date in high school.

As she drove, I filled her in on the trip to Silver Wells. It took six tries before she stopped interrupting me with questions about Ritter.

"You should have told me he asked you out. I would have understood. God, Ellie!"

I shook my head. "I don't think he was asking me out on a date. I like Ritter. I really do. But I'm not going to start anything, even just a friendship—with him or anyone else—by standing you up. Besides, I want to see that house."

She was silent for several seconds, and I thought she might be so frustrated with me that she couldn't think what to say. Then she looked over at me, and I saw her eyes were a little glossy.

"Thanks, Ellie. I want you to be as happy as you can be. But I really missed you when you were married to Harris."

"I feel terrible about that. I don't think I ever told you how sorry I am. I never should have let him become a wedge between us."

"Oh, pooh," she said brightly. "All's well. Ritter is no Harris—that's for *sure*."

We both laughed. It felt great.

"Okay, now tell me more about Josie's brother."

She nodded her understanding when I tried to explain Vance Overland's mixed-up feelings about his sister's death. "I hope he'll be able to reconcile his feelings in the long run," she said.

"Me, too." *If he didn't kill his sister, that is.*

The terrain undulated, then flattened again, then rose again. Ten minutes later, we rounded a cliff to find a solitary house that looked as though it had risen directly from the earth.

It sat on a ridge, and while I'd seen it many times from far below, the house was remarkable up close. The colors reflected the landscape: browns and creams, grays and muted greens. It was a solid building made up of so many horizontal lines I had to search for the verticals that held it up. Two bands of windows delineated the ground and top floors, and broad eves reached out from the flat roof.

She parked in the circular drive and let Alexandra out. I struggled out of the seat and thankfully caught my breath on solid ground.

Arms folded, Astrid leaned her tush against the side of her car and took in the view.

I joined her, breathing in the cooling air with appreciation. "Nice place."

"Sure is." She pushed away from the car. "Come on."

There was no garden, not even near the foundation. Or at least that's what I thought at first, but when we got closer, I saw the plantings were indeed deliberate. It was subtle landscaping, indeed, made up entirely of native species. Goldenrod and monkey flower brushed the edge of the steps, and pineapple weed, a tiny version of chamomile,

padded the cracks between the stones in the pathway leading to the door. As we walked, our steps released the gentle,
fruity spice to whirl around us in an olfactory haze. The
only nonnative plants I saw were the three varieties of flow-
ering thyme in an urn by the door.

The wooden slats of the narrow porch creaked as Alexandra bounded to the door, her brushy tail waving like a
sentinel's flag. The screen opened, and a white-haired
man stepped out.

"Hey, baby," he said to the dog, kneeling to ruff her
neck. "Who's a good girl? Did you miss me?"

She answered with a slurp of her big tongue on his chin,
and he laughed. Standing, he waved us forward. Smiling
brown eyes greeted us from behind silver-framed glasses.
He had a square jaw and weathered skin, and wore jeans
with a crisp collared shirt.

"Astrid! It's so good to see you." He stepped forward
and they hugged.

The shepherd ran off the porch and began an examination of the property, no doubt to make sure nothing untoward had happened in her territory during her absence.

"Ellie, this is John Trace," Astrid said. "John, my friend
Elliana Allbright."

He stuck out his hand. "Welcome to the homestead,
Elliana."

I shook it. "Thanks. You have a beautiful house here,
kind of a hidden secret."

John looked pleased.

"I've seen you around Poppyville," I said. "At the
library. And the community theater. They were putting
on *Winesburg, Ohio*, I think."

John looked to the sky and then back at me. "Boy, that was a fiasco. Talk about drama, and I don't mean on the stage. Still, I enjoy working on the sets. You own that perfume shop at the end of Corona Street, don't you?"

I nodded. "Scents and Nonsense. Have you been in?"

"Not yet. I'm planning on it. Heard you know your business when it comes to aromatherapy, young lady. And Gene desperately needs something to help him sleep. He won't take pills."

"Oh, it's not that bad," said another man, joining us on the porch. He was taller, thin as a rail, with a hooked nose and a mop of graying blond hair. He wore a polo shirt with jeans and sneakers. The dark circles under his eyes contradicted his protests. My guess was that this man hardly slept more than a few hours a night, and it was wearing him down. I had the feeling it wasn't normal insomnia, either. Something was bothering him enough to keep him up at night.

Maybe Gamma's cowslip cordial would help.

"I'm Gene." He stuck out his hand. I handled my own introduction, while Astrid returned their house key to John. I heard her updating him on Alexandra, including the jogging schedule and a slight change that she'd made in the glucosamine supplement for the dog's arthritis. Gene invited me inside as John arranged for Astrid to take care of the shepherd again in a couple of weeks. As I crossed the threshold, I heard him say he was slated to give a talk at UCLA on practical ways to help the homeless.

The interior of the house reflected the simple lines of the outside, and the furniture had a practical Shaker appeal. The verticals in the windows were more obvious from the inside, though they were cut sideways with slatted shutters. I took it all in with a sweeping glance, but my attention was immediately drawn to the cluster of photos on one wall. The composition reminded me of the ones on Josie's walls. I walked over to them. The subject matter was also similar. I was about to ask if they were hers when I saw one that made the question moot.

It was an arty shot, different from anything I'd seen of hers so far. Less sophisticated, but also full of a wild energy. But the thing that gave it away as one of Josie's was that she was one of the subjects. She and the other woman were both scantily clad in identical off-the-shoulder cleavage-emphasizing shirts that made me appreciate the androgynous uniforms at the Roux Grill. Josie's hair was much shorter, with chunky blond streaks, and she had on more eyeliner than Cleopatra, yet looked much younger than the twenty-nine-year-old I'd known. The other woman had her eyes closed, her head back, and had been caught in an open-mouthed laugh, her bright red lipstick contrasting with her white teeth and glossy black pageboy haircut.

After talking with Josie's brother, my guess was that the brightly lit area behind them was a stage. It was empty, but surely this picture had been taken in the Calla Club. However, Josie had cropped the shot and changed the shading and color quality so that it looked like a classy vintage shot à la Marilyn Monroe. I noticed something on Josie's shoulder then. It was a small tattoo, right about where a bra strap might fall. I leaned in closer.

It was a daisy.

For innocence. In the Calla Club. *Calla lilies for beauty.*

Then I saw the other woman had one, too. They must have visited the tattoo parlor together.

"Aren't these lovely?" Gene said, coming to stand next to me. He pointed to a stream running beneath a low cliff, the shine of the moving water caught in time but still appearing to dance on the paper it was printed on. A series of mare's tails floated above the cliff as if streaking to the far horizon. "That one is my favorite."

"Stunning," I said. "Josie had a lot of talent."

"You knew her?" Gene's expression saddened. "It's a small town. Of course. You know what happened, then."

"She worked for me," I said. Then, after a moment's hesitation, I added, "Actually, I found her body," watching his face to see if there was any reaction.

"Oh!" He put his hand on my shoulder in a gesture that at one time I would have found intrusive but now felt comforting. "I'm so sorry, my dear. What a horrible thing."

I nodded in silence, setting my jaw and focusing on the pictures to keep away the tears.

"I bought these pictures from her, and we were trying to get her a show in a gallery in Sacramento," he said, politely looking at the photos again so I could collect myself. "We almost had the owner convinced. Now I suppose we'll have to scrap the idea. It's too bad. We have all the photos she was going to show in the basement, matted and ready to hang."

A little surprised, I turned to him. Compassion filled his basset hound gaze. Behind us, Astrid and John came inside.

"Didn't Josie clean your house for you?" I asked.

"Sure," Gene said, looking back at the photos on the wall. "But she was our friend, too." He turned to John. "We truly believed that with a little funding and support, Josie could have gone far. We planned to provide some of that funding through our foundation."

I sighed. "She was a good photographer. And determined. She worked hard. I'm glad to hear she had you guys on her side. What is your foundation?"

John smiled. "It's the Trace Foundation. Original name, huh? It funds a number of things, but primarily it supports advocacy groups for the homeless."

"Ah. The university lecture I heard you mention to Astrid."

Gene nodded. "We've had some difficult times. Now we want to give back."

My head cocked to the side, I asked, "Are you familiar with the homeless who camp behind the stables in Poppyville?"

Together, they nodded. "Sure," Gene said. "We've gone out and talked with them several times. And we work with Gessie King to make sure that the half dozen people or so who more or less live on her property get regular medical care at the Poppyville Clinic."

Astrid, who had been examining Josie's photographs as we talked, turned around with a sour expression. "You know Bongo Pete, then?"

"God, yes." Gene's face lit up, and for a second I saw the energy he would have if he got a good night's sleep. "What a character! And not a bad bongo player, it turns out." He chuckled.

"Do you think he would make a credible witness in court?" I asked.

Gene looked puzzled, glanced at John, and then back at me. "I don't understand. What court?"

I shook my head. "Never mind. Listen, I have a suggestion for you."

Still frowning, Gene asked, "What's that?"

"Tonight, take a sprig of each of the thyme plants you have growing on the porch there—woolly, mother of thyme, and the variegated lemon thyme—and crush them enough to smell their fragrance. Then put them under your pillow. It might help you sleep until you can get to Scents and Nonsense for one of my custom blends."

He stared at me. "Well, I guess you do know your business." He glanced at his partner, who was nodding at him. "I'll give it a try."

CHAPTER 16

W E bid our farewells. Outside, John, Gene, and
Alexandra the German shepherd watched us
screech out of the driveway toward the winding road back
to town.

"So Bongo Pete really plays the bongos," I mused,
absently holding on for dear life. "Who knew?"

My friend shook her head and tromped on the gas
pedal. "I can't believe he's going to testify against you."
Her eyes cut my way. "If it comes to that, I mean. It's not
going to, is it?"

Stomach twisting, I closed my eyes against the thought.
"If Lang has his way, it just might. There are a few other
suspects, but those two guys I just met don't go on the list."

I held up my hand, ticking off my fingers as I had in the
garden with Ritter and Thea earlier in the day. "So far that
list includes me—at least if you're asking Max Lang—plus

Josie's creepy apartment manager, her brother who thinks she ruined his life but still seems to miss her, and a waitress she worked with who didn't like how the cook flirted with Josie." My hands dropped. "Weak, weak, weak."

"And Harris," Astrid added. "It's usually the husband or boyfriend, you know."

"Whatever the statistics might say, he's just not a violent guy," I insisted.

"He's fooled you before," she said, yanking on the steering wheel and nearly sending the car into a skid as we entered Poppyville.

Hard to argue with that, I thought as I grabbed for the oh-my-God handle above the door.

I T was past eight when we got back. I fed Nabokov some fancy wet food and sprinkled a few granules into Leonard's tank before heading out to the garden. The mnemosyne had another bloom open, but there were five more buds to go. The first bloom still looked fresh, so I decided I could risk another day before I distilled the bewitching fragrance. All the other plants in the Enchanted Garden looked healthy and happy, even though I'd had little time to attend to them over the last few days. I felt the frustration of my fruitless investigations fall away as I locked the back door and slowly walked down to my tiny house.

Dash padded down the path behind me, toenails clicking on the stepping stones. Once inside, my stomach growled, surprising me. I'd been sure Raleigh's enormous grilled cheese would carry me through a couple of meals. For a moment I considered calling Ritter to see if he was still interested in dinner.

"Nah," I said.

Dash peered up at me expectantly.

"Yeah?"

He woofed.

"I guess it can't hurt to try." Leaning my hip against the counter, I dug out my cell phone and called Thea.

She answered on the third ring, sounding worried. "Ellie? Everything okay?"

"Sure," I said. "I was just trying to get ahold of Ritter."

"He's out with someone. Not sure who. Do you want his number?"

My shoulders slumped. Was he out with Cynthia again? "That's okay."

"No, really. In fact I'll text it to you."

"All right." My voice was flat. I'd really thought Ritter and I had hit it off that afternoon. Maybe I'd missed my chance.

Oh, well.

"Honey," Thea said, "why don't you just get it over with and ask my brother out?"

"I was going to," I said, sounding grumpy.

"Though, you know," she went on without noticing, "he's going to be leaving again pretty soon. Still, it might be good practice."

"Practice?"

"For getting back in the dating scene."

"Dating scene. Lord, Thea. That sounds like something I can do without."

"Yeah. We'll see. Pretty soon you'll be out on the town every night."

I gave a little laugh. "Thea, I can't even imagine being out on the town in Poppyville every night."

She laughed, too, and we said good-bye. Seconds later my phone buzzed to let me know I had a text. Sure enough, it was Ritter's number.

Which I was not about to call.

I straightened my shoulders and considered my options. It had been too long since I'd been to the grocery store, but I had fresh eggs from the weekend farmers' market, along with some artisanal cheese and the loaf of heavy peasant bread that had hosted my sandwiches for the last few days. Returning to the garden, I cut sprigs of tarragon, parsley, and chives, all of which combined nicely with the sharp flavor of the cheese for a simple omelet. I took my plate and a tall glass of chamomile iced tea outside to the back porch and settled on the porch swing.

Two actual meals in one day. That's progress. My sporadic eating habits were a symptom of my life being out of balance. Adding a murder investigation to the mix hadn't helped.

And I was neglecting my business. That was unaccept- able. After dinner, I dragged out my laptop to try to check a few more things off my list as the sun set over Kestrel Peak, and the mule deer began to sift out of the stand of trees at the edge of the meadow.

My in-box contained a request for perfume from a local woman I'd supplied since Scents & Nonsense opened. In fact, hers was one of the first blends I'd dis- tilled with my special method. All the scents in it originated in the Enchanted Garden, the flowers and leaves picked mere moments before processing.

See, most essential oils are distilled from mass quantities of the same kind of plant material. The way I did it was considerably more targeted, and therefore done on a very small scale. I used a three-liter copper alembic still which, other than her garden journal, was the only thing my gamma had passed on to me. It was tiny in comparison to any type of commercial equipment, but perfect for what I used it for: customized, one-of-a-kind scents. In addition to creating the essential oils on demand, I didn't distill one species at a time; I combined all the types of flowers and herbs I'd selected for any given perfume and distilled them *together*. The result was an interlacing of scents that created fragrances that couldn't be achieved any other way.

I put the perfume request on my task list and checked the next e-mail. It was a request for wedding favors. I'd hired out the garden to a couple of small wedding parties in the last year with success, but I was leery of having too many people around the delicate miniature gardens at once. Wedding favors were a different matter. The bride didn't have anything particular in mind, just something that smelled nice. I suggested a few things that might appeal to her guests, including the men: peppermint travel candles, fir-scented soaps, and the chocolate-scented lotion bars in which I used the raw cocoa butter I'd sold to Detective Garcia. I quoted pricing on each and logged out of my e-mail.

I'd forgotten to answer the e-mail about the custom perfume, and switched the e-mail screen back on. The program had saved my password, so it was easy to . . .

Hang on.

The week before, Josie had checked her e-mail on my laptop in the office of Scents & Nonsense. On a hunch, I entered "jos" in the username field. Sure enough, the rest of her username filled in, and her password appeared as a series of asterisks.

I clicked ENTER.

There were loads of newsletters and blog subscriptions having to do with photography and stock photo sites waiting in her in-box. I noted there was an e-mail from her brother that hadn't been opened even though she'd responded to e-mails more recent than that one. One e-mail that had been delivered in the last day was from someone named Bob Farsen. I hesitated, my finger over the mouse button, but didn't open it. I already felt too creepy about snooping into her private life.

Still, I needed more information if I was going to clear my name and see her killer punished, so I soldiered on. There was a folder called HOUSEFAIRY. I opened it and found correspondence with her different clients. From what I could tell, there were only the four I already knew about.

I returned to the in-box, hesitated, and went ahead and opened the e-mail from Bob Farsen. When I saw how it started, I cringed all over again.

Josie, I'm so, so sorry. I know you say you're done with me, but I have to keep trying. Back then, I just misunderstood about the Calla Club. And you were right—I never should have accused you of doing anything wrong, and I shouldn't have asked you to quit. I won't apologize for asking you to marry me, though, and I'm going to try again. And again and again and again. Things didn't work out with Cindi, and I know now that you are the only one for me. Please, please come back to Silver Wells. Or let me know where you are now, and I'll move there, no matter where it is.

Bob.

p.s. Where ARE you?

Ugh. So not my business! But did this intense-to-the-point-of-creepy guy even know Josie was dead? My guess was that he didn't. The police wouldn't have known to tell him unless they'd taken Josie's address book . . . *Oh, heavens. They have Josie's laptop.*

Quickly, I marked the e-mail as unread. Suddenly afraid that they might know I was looking at Josie's e-mail that very moment, I logged out and slammed my computer shut.

The sun had gone down, leaving behind a few pink-lit clouds above the foothills. I could see the silhouettes of the deer, which had fanned out to nibble at the tender greens and yummy wildflowers in the meadow.

"What do you think, Dash? Should I call this Bob Farsen guy and tell him the bad news?"

He made a sound in the back of his throat and thumped down at my feet.

"Well, just to let him know. I mean, he deserves that, even if it's awful news—don't you think?"

Dash sighed.

"And maybe I can ask him about what Josie did at the Calla Club."

A breath of air seemed to laugh through the oak leaves. I gazed skyward, but it was only the breeze.

Still, as long as I'm taking the appearance of Gamma's mnemosyne flower as a sign, I might as well take that as one, too.

I pulled my cell phone out of my pocket. Information had a number for Bob Farsen in Silver Wells and offered to connect me. In seconds he was picking up the phone, and I was scrambling for what to say.

I explained who I was and fumbled through the bad news.

After a shocked silence, he said, "I can't believe it. I just can't believe it."

"I know," I said. "It's terrible." I wanted to give him a dose of eucalyptus to help release his attachment to Josie and a swig of the chamomile tea in my hand to help with acceptance.

A pause. "Killed? How was she killed?" he asked.

"Someone, um, stabbed her." I grimaced to myself.

"Really? Do they know who did it?"

I was getting a bad vibe. Bob Farsen sounded way too excited and not nearly upset enough about Josie's murder.

"Not yet," I said carefully.

"What kind of knife? Do they know?"

Ew. What was wrong with this guy?

"Not sure," I answered shortly. "When was the last time you saw her?"

"Oh, gosh. It's been a long time. Since she moved."

So a few years, at least. And he was still sending her fervent electronic love notes?

"Where did you say she lived?" he asked eagerly. "And what's your name?"

"I'm very sorry for your loss," I said, instead of answering his questions. "I'm just letting people know what happened."

"How did you know about me? Did she talk about me? I bet she talked about me."

"Um, no. Sorry. Your name was in . . . her effects," I said. "I just thought you should know."

I was about to hang up when a possibility flickered in my mind. Maybe Bob Farsen could help me after all.

"Do you know any of her friends from the Calla Club that I should contact?" I asked as casually as I could.

"That place is closed," he said. "Has been for a while."

I waited.

"She bartended there." A pause and then, "Nothing else, you hear? No dancing. Just bartending. I told her she had to quit the place, though, if we were going to get married. Did you know we were going to get married? Well, not right away, but she would have come around." Bitterness infused his next words. "But she still broke up with me, and then she quit the Calla anyway. I tried to get her back. I did. Over and over. But she left town and wouldn't tell me where she moved." He sounded angry.

I moved the phone away from my ear. *Time to end this.*

"She said she was tired of men telling her what to do—" he began.

"I'm sorry," I interrupted. "I have to call a few more people. I'm very sorry for your loss. Good night, Mr. Farsen."

I hung up and found my hands were shaking. Well, at least I'd found out that Josie was a bartender at the Calla Club, and nothing else.

Tired of men telling her what to do. That sure didn't fit with her dating Harris—though to be honest, I'd learned that I could just ignore his bossiness most of the time. I wondered whether Josie was the kind of woman who was just attracted to the wrong kind of guy.

Which, unfortunately, made me wonder the same thing about myself.

CHAPTER 17

THE chamomile iced tea hadn't calmed me at all. Though I was dog tired, my thoughts were in a flurry, circling around the day's revelations about Josie, not to mention the talk of secrets and hidden memories. Besides, I had a perfume to make. My clients paid me well for custom blends, and it wasn't even ten o'clock yet.

Might as well do it now.

I went inside and up to my bedroom. With ritual reverence, I lifted out the three-liter copper distiller from its special cabinet, my hands cupping the spherical water pot at the bottom. The reddish metal was shiny and bright, carefully polished over the years, first by Gamma, and then by me. I carried it down the spiral stairs and outside to an open graveled area at the back of the garden that I'd set aside for just this purpose. Then I retrieved a small camping stove from a cubby on the back porch, and a gallon jug of spring water. Back in the distilling area, I readied the camping stove. Gamma would have used a grate over an open fire, but I wasn't that much of a traditionalist, and the stove was faster and safer.

Out in the Enchanted Garden, I gathered fragrant rose petals from the scarlet Don Juan climbing the fence, three sweet-scented gardenia flowers from a pot on the patio, and a handful of apple mint from one of the tiered herb beds. Finally, I added a sprinkling of soft yew needles—they didn't have a discernible scent for most people, but I knew they'd add an indefinable touch to the finished perfume.

Yew for sorrow.

Yes, sometimes a balanced scent required sorrow as well as joy.

I didn't measure, simply sniffed and adjusted the combination until the ratio felt right. Then I placed some of the plant material in the round pot, or *retort*, along with spring water. I added more flowers and leaves to the onion-shaped vessel that served as the lid of the retort and acted as a condenser. I attached the tube, delightfully known as the bird's beak, to the condenser and filled the lid with cool water.

The steam from the boiling liquid, laden with volatile plant oils, would recondense after traveling through the serpentine copper pipe, and separate the precious drops of essential oil from the floral water. The oil I would capture from the extended tip of the bird's beak tube, and the intensely fragrant liquid, or hydrosol, would stay in the pot. I preserved the hydrosol with a dash of vodka and sold it separately. It was ideal to use in laundry rinses, irons, or to spray onto clothes to freshen them.

As the water came to a boil, the moon rose high into the sky, and the garden took on a charmed atmosphere. The moonflower tumbling over the wooden obelisk in the center of one of the herb beds glowed as bright as its namesake. Night birds called and cheeped. A sound of flapping and the faint scent of guano made me look up in time to see a wave of bats swooping and diving on their nightly quest for a dinner of tasty insects.

Nature had always felt magical to me. So much so that I'd stopped noticing after a while. Only after being stuck in the restaurant day in and day out had I realized how it was part of my lifeblood. Without exposure to plants, the air, the very thrum of the earth, I was only an anemic version of myself. I'd started getting headaches and had no energy.

All that had disappeared as I'd planted and hoed and weeded and coaxed new life into this space behind my shop. Now, that I was back among growing things, I wasn't ever going to take them for granted again.

Perhaps that was why so many strange things had happened in the Enchanted Garden lately. And maybe it wasn't just lately. I could remember feeling *enchanted* in the garden, playing with Mama and then working with Gamma. That was the reason I'd called the area behind Scents & Nonsense the Enchanted Garden. The reason I'd infused it with whimsy—the doors, the miniatures, the fairy figurines—to try to capture that feeling I'd had as a child.

As I watched, a glimmer of light traveled through the air above the boiling copper pot.

I smiled to myself.

Perhaps I didn't have to try so hard. Perhaps the enchantment was already here.

The copper pot hissed as the concoction came to a boil and the steam separated into oil and water. I brought a bottle to the tip of the ornate bird's beak tubing and watched as the oil slowly, slowly dripped into the opening. Some of the fragrance danced out into the air, and I inhaled it with appreciation.

One last drop of oil quivered at the end of the tubing. I captured it and was corking the perfume for my customer when I heard footsteps. Whirling in alarm, I searched the moonlit path. Beside me, Dash didn't make a sound.

"Ms. Allbright? What on earth are you doing?"

I bolted to my feet, heart pounding, a gasp in my throat.

"Sorry. Didn't mean to scare you." Lupe Garcia stood at the edge of the gravel. She wore dark pants and a long-sleeved T-shirt. Her sneakers glowed neon orange in the lunar light.

Palm on my chest, I said, "Well, you did scare me." The adrenaline was still winding through my veins. "What are you doing back here? Good heavens, it's after ten."

She approached and squatted by the cook stove. Delicately, she touched the copper alembic with the tip of her finger.

"Careful," I warned. "That's hot."

"There's no other access to your house without circling back through the meadow. I wanted to talk to you," she said, looking up at me from under her brow.

"You could try the telephone." I bent to turn off the stove. The slight hissing faded into silence.

She nodded, her attention back on the distiller. "I could have. I wanted to talk to you in person. That thing you did this morning, combining the cinnamon and cardamom and chocolate in just the right amounts to smell like my great aunt's *champurrado*—did you already know the recipe? Or was it something else?"

I shrugged. "I'm good with scents."

She stood. With a wave of her arm that included the stove and the elaborate old-fashioned still. "And this?"

Was that suspicion in her voice? Or curiosity? I couldn't tell. "You know I make perfumes, right?" I asked.

"Right."

"This is how I do it. This one is for a longtime client, a woman I developed this particular blend for. I distill the essences from plants here in the garden—or sometimes I get them from other sources—and sell them to my customers."

She looked at me, then at the copper pot, then back at me. "Distill? Like with booze?"

I laughed. "Exactly like with booze. Only I don't distill alcohol, just essential oils and liquid hydrosols."

"That's fascinating," Garcia said.

"I think so. My grandmother showed me how when I was very young. Is the hot chocolate really why you came to talk to me?"

I felt her assessing gaze. "That, and I wanted to see the inside of your tiny house. It's—" She looked away as if embarrassed. "I've thought of downsizing to something like it, but I've never seen inside one."

"Do you have a warrant?" I asked.

"Nope."

"Well, I'm a murder suspect. It doesn't seem very smart to let you in without a warrant."

"Do you have anything to hide?" she asked.

"Nope. Should you really be here?"

A beat, then, "Probably not." She knelt by the distiller, her eyes roving over the sensuous contours of the copper.

The silence filled with the sound of nearby Raven Creek and the leaves of the oak tree rubbing together. I wrestled internally with whether or not to tell her what I'd learned about Josie. Glancing down, I saw one of the engraved river rocks reflecting the lunar shine. It read HONESTY.

At least I'd actually ordered a rock from the engraver that said that. Still, it was good advice. I knelt down by her. "Can I ask you something?"

She glanced over at me. "Like what?"

"Do you think I killed Josie Overland?"

"There was a witness."

"Not to the attack," I said. "And that witness is not the most reliable timekeeper in town. I'm sure you know that. Plus, Max Lang and my ex-husband are old friends. Lang doesn't like me."

"I'd figured that out."

"So?"

She stood. "So I'm open to other ideas if you have them."

Honesty.

I hesitated. "Has anything about a strip club come up in your investigation?"

She nodded. "The Calla Club. The victim used to work there. Bartender."

I whooshed out a breath. "You *have* been investigating."

Garcia laughed. "As have you, apparently. Do you have any more of those cookies from this morning?"

"I think there are a few left in the shop. Follow me."

Automatically, Dash moved to my heel. As we walked, the detective asked, "What else have you been up to?"

I inhaled, debating. *In for a penny, in for a pound.* "I went to Silver Wells."

She looked surprised.

"I know I wasn't supposed to leave town, but I just had to talk to Josie's brother."

"And?" she asked with mild interest.

"He thinks that Josie ruined his chance to be hired at a highfalutin law firm. At the same time, he's more upset about her death than he wants to let on."

"And he has an alibi," Garcia said, her hand on the back of one of the rocking chairs on the patio while she waited for me to unlock the door to Scents & Nonsense. "His boss confirms that he was working with a paralegal on an emergency motion or brief or whatever until nearly three in the morning on Monday. Time of death for Josie Overland was around two a.m., so she had to have been attacked in the park before then."

Three in the morning? Jeez. No wonder Vance Overland hated his job.

I twisted the key in the lock. "What about Josie's laptop?" I looked over to see Garcia watching me. "You did take it from her apartment, right?"

"Of course. It's in the state lab." She made a face. "It'll probably take another couple of weeks before the techs get to it, though. I don't think Poppyville ranks high on their list of priorities."

Taking a deep breath and sliding the door open, I said, "I looked at her e-mail."

Garcia's gaze sharpened. And there was something else in it. Was it—could it be—admiration?

"And?" she asked.

"I think you might want to check into a guy named Bob Farsen. In Silver Wells."

"Because . . . ?"

"Let's just say he seemed way too interested in Josie—both dead and alive."

"I see. Okay, I'll look into it."

We stepped into the shop, and I flipped on the light. Nabokov had returned to his bed, and apparently didn't see either of us as any threat to Leonard because he stood, stretched, and lay back down.

"Did you talk to anyone else?" Garcia asked.

"Some people at the Roux Grill." I couldn't keep the frustration out of my voice. "What about the guy who manages Josie's apartment complex? He's totally creepy."

Garcia held out her hand. "You have good instincts. He's a registered sex offender."

Eyes wide, I took the plastic wrap off the last two ginger softies and offered the plate.

"He exposed himself to a tourist on Corona Street a while back," Garcia said, taking a cookie and nibbling on the edge.

I winced. "That's terrible."

"It is," she said.

"Josie complained about him to the owner of the building," I said.

"He's unpleasant, but from what we can tell, not violent. Yet."

Yet. As far as anyone knew.

"What about the people Josie cleaned for?" I asked.

"We found four clients," she said.

I nodded. "Me, too."

"Lang doesn't see them as suspects. Two were out of town, and he hasn't been in a hurry to talk to the others."

"Lang," I muttered.

She didn't say anything.

"And you know that Harris and Josie had a big fight, right?" I asked.

Her eyebrow lifted. "You mentioned that when we released the crime scene, so I checked back with a couple of people at the Roux Grill this afternoon. They confirmed it." Watching me with a speculative expression, she asked, "Do you think he killed her?"

After a moment's hesitation, I shook my head. "I really don't. He's not the type." I held up my hand. "I know, I know. I should be happy if he's considered a suspect, but I just can't see it." My hand dropped and a rueful expression crept onto my face. "I sure hope it wasn't him, because I'd really be in trouble then. Your partner would never go after Harris."

Garcia frowned.

"There is someone at the Roux who seemed to hate Josie, though. One of the waitresses. Her first name is Shyla, but I don't know her last name. Did you talk to her?"

Slowly, she shook her head. "She must not have been on shift. So: Shyla something and Bob Farsen. I'll look into them both."

For the first time in days I felt as though I could take a full breath. "Thank you."

"Let me know if you think of anything else, okay?" Garcia said as I led her to the front door and let her out. She stopped and snagged my gaze. "If you did kill Josie Overland, Ms. Allbright, we will nail you to the wall." Her head cocked to the side. "But if you didn't, I want to get this right. Just so you know."

She left before I could answer. Still, I felt better. Lang might be delighted to see me behind bars, but at least Garcia was willing to give me a fighting chance.

That night as I fell asleep with Dash sprawled beside me on the bed, I wondered if Lang was just going to ignore Josie's other cleaning clients. Inga had told me her family had just returned to town, and she hadn't seemed to know anything about Josie's murder. And I agreed with Astrid that the Traces weren't suspects—especially after meeting them. But what about the other two? Was he ever going to question them? Would Garcia talk to them without her partner?

I considered how I might go about it. Thea might be able to get me access to Rance and Sophia. But what about the ice-skater, Missy Renault? How could I get her to talk to me?

I fell asleep without thinking of a good answer.

CHAPTER 18

CONSIDERABLY cheered by my conversation with Detective Garcia the evening before, I hummed to myself as Dash and I walked through the Enchanted Garden to Scents & Nonsense. My light floral skirt swirled around my knees as I topped off the birdbath with water. As I emptied the water can into the vessel, I noted that a total of five flowers had opened on the mnemosyne. There were two left to go.

Tonight, I'll distill its essence. That was one bloom I wouldn't mix with any others. I wanted the oil to be as pure as possible.

Hidden memory,
Unbound

Had Gamma meant that literally?
It wasn't a question I could answer, so I turned my

attention to the more mundane aspects of my life, the few things I had some control over. I fed Nabby and let him out, gave Leonard his breakfast, checked the water level on his tank, and started the coffee. Then I ran a lamb's wool duster over the tops of the display tables. Back in the office, I retrieved my inventory list and took it out to assess the depleted stock of soaps and body oils on the shelves. By the time those items had been tidied and rearranged, Astrid was sliding her key into the lock on the front door. The smell of chocolate preceded her, and I eyed the covered plate in her hand with interest.

"I told you I'd make chocolate cookies today. Chewy double chocolate chunk and hazelnut cookies, as a matter of fact."

"Also known as breakfast," I said with a laugh. "The coffee's ready. Let's go outside. Is Tally with you? She can come with us." I craned my neck to see if the big Newfoundland was waiting on the boardwalk in front.

"I'm happy to say Tally was adopted yesterday by a family with three little ones. It's a good fit—she's gentle as a lamb with kids."

"Ah." I smiled. "It's nice to hear good news."

On the back patio, we settled into the rocking chairs with steaming mugs and sweet treats for breakfast.

I filled her in on what had happened since I saw her last. She grimaced when I told her about Bob Farsen's creepy interest in the murder weapon. The news about Tom Steinhart flashing a tourist didn't seem to surprise her at all.

"That guy is off," she said. "Someday we're going to hear he did something awful."

"You know one thing that's upsetting about this whole business, besides, you know, the murder itself?" I asked. "I'm running into a lot of pretty icky people as a result of trying to figure out what happened."

She took a bite of cookie and washed it down with a swig of dark roast. "I take it you wouldn't want to be a detective full time, then."

"Good heavens, no." I shuddered.

The blue butterflies had started to gather around Nabby, who sat on the edge of a retaining wall. Thea had created a spiraling mosaic in the center of it, which added yet another stunning design element to the Enchanted Garden. Dash put his chin on the stone next to Nabby, who reached over and laid a soft gray paw on the dog's nose. For a moment it looked for all the world as though they were having some kind of conversation. Then the corgi lay down at the base of the wall, his sleepy brown eyes watching the fluttering azure wings above. A hummingbird buzzed in, paused in midair for a moment, and then zinged to the vermilion bee balm for a sip of nectar.

I pointed to the scene. "That is what I want to do full time." I pointed to Scents & Nonsense behind us. "And that. And this." I toasted her with my last bite of cookie and placed it on my tongue to savor. "I can hardly wait for the whole mess to be over with, the killer safely behind bars, and for life to get back to normal."

"No kidding," Astrid agreed. "At least it sounds like Detective Garcia is on your side."

"Well, she's on the side of the truth, and that's good enough for me. She didn't seem too upset that I'd done some investigating on my own, either."

"Can you imagine working with Max Lang day in and day out?" Astrid asked.

"Ugh."

"So what's next, Nancy Drew?"

I stuck my tongue out at her. "Now that I know who Josie's other two clients were, I'm going to try to talk with them. With my luck, they were both out of town, too." I rolled my eyes, then smiled. "At the Greenstockings meeting, Thea said she was going to meet with Sophia Thelane about doing more landscape work on their place, and I'm going to see if she'll let me tag along. I have no idea how to get to Missy Renault, though."

"She has quite the reputation as a diva," Astrid said. "Probably wouldn't talk to you if you just showed up on her doorstep. And you sure won't run into her at the Roux. She's famous for being a staunch vegetarian."

"Good, because the last thing I want to do is hang out at the Roux Grill waiting for her to show up." I sighed. "I'll figure something out."

"You always do."

A blue jay landed on the edge of the birdbath, hopping in enough to get his feet wet. Below, the mnemosyne looked almost garish. Astrid hadn't commented on it, which kind of surprised me. She wasn't a huge gardener, but she was extremely observant. I thought for a split second about mentioning it, but couldn't bring myself to. That flower, that plant was *mine*.

At least until I learned more about it.

Our impromptu breakfast finished, Astrid left for a round of dog walking and cat feeding. I readied the register and flipped the sign in the front window of Scents

& Nonsense to OPEN. A few people were wandering the boardwalk, but it was early, and the weekend crowds hadn't started to filter into town yet.

I reached for the phone and called Thea. Her cell rang three times before it was answered.

"Elliana! Did you know Thea has a picture of you that shows up when you call?" The voice was deep and instantly recognizable. The sound of it made me shiver. "You're sitting next to a pile of compost."

Wonderful.

"Hi, Ritter. Where's your sister?"

"Out talking with a delivery driver. She left her phone on the desk, and when I saw it was you, I grabbed it."

I said, "Listen, could you take a message for Thea?"

"Sure thing."

"She mentioned that Sophia Thelane wanted to talk to her about a landscaping project. Would you tell her I'd like to go with her when she meets with Sophia?"

"Fan girl, huh."

I snorted. "Not exactly. Josie Overland helped the maid at Sophia and Rance's house. I just want to get a feel for how they got along with her."

"Elliana Allbright, intrepid detective."

"Hush, you."

He laughed. "Okay. I'll pass on the info to her."

A customer came in then, and I got off the phone to help her. A tall woman, with angled features and a stooped gait, she waved me off. After browsing for a long time, she finally selected a neck pillow filled with flax seeds and cloves. I rang her up and got back to work on inventory.

Traffic increased. I was wonderfully busy for an hour;

then business slowed. I was pouring myself another cup of coffee when the door chimed again. I turned to find Ritter coming into the shop. Today he wore a T-shirt that left nothing to the imagination, and what I was starting to think of as his trademark jeans. As I watched he brushed his hair straight back from his forehead with one hand, but it bounded back around his handsome face as if it had a life of its own.

"Hey."

"Hey, yourself," I said, managing not to fan myself. "What's up?"

"You know the landscaping Sophia Thelane wanted to talk to my sister about?" He lifted a shoulder and let it drop. "Well, I'm a fair hand at such things, and Thea's swamped at the nursery, so she asked me to meet with Sophia to find out a little more about what she has in mind. This afternoon." He grinned. "You still want to come with?"

I smiled demurely. "If that works for you."

He laughed. "Apparently she wants a retaining wall built by her swimming pool. I want to check out the one I saw out in your garden before I go up to her place this afternoon."

"The one with the mosaic?" I turned and pointed out the window to where Nabby sprawled on top of the wall. The butterflies had dispersed, but Dash was still tucked into the shade at the base, now seriously snoozing.

He came to stand by me, his gaze following my finger. "That's the one."

"Thea built that. It took her three days."

Ritter must have heard the skepticism in my voice, because he sounded a little defensive when he said,

"Today, I'm just going to show Sophia a few pictures. That's why I'm here, to take some pics. Thea will create the actual wall."

He stepped to the open door and went outside, then turned. "You don't mind, do you?"

I gulped. "Of course not." I glanced out front, but no one seemed on the verge of coming into Scents & Nonsense, so I joined Ritter in the garden. "Take as many pictures as you want."

Taking his phone out, he did just that, varying the angles and level of detail with each one. Then he stepped back and stood next to me. He leaned toward me and asked, "When do you want to go?"

I could feel his breath on my cheek. Unaccountably, he smelled of ocean and petrichor, that unique scent that fills the air when it rains after a long dry spell.

He spoke again. "There is something about you, Elliana. I don't know what it is."

A gust of air blew a swirl of petals off the Don Juan rose. They skittered around the stones at our feet, diving and dipping, then settled to the side of the path as the wind died down.

Ritter watched them, then looked back at me with a surprised expression.

A sign? Or the wind? I couldn't help but grin. "How about two thirty, then?"

THE woman who wanted scented favors for her wedding reception had decided on the chocolate lotion bars. I was happy to oblige—working with the fragrant cocoa butter was a joy. Since Josie's death, I'd fallen behind on so many things, but a glance at my watch told me I'd have plenty of time to make the bars before Ritter came back to pick me up.

Moving to my production counter, I hauled out a single-burner hot plate from beneath it. I plugged it in but didn't turn it on yet. Out came a battered, stainless steel pot, big stirring spoon, and a scale I'd originally bought for the restaurant but ended up confiscating for myself. In the office, which also served as a storeroom, I grabbed a chunk of beeswax, the container of raw cocoa butter, a gallon jug of olive oil, and some light almond oil that had been infused with Tahitian vanilla pods.

Back at the counter, I measured and weighed out the first three items in a 1:1:1 ratio and added them to the pot. Once the mixture was warming on the hot plate, I opened the drawer under the counter where I kept all my soap molds, and selected two dozen aspen leaves, sunflowers, and sea-shells. Laying them on the counter, I stirred the melting oils and wax, inhaling the chocolate scent until my mouth watered.

Luckily, I had Astrid's cookies to take care of that.

A family came in, and the father and two teenage girls were soon gathered on the other side of the counter. I explained what I was doing.

"The cocoa butter is already a solid, but the olive oil is emollient, and soaks deeper into your skin. It's too liquid at room temperature for a solid lotion, though, so the beeswax serves to firm it up. Also, beeswax is terrific for your skin."

Hearing me, the mother joined them. "Do you have any of those for sale?"

I pointed out the shelf where they were arranged, and she left to take a look. From the corner of my eye, I saw her examine the different "flavors": vanilla, cherry, orange, and cinnamon—all scents that melded well with chocolate. I'd chosen the vanilla for the wedding favors because it was both calming and romantic—perfect for the occasion, I thought.

Another customer came in from the boardwalk, and then two women. By the time I added the vanilla-scented oil to the mixture, I had quite the audience.

With great care, I ladled the warm mixture into the molds, ending up with six dozen lotion bars.

"And that's it," I said. "When they've cooled, I'll unmold them and package them in boxes like you see over there." Only I'd add pretty ribbons and a custom label to this batch.

Everyone dispersed, but remained in the store or wandered out to the Enchanted Garden, munching on cookies and drinking tea or lemonade. By the time Maggie showed up a few minutes after one, I'd made several sales and was feeling quite pleased with myself.

"Wow, Ellie! It smells amazing in here." She headed to the office to stow her purse. Today she wore white slacks and a pink blouse with a silk scarf. It was nice to see her in something besides the Roux Grill uniform. "You should open the front door so people can smell it from the street. Like with the bakery, you know?"

Pointing my finger at her, I said, "You are a genius."

She laughed and went to prop the door open. Sure

enough, within a few minutes an older couple had wandered in off the street. Maggie invited them to have some cookies and look around, and once again I felt lucky that she'd wanted to work at Scents & Nonsense.

Leaving her to watch things out front, I quickly made up the wedding-centric labels with the names of the bride and groom and the date of the ceremony using the graphics program I used for all my labels. Then I printed them out and set Maggie to affixing them to the boxes that the lotion bars would nestle into.

"When you're done with that, tuck some of this excelsior into each of the boxes for the bars to sit on."

"You've got it."

My cell rang. I ducked behind the counter to retrieve it and saw it was Astrid.

"I've solved your problem!" she exclaimed by way of greeting.

I went into the office and closed the door partway to get a little privacy. "You know who killed Josie?"

"No, not that problem. The one about how to talk to prissy Missy the ice-skater."

Leaning against the filing cabinet, I said, "Do tell."

"I'm sitting here at my desk, calling clients to remind them of their pet's appointments tomorrow, when I see her go into the gym across the street."

"And . . ."

"And she's dressed to work out! She's going to be there a while, Ellie. You need to get over there and take advantage of that."

I hated the gym. The very idea of sweating without actually accomplishing anything was almost offensive to me. I would rather work in the garden all day long than hit the treadmill for half an hour. However, Astrid had a point. This might be my only chance. I looked at my watch. It was one fifteen. I had until two thirty before Ritter picked me up.

"I'm not a member of the gym," I said.

She laughed. "Just go in and ask for a tour. They do that all the time. They'll let you try out the equipment, hang around for a while. Start up a conversation or two with someone else who's working out there—like a certain former Olympian. . . ."

"I guess I could do that," I said.

"You might get a sales pitch, of course."

"Believe me—I can resist any pitch that tries to get me to go to that place over and over again. Ugh."

"It's good for you," Astrid said.

"Gotta go," I said. "Thanks for the heads-up." I hung up and went back out to where Maggie was working. "I'm going to have to leave you in charge again this afternoon. I'm going over to the gym right now, but I'll be back—before leaving again."

"No problem. I don't know how you managed with help only two days a week, though."

I shook my head. "I'm starting to wonder that myself."

Of course, I hadn't been investigating a murder then, either.

"Well, I'm willing to work as much as you want me to. It's a joy spending time here."

CHAPTER 19

I N my loft bedroom, I shuffled through drawers searching for something that looked like workout gear. There: yoga pants and a T-shirt. It would have to do. And honestly, I'd been known to actually use the yoga pants for their intended purpose. I changed and went out to Corona Street through the garden gate.

Boomtown Gym, or, since there was only one fitness center in Poppyville, simply "the gym," was on Cooperhawk Way, a block off the main drag. It was a small classy place housed in a brick building that had originally been a feed store. Located on the corner, it was directly across from Dr. Ericcson's vet office. Sure enough, I saw Astrid sitting at her desk. When she saw me through the window, she waved.

My phone buzzed in my purse, which I'd brought along,

since yoga pants don't have decent pockets. I pulled it out
and saw Astrid had texted.

If you join, I'll come work out with you!!

I turned and gave her a sarcastic smile from across the
street, turned toward the door of the gym, and went inside
for the first time in my life.

The air vibrated with a driving dance beat. To the left,
a bank of cardiac machines marched down the wall: ellip-
ticals, stationary bikes, treadmills, and stair climbers.
About half of them were in use. Straight ahead, two rows
of weight machines filled the space to the back wall and
locker rooms. To the right, three other rooms opened off
the main area. One had ropes and straps and other devices
of torture hanging from above. The second contained tiny
tables and lots of toys—day care for busy moms.

In the third area a class was in session. A group of
women—not a single man from what I could tell—
bounced and stepped and swayed and stomped to the beat
of the music, waving their arms in synchronicity and
having a great time. With a sense of dread, I craned my
neck to see if Missy Renault was one of the masochists
taking part. If she was, I was out of luck.

I hated classes like that. I hated anything that took a
lot of coordination, especially if it was in front of other
people. Harris had assured me throughout our marriage
that I had two left feet. I couldn't argue with him. I'd even
messed up the first dance at our wedding.

"Can I help you?"

I turned to see an extremely buff guy with a shaved

head and eyebrow ring. I recognized him as a clerk at the hardware store. *Lots of moonlighting in Poppyville,* I thought. He'd come into the Roux Grill with his wife on occasion.

"I don't think you're a member here, are you?" He had kind eyes.

"No. I was hoping maybe you could show me around." I took a breath. "Maybe let me try some of the equipment?"

"You're Ellie, aren't you? I remember you from the restaurant."

"That's me. I'm sorry, but I don't remember your name."

"Mark Kittery. And I'll be more than happy to show you around. Here we have the TRX suspension training room. You use your own body weight to work out with these straps, and . . ."

My attention wandered, as did my eyes, searching for Missy Renault. Finally, I saw her toward the back of the room, running on a treadmill. And on the other side of a stair stepper, Inga Fowler spun away on a stationary bike. They were chatting to each other over the empty stair stepper like old buddies.

Which, perhaps, they were. I hoped so, because Inga might be my way into a conversation with Missy.

Mark showed me the class schedule, invited me to check out the women's locker room on my own, and led me to the day care room I'd already noticed. Inside, I found Inga's two children putting together an oversize puzzle. I waved to them, and they waved back. The teenager who was watching them looked up and waved at me, too.

Friendly place.

"Are you familiar with pin-loaded weight machines?" my guide asked.

My blank look must have been answer enough, because he beckoned me over to a contraption that consisted of a series of pulleys and weights. I could tell right away it was going to kick my behind.

"Come sit here," Mark said.

"Oh, I think I've seen enough," I said. "Maybe I could just look around a little more on my own?"

"It's no trouble," he assured me. "Grab this bar."

Suppressing a sigh, I did as I was told, watching Missy and Inga out of the corner of my eye.

"Pull it down," Mark said.

I pulled.

"Wow! You're strong for such a little thing. Here." He added more weight.

I pulled the bar down again. Inga had slowed and was punching buttons on the console of the exercise bike.

"Jeez. That's amazing!" he said, moving the bolt down in the pile of weights on the machine. "Try this."

I stood up. "Do you mind if I go talk to my friend over there? Maybe she can tell me how she likes it here."

He looked disappointed, then saw I was pointing toward Missy and brightened. "Oh, I'm sure you'll get a good review from her."

Thanking him, I made my way through the machines toward the two women. Then I realized my new friend had decided to come with me.

Dang it. How am I going to get him to leave me alone?

Someone came in and stood by the front counter. Mark

saw them, and with a moue of apology said, "Sorry, Ellie. I'm on the desk right now. I'll check in with you when I can."

"Okeydoke," I said, trying to keep the relief out of my voice. "Hi, Inga!" I interrupted their conversation.

Missy scowled, but Inga looked over at me. I saw that she had thirty minutes left on her virtual ride. She looked exhausted and too thin in her racer-back tank. I wondered what she'd eaten that day.

"Well, hi, Ellie. I didn't know you were a member here," Inga said.

"I'm not. Just checking it out. You know. Not getting any younger and all that."

She made a face, and I sensed her familiar anxiety. Because I'd made a crack about age? Inga had to still be in her twenties—unless she'd had work done.

I smiled a big smile at Missy, who had been watching us from her treadmill with a sour expression. "Hi. I've seen you at the salon, but don't think we've actually met. I'm Ellie." The music suddenly stopped as I spoke, so my name echoed throughout the room. I ducked my head and tried to will myself to stop blushing.

"Missy," she said. Her black hair was pulled back in a ponytail, and her forehead was shiny with sweat. She was a substantial woman—not overweight, but seriously muscled. Still, she ran easily along the treadmill, her rapid footfalls light and silent.

I climbed onto the stair stepper between them and peered at the control pad. I could feel their eyes on me, so I took a chance and punched a button at random. The steps began moving under my feet, and I had to start climbing to keep from being dumped backward onto the floor. Within seconds, I was panting and sweating.

Great.

I plodded on, thighs burning. Inga and Missy had stopped talking once I'd unceremoniously elbowed my way in between them. How was I going to start a conversation about Josie when Missy didn't seem to want to talk to me at all?

Artlessly, that was how. "So Missy, Josie Overland told me she used to clean for you. She was such a sweetheart. What happened is so terrible."

Inga shot me a surprised look.

Missy's lip curled. "Used to, is right. I fired her."

My jaw slackened in surprise. Then the stair stepper got away from me, and I had to scramble to keep up.

What button did I push, anyway? I squinted at the control panel, but all I saw was a series of lines that looked as if they belonged on an EKG.

I'm going to need an EKG by the time I'm done here.

"You fired her?" I panted. "She worked for me, too. Bartending and also in my retail store. I thought she did a good job."

"She was a snoop," Missy said flatly. "And I think she stole some of my jewelry."

I flat out gaped at her. I punched the STOP button, and the stairs mercifully ceased their movement. "Stole? Holy cow." I looked at Inga. "Did you have any problem like that with Josie?"

Inga shook her head.

Now that I wasn't trying to climb the Eiffel Tower, I

could sense something beyond the bitterness Missy Renault projected. I took in her defiant expression, the determined set of her jaw. Despite all that, this woman was deeply lonely.

Well, no wonder. She probably drove everyone around her away. I tried to dig up some compassion, but the last few days had tapped many of my resources. Maybe I could try to help her another time.

If she even wanted help. That, I felt, was probably the crux.

Concentrate, Ellie. You're here about Josie.

Inga's anxiety was rising, too. Standing between the two of them, I felt buffeted by emotion.

"I guess maybe I didn't know Josie that well." I reached for one of the antibacterial towelettes available in containers all over the gym, and swept it over the stair stepper as an excuse to stay where I was. "I wouldn't have thought she was a thief, though. How long did she work for you?"

Missy shrugged. "A year, maybe."

I looked at Inga.

"Same," she said. "It wasn't my idea to hire her, though. I didn't like having a maid."

I remembered the computer file labeled HOUSEFAIRY. Josie hadn't exactly considered herself a maid. But all I said was, "Why not?"

Inga shrugged. "I just don't like having people I don't know in my home. It's one of the reasons I don't have a nanny. I like being a mom."

"But no one likes to clean," Missy pointed out as her treadmill slowed and she began to walk.

"Maybe," the other woman said. "But I love my home.

I like taking care of it. I didn't grow up rich, you know. It feels wrong to ask someone to scrub my floors. My husband insisted, though. He's the one who hired Josie."

I smiled at her. "I saw your kids are over in the day care. They're terrific."

Inga's face brightened, and a calmness took over. "They're sweethearts. I'm so lucky. I love my life," she said.

"With all that money?" Missy asked with a laugh. "I bet you do."

"That helps," Inga admitted, turning off her bike with twenty minutes still left on the timer. She looked at her children through the open door of the day care. "But mostly, it's about them."

She got off the bike and gathered her water bottle and a towel. "I'll see you two later. Ellie, maybe I'll run into you here again?"

"Maybe," I said brightly. *Not on your life.*

She turned, and that's when I saw the tattoo of a tiny daisy on her shoulder. A normal tank top would have covered it, but the racer back left it exposed.

"Wait up," Missy said. "I'm coming with." She followed Inga back to the locker room without so much as a toodle-oo to me.

I took one last look around the room, my thoughts racing. Then my eyes found the digital clock on the wall.

It read two fifteen.

Darn it! Ritter was going to be at Scents & Nonsense in fifteen minutes, and thanks to my foray into the world of fitness, I smelled like a goat.

I jogged to the door and called to a puzzled-looking Mark, "Thanks for the tour. I'll let you know!"

Thankfully, Astrid wasn't at her desk by the window anymore, so she didn't see me jog by—or all the way home. On the way, I kept trying to remember what the woman in the photo with Josie had looked like at the Trace's. Black hair, red lips, white teeth—and that daisy tattoo. That was all I could come up with. So why would Inga have the same tattoo? Had she seen Josie's and wanted to copy it? I had to admit, it was pretty cute.

When I got to the store, I was sweatier than ever—and a mint green truck was parked right in front.

I tried to sneak around back, but Ritter stepped out to the back patio of Scents & Nonsense right as I hurried by. I nearly bumped into him, then backpedaled away.

"Hey!" I said in a cheerful tone. "You're early! And I was just at the gym. I'm going to grab a quick shower, okay?"

"Sure," he said easily. He grinned and sat down on a rocking chair. "I'll wait here."

I scurried down the path to my house. He hadn't blinked an eye when I said I'd been to the gym, and I had to look a sight. As I dashed through the shower and threw on a pair of shorts and the first shirt that came to hand, I wondered if I seemed like the sort of woman who worked out. Giving myself a once-over in the mirror with an assessing eye, I had to admit I was in pretty good shape. I could hardly avoid it. *Gardening is the best exercise—for the body and the soul,* I thought, reaching for the blow dryer.

Then I put it back on its hook. *No time for that.*

No time for makeup, either. But Ritter still gave me an appreciative look when I came back to find him playing fetch with Dash and a ratty old tennis ball.

"Sorry about that," I said. "Hope I didn't make us late."

"Nah," he said in a mellow tone. "I like your hair all wet and wild like that."

"No time to dry it," I said, blushing.

"It'll dry on the way," he said.

I checked in with Maggie and set her to unmolding the now-cooled lotion bars. Out on the boardwalk, I eyed the truck.

"Are you planning to get your own car, or just keep borrowing your sister's ride?"

He shrugged. "No reason to get my own car. I might be leaving in another month, and then what would I do with a car?"

Lead settled into my stomach.

He turned to face me. "You know I'm here because I'm waiting for a grant to come through for my work, right?"

I nodded. Thea had warned me. "Come on," I said. "Let's go."

CHAPTER 20

I KNEW it was a long shot, hoping for useful information about Josie from the fashion model we were going to see. Other than Missy's accusation that Josie had stolen her jewelry—something I didn't believe for a minute—no one Josie had cleaned for had provided any real helpful information. I crossed my fingers that Detective Garcia would do what she could in an official capacity, but my Chatty Cathy attempts to elicit information sure hadn't garnered much.

Still, I was happy to take a drive on a sunny afternoon, and I'd always been curious about what the Tillman-Thelane gardens looked like. So I sat back and tried to enjoy myself in spite of my worries. Ritter didn't know where the estate was, so I directed him to the west side of town and into the only neighborhood Poppyville could call fancy. The other houses were nothing compared to our destination, though—a rambling seven-acre spread behind a high stone wall that I'd never been on the other side of. At least not since the couple had moved to town and built their big house. When I was a child, that area had been an open space popular with birders and butterfly hunters.

Ritter guided the truck around curves with smooth ease, blue eyes narrowed against the wind coming in the window and sun-streaked hair blowing around his face. He didn't seem to mind, indeed had a small smile for the entire trip. With all the air rushing though the cab, we didn't talk much.

He was right; by the time we arrived, my hair was completely dry. I checked in the mirror, and was not impressed with my tangled tresses, but at least they were clean.

Ritter pushed a button and looked into the camera set outside the wall. Moments later, the big iron gate was rolling to the side, and we drove through. I unfastened my seat belt and sat forward, taking in every detail as we wound up the narrow drive to the ginormous house on the hill. Maples lined the road on both sides, reaching up behind precise boxwood hedges.

"Those need a lot of water," I said. "In fact, all this greenery does."

"They can afford it."

"Yeah—but can the rest of us?" I asked.

"Good point."

The drought that affected much of the state hadn't hit Poppyville as hard. My garden was close to Raven Creek, and the underground springs that supplied the town were still in good shape. We knew we were lucky. Beyond lucky, actually. So many people were suffering from a lack of water.

And places like this weren't helping any.

We reached the front of the house, which looked like something out of *Downton Abbey*. Not as large, of course, but ornate and very, very formal. I expected a butler to come out, or better yet a footman, but instead, Sophia Thelane herself came running out of the house as Ritter parked the car.

"Oh, you're here!" she said unnecessarily. "Thea called and said she was sending you two." She did a double-take when she saw Ritter. "Well, hello. I'm Sophia."

"Ritter Nelson," he said, sticking his hand out. "I've got some pictures for you to look at, and I'd like to see where you want the wall built. This is Elliana Allbright. She's assisting me today."

"Hi, Ella." Her eyes flicked to me for a split second before returning to Ritter. "Come on back, and I'll show you what I have in mind."

I tried not to feel slighted—or like an ugly duckling. Sophia was indeed beautiful, but without artifice. She wore not a single bit of makeup, her expensively streaked hair was arranged in a messy pile on her head, and she had on a light off-the-shoulder sweater and cutoff jeans with holes in them. Yet everything about her exuded a sort of natural sex appeal. It was as if something that ran through her veins made her move like a cat and throw sparks when she laughed. She wasn't *trying*, though.

Wow. What I wouldn't give for a little of that.

She led us around the outside of the house to another gate, which she opened to the pool area. I'd been noting

the landscape and admiring Thea's work. At the same
time, it was unsettling.

For one thing, there were a *lot* of chemicals in use on
this piece of land. Pesticides and herbicides and artificial
fertilizers. I could smell their subtle sickening sweetness.
And the plants were, for want of a better way of putting it,
overtended. There were no spent blooms. Not even fading
ones. No weeds. Nothing too large or too small for its
delineated space. The roses were beautiful, but climbed
their trellis in exacting rows. *Rows.* Someone took care of
this garden full time. They took such good care of it they
cramped its style.

It felt as if the garden was full of beautiful birds that
had had their wings clipped to keep them tame. I thought
of the pieces of driftwood, the rocks, and other natural
items Josie had collected on the shelves of her apartment,
and wondered how she'd felt on this fancy estate.

We reached the pool, and I adjusted my assumption about
a gardener. There were actually three men working along
the edges, not just one. Sophia approached and gave a few
instructions. One of the men asked a question, and she
shrugged and laughed. She wasn't the one who was the control freak. Maybe it was her husband.

"Come over here," she called to Ritter. I followed along
like a puppy.

We wended our way over the stamped concrete, past
an elaborate fountain—more water waste—and around
to an adorable grotto set into a tall hedge. The inside was
hidden from the pool and most of the surrounding area.
It felt private and wilder than anything I'd seen since
coming inside the gate, with ivy winding up the bay

laurels and a lopsided table and mismatched chairs teetering on the mossy stones.

"I love this," I exclaimed.

Sophia laughed. "Isn't it wonderful? My husband loathes it, of course. He likes things just so. I don't care, though. Rance is hardly here, anyway. He's been working in Scotland for the last four months. Anyway, this little space is mine, all mine, and it's where I want Thea to build my mosaic wall."

"Here?" I asked, pointing to the open spot beside the hedge.

"Exactly. And I want it to curve around here." She walked along the line she had in mind.

"Got it," Ritter said. "Let me show you some pictures."

They sat at the rickety table and bent their heads over Ritter's phone. He began flipping through the pictures he'd taken of my mosaic wall, and Sophia oohed and aahed at each one.

Feeling a little awkward just standing there, I went out to the pool to take a look around. Slowly, I strolled the perimeter, smiling at the gardeners, and trying not to breathe the strong scent of chlorine that had joined the other chemical smells.

As I rounded the far end, I saw Ritter and Sophia in the grotto. They weren't looking at his phone anymore. Sophia leaned in close and whispered something in his ear. He stepped back, looking startled. With a little shake of his head, he said something to the model. They rose and came out to meet me.

"Ella, Ritter tells me these pictures are of a wall in your garden."

I nodded, feeling more awkward than ever.

"Elliana," Ritter corrected.

"Right," she said. "And your garden is open to the public? He says it's really something."

"It's behind Scents and Nonsense, the shop at the end of Corona Street. It's open whenever the shop is open," I said, trying to smile. "I'm sure Josie Overland told you about it. She worked there. Here, too, from what I understand."

Sophia closed her eyes and shook her head. "Josie. That poor girl. I cannot believe what happened." She sounded sincere. "But I'm afraid she didn't talk to me about your adorable gardens and store. She only came in when my regular housekeeper was off, but only for the last six months or so." Her hand went to her throat. "Have they caught whoever did it yet?"

"I'm afraid not," I said.

Ritter promised to pass on the notes he'd taken to Thea, who would contact Sophia soon. The model walked us back to the truck and, watching her move, I wondered about her effect on Ritter. He couldn't possibly be immune to her charms.

I pushed the thought out of my head and got in the truck. Sophia's good-bye dripped with disappointment, and as she turned away from Ritter, her fingertips trailed slowly down his arm.

Just like Cynthia's had, in the Roux Grill. Was that a thing? Maybe I'd have to try it sometime.

Nah.

He watched her walk away with a bemused expression, then raised his eyebrows. "She's something, isn't she?"

I nodded. "I'll say."

He got in the truck. "Did you enjoy the show?" Sarcasm laced the words.

My eyebrow rose. "What show?"

The truck started with a rumble that quieted to a purr. "The famous fashion model licking my ear."

"I . . . she *licked* it?"

He laughed, reddening. "She sure did." He put the truck into gear. We drove back along the winding driveway. "She suggested that I might want to come visit her, um, grotto, at a later date, too."

"She's married!"

"Hmm. I don't think that really matters to Sophia. At least not when her husband is gone, and, as you heard, he's been away for a long time. If you think I'd be the first affair she's had, you'd be one hundred percent wrong, Elliana. I bet your friend Josie knew that, too. However, I doubt it got her killed, because I bet everyone who works there knows. As you can see, Sophia isn't all that subtle with her advances."

I stared at him. "When are you going back?"

His response was a surprised look. "I'm not!"

"Good Lord. You're going to pass that up?"

"Why . . . you actually . . . Listen here—just because she doesn't care that she's married doesn't mean I don't care. And besides, I'm interested in someone else."

"Oh," I said quietly. It had to be Cynthia.

Ritter eyes narrowed, and he spared a glance away from the road. "Thea said you called last night, trying to get ahold of me."

I nodded.

"Because . . . ?"

I was saved from having to respond by the approach of another car.

A police car, actually, with the Poppyville town logo on the side. Detective Max Lang was driving, and Detective Garcia sat beside him.

Though the two vehicles could have scooted by each other, Lang swerved to block the drive. He threw his car into park and got out, glowering at us both.

"What in blazes are you doing here, Allbright?"

Garcia exited from the other side of the car.

"She's helping me out with a job for my sister," Ritter said.

"Who the heck is your sister?"

"This is Ritter Nelson," I said, getting out of the truck. "Thea Nelson's brother. Don't you recognize her truck?"

"Who told you to exit your vehicle?"

"Oh, for heaven's sake, Max!" I said. "What is your problem?"

He glared at me, then barked at Ritter. "License and registration, mister."

Looking an apology at Ritter, I sidled around to where Garcia stood by one of the über tidy boxwoods.

"You learn anything from Ms. Thelane?" she asked in a low voice.

A little surprised, I said, "Nothing that seems helpful. She's probably had a few affairs with her husband gone, but it doesn't seem to be that much of a secret."

"Don't bother with the ice-skater," Garcia muttered. "I checked her alibi. Her sister was visiting. They went to Fresno that night."

"Jeez. Doesn't anyone stick around Poppyville anymore? Does Lang know?"

"He does now. Not that he ever suspected her, you know."

"Right. He only suspects me."

"I have a call in to the Silver Wells police about Bob Farsen." She spoke quickly, seeing that her partner was almost finished harassing Ritter. "They haven't gotten back to me yet."

"Thanks," I murmured and moved away from her.

"You'd better not be interfering with official police business, Ellie," Lang warned as we all got back in our vehicles.

I schooled my expression to hide my anger until after Ritter and I were out on the road back to downtown Poppyville. Then I banged my fist on the dashboard.

"Sorry," I said.

"Close your eyes," he said. "Let the wind blow all thoughts of that jerk right out of your mind."

It was good advice. By the time we got back to Scents & Nonsense, Lang felt like a distant memory.

B EFORE Maggie left for the evening, I asked her if she'd heard anything about Sophia Thelane having an affair.

"Oh, Lordy, yes. You didn't know?"

"Had no idea. Of course, people don't talk here like they do in the Roux Grill—especially after a few drinks."

"Well, she goes through men like water. But that actor husband of hers isn't any better, from what I hear."

"Did Josie tell you about them?" I asked. "She covered for their housekeeper on her day off."

"No." Maggie went into the office and retrieved her purse. When she came back out, she said, "See, Josie didn't talk about the people she cleaned for. Once said, 'What happens in a client's home, stays in a client's home.' Said 'Housefairies don't tattle.'"

I gave a little laugh. "I like that she called herself a house-fairy."

Maggie took off, and I checked the day's receipts. They were decent, which I found encouraging. Maybe business was getting back to normal, even if nothing else was.

I opened the back door and saw that the final two blooms on the mnemosyne had opened.

Tonight, then. Tonight I distill those flowers to their bare essence. And then I find out what Gamma was talking about in her journal.

But for now it was only five thirty. Usually I kept Scents & Nonsense open until six in the spring and summer. That last half hour of traffic was light to nonexistent, though.

Perhaps I should consider closing earlier.

On the other hand, if I could stay open later in the summer, the after-dinner crowd wandering the board-walks of Poppyville might be worth it. *Maybe just on the weekends.* Hiring Maggie for more hours might make that possible.

But I couldn't stop thinking about distilling the mnemosyne. Finally, I checked out on Corona Street to see if it looked as if anyone was about to come in the shop. I didn't see anyone out front, though shrieks of children's laughter echoed from the direction of the park.

Guess that crime scene has been released, too. I shuddered.

Back out in the Enchanted Garden, I raced down to my tiny house and retrieved Gamma's garden journal. After checking the shop again and finding it empty, I took the journal over to the purple blooms and opened it to the central page.

CHAPTER 21

T HE plant on the page and the plant under the bird-bath were identical, down to the number of petals and the angle of the corkscrew stem. It was downright weird, as if Gamma had drawn not just *a* mnemosyne, but *this* mnemosyne. I tentatively reached out and ran the back of my hand along the outside of the latest flower to open.

A tingle ran up my arm, and I dropped the journal. Blinking, I saw that it landed spine-side down, still open to the drawing. A rustling sound rose into the air. It seemed to come from all directions, from every plant in the garden. I remembered Gamma's singsong voice:

This is Lily, Elliana. See how she flirts in her yellow dress? And this is Snapdragon. So gracious. But you lie, also, don't you, dear? Deceitful Snapdragon. Look closely, Elliana, deeper than the colors, deeper than your eyes alone can see. Close your eyes in order to see them better. Can you detect their spirits?

She'd always talked like that, as if the plants had souls and personalities. As if you might want to invite some of them for dinner, but others not so much.

I closed my eyes.

Of course you can, Elliana. If you try.

The rustling faded, replaced with birdsong and the chattering of our resident squirrel. I opened my eyes and looked around.

The picture of the mnemosyne still shone forth vibrantly from the page of the book I'd dropped. Slowly, I stooped and picked it up.

If that was what happened when I *touched* the flower, what would the distilled essence be like?

Guess I'll find out soon enough.

I turned and went back to Scents & Nonsense and checked the time. The whole episode had happened in less than five minutes. It had felt like more, but I still had twenty minutes before I was supposed to close.

I went over and sat in my favorite rocker, eyeing the mnemosyne. I often remembered snippets of what my grandmother had said when I was working in the Enchanted Garden, but I hadn't remembered that conversation before. How was I supposed to see with my eyes closed?

With my ear cocked toward the open door to the store, I rose and strode to a bright orange snapdragon that towered over the roof of a tiny stone fairy cottage. Bending at the waist, I stared at it, long and hard. *Gracious,* Gamma had said. *And deceitful.*

The snapdragon didn't seem to have anything to say about that, though.

I heard a noise behind me and turned, expecting to see that a customer had come into the shop, but it was Ritter. He waved my wallet at me from the doorway.

"This must have slipped out of your purse," he said, and stepped outside to bring it to me. "I found it on the floor of the truck."

"Oh! I'd hate to lose that. Thanks for bringing it back." I smiled.

"No problem." He smiled, too, and bent to pet Dash. "I brought you a present, too."

I tipped my head to the side. "Present?"

He turned and went back inside. When he came back out to the patio, he was carrying a small bowl that held the tiniest juniper tree I'd ever seen. It looked ancient with its dark gnarled trunk and the minuscule bits of lichen adhering to the branches.

I looked up, eyes wide. "You bonsai'd this?" I asked Ritter.

He shrugged, but looked pleased. "I found it growing out of a rock face yesterday and brought it home." He thrust the exquisite little tree toward me.

"Where did you find it?"

"Up on Kestrel Peak. You know Mark Kittery?"

"From the gym?"

He nodded. "He's an old friend of mine. We went for a hike last evening, and that's when I found this."

I stared at him.

"What?" he asked.

"I thought you were out with Cynthia." I wanted to clamp my hand over my mouth the second the words slipped out.

"You . . . Oh, Elliana. Of course. You saw us together at the Roux Grill." A small smile tugged at his lips. "For the record, Cynthia Beck and I are old friends. Nothing more. At least not on my end."

I ducked my head to hide my relief and examined the little tree.

Reverently, I cupped my hands around the shallow ceramic bowl. The soil surrounding the tree's trunk was covered with shreds of moss and a few strategically placed stones.

"I didn't really do anything to it," he said, watching me. "It was already stunted—wind-whipped and surviving off nothing but the moisture in the air and the occasional dribble of rain. No idea how old it is. But as soon as I saw it, I thought of your garden." He gestured toward the verdant beds and winding pathways. "And the miniature tableaus you have out here. I couldn't help but think this little guy would fit right in."

With the tip of my finger, I stroked a twisted branch, marveling at the small miracle of it. This hardscrabble little juniper could have died—probably would have died—but now it was a piece of living art, carefully tended and given to me. My vision grew watery, and I blinked away the sudden emotion that the simple act of such thoughtfulness had evoked.

Swallowing hard, I looked up at Ritter. "Thank you."

He grinned, his relief tangible. That last surprised me. Had he been afraid I'd turn the gift away?

"Ritter?" I started to look at the ground, but made

myself meet his eyes. Swallowed hard. I was really out of practice with this kind of thing. "Do you think you might want to go out to dinner with me?"

He grinned. "Why, Elliana. I thought you'd never ask. How about tonight?"

"Oh!" The mnemosyne. "Would tomorrow night work instead?"

He nodded. "Sure. I'll pick you up at seven."

"Ellie! Ellie, where are you?"

My stomach twisted as I recognized the voice.

We turned toward the shop.

"Harris," I said as he loomed in the doorway. "What are you doing here?" Whatever it was, he looked mighty unhappy.

"I'm surprised you're still in business, Ellie," he said, his hands gripping the sides of the frame so hard that his knuckles had turned white. "Leaving your little store open to the street like that, allowing anyone to just walk in and take your money, or steal that *nonsense* you sell in there."

He'd always called my interest in aromatherapy "nonsense." His derision had inspired the name of the store, a detail that was utterly lost on him.

"But that's not my problem." He stepped outside.

Dash moved closer to my leg and growled low in his throat.

"Stay," I murmured.

"You deserve anything that happens to you," Harris said.

Ritter moved to stand by me at the far edge of the patio.

"Elliana?" he asked in a low voice. "Who is this guy?"

My heart was pounding, but I kept my tone mild. "What brought this on, Harris?"

Instead of answering, he glared at Ritter. "Who're you?"

"Harris! He could very well be a customer! What's wrong with you?"

"Elliana?" Ritter asked again.

"He's my ex-husband," I muttered, and sighed. "Now, what bee got into your bonnet, dear?" I couldn't keep the sarcasm out of my voice. "Because I've been up to my ears in crazy lately and, frankly, your act is getting old."

Beside me, Ritter smiled.

Harris, on the other hand, turned pink then red. He walked toward us.

I felt my eyes grow wide, and Dash bounced on his feet. One word from me and he'd go after Harris. That was the last thing I wanted, though. Somehow, I had to keep this situation under control.

"First you stole Josie from me, and now Maggie," he spluttered. "I wanted Maggie to cover Shyla's shift this afternoon, but noooo, she couldn't because she's here working for *you*."

I relaxed. "Is that all? Harris, you can't cut everyone's hours to the bone and also expect them to be available on a moment's notice."

"And that!" He pointed a finger at me. "You filled Josie's head with ideas like that, and then you turn around and tried to shift the cops' suspicions onto me when we both know you killed her."

"Oh, for Pete's sake," I said.

Ritter took another step. "Elliana didn't kill anyone."

"She told that woman cop about a silly little disagreement Josie and I had, and now she's asking all sorts of questions." Harris' face was purple. I hoped he wouldn't drop dead right there in front of us.

I'd had my fill of dead bodies.

"How do you know it was me?" I asked. "I wasn't there, but a lot of people were. In case you haven't noticed, you're not exactly quiet when you 'disagree.'"

"I still think you killed her," Harris tried again, but he was losing steam.

"That's enough," Ritter said, stepping forward.

"You stay out of this!" Harris met him halfway and, to my utter astonishment, swung his fist at Ritter's chin.

Ritter easily jerked his head out of the way, but I was trembling down to my toes. This was the first time I'd seen my ex be physically aggressive, and it changed everything. Should I rethink whether he could have killed Josie? Was that why he was so determined to pin her murder on me?

"Hey, everyone!"

Now Maria Canto from the library stood in the door. I took back what I'd been thinking about closing early. Tonight, Scents & Nonsense was hopping. Her dark eyes scanned the scene, flicking from face to face, finally landing on mine with a questioning look.

"Um, I can come back later," she said.

"No, no. Harris was just leaving," I said, giving him a meaningful look.

Harris rolled his shoulders and stomped to the garden gate. Without another word, he opened it and went out to Corona Street. His last statement was to slam it shut so hard the whole fence rattled.

Ritter followed behind him, pausing before lifting the latch. He looked back at me. "See you tomorrow night!"

I lifted my hand with a smile. Even Harris couldn't ruin the fact that I had a dinner date with Ritter Nelson.

Maria watched them both go, started to say something, then seemed to let it drop. "Do you still carry that sugar scrub that smells like pine trees?"

"Over here."

I CLOSED the shop and went to scrounge something from my kitchen. Standing in front of my slide-out pantry, I considered my options: sardines, peanut butter, olives, salsa, and a mysterious can of creamed corn I couldn't remember buying.

Then I spied the pasta canister, and pulled it out. A can of artichoke hearts. The cheese I'd used in the omelet the night before, and heck, why not an egg, too? Outside, I snipped more chives and gathered a handful of sage flowers. I picked several leaves from the dandelions I let grow back by the compost bin, took them inside, and rinsed them in the kitchen sink. Then I tossed them with a simple dressing of olive oil, balsamic vinegar, and brown mustard while the corkscrew pasta boiled on the stovetop. I mixed all the other ingredients with freshly cracked pepper. Adding the hot pasta and a bit of starchy water to the sauce, along with a knob of butter, I mixed it all together until the egg was cooked and the cheese had melted. A bit more pepper, another grating of cheese, and dinner was served.

Opening my last bottle of hard cider, I took my meal out to the Enchanted Garden rather than the porch. It was earlier than I usually ate, but I hadn't eaten anything but chocolate cookies all day. Come to think of it, I'd climbed a bunch of stupid virtual steps at the gym, too. No wonder I was famished.

I dug in, dropping the occasional nugget of pasta to Dash, who was stationed expectantly at my feet—exactly the way a good dog owner shouldn't. Halfway through, I slowed down and sat back to take a pull from my cider.

Soon I'd be distilling those strange flowers. After dark. I wasn't sure why, but I felt sure it should be after the sun had set. Taking another bite of pasta, I imagined placing them in the copper pot. *Better use gloves,* I thought. And then I pictured the camp stove beneath it.

Oh. No. Not for this. This time I needed a fire like Gamma used to make, with a grate set over the top.

Except . . .

I didn't exactly keep firewood around. And I didn't have a grate.

There might be some wood out in the meadow, by the stand of pines. And I can build the fire right in the center of the gravel.

Finished, I carried my plate back to the house. On the step, I looked up at the oak tree that stood guard at the corner. A dead branch with a lot of twigs hung down.

Oak for wisdom, strength, and endurance.

I hadn't noticed the dead branch before. Probably too distracted by investigating Josie's murder. Sure was convenient, though.

I washed my dinner dishes and went back outside. The branch came off easily in my hands. It snapped into six-inch lengths as if perforated.

Really convenient.

Carrying it all to the distilling area, I dumped them into a pile and called Astrid.

"Hey," I said when she answered. "Do you still have that little hibachi?"

"Ellie, I haven't had that for a long time. Why?"

"I'm looking for a cooking grate. That would have been kind of small, but it would have worked."

"Try Gessie. I bet she's got a big ol' grill at the stables, for the campfires she holds after the trail rides."

"Thanks. I will."

But after we hung up, I reconsidered. The grills I'd seen at Gessie's were, indeed, big. I needed something smaller.

Not too big and not too small . . . Then I remembered where there were grill grates that would be just right.

"Come on, Dash. Let's go for a walk."

He sat still while I fastened his leash onto his collar. Together, we went out the gate to Corona Street and turned left, toward the park. As we walked, we passed a father and son playing Frisbee, a ponytailed man walking his dog, and an older woman setting up an easel and glopping paint onto a paper palette. Farther along the fitness trail, a middle-aged couple sat on a blanket with a picnic spread out between them.

We rounded the far end of the loop and entered a part of the park that was unoccupied. I eyed the enclosed grill areas we passed. There were big ones you could have cooked a dozen steaks on, but also small ones designed for just a few burgers or hot dogs. I wanted to steal one of those smaller ones.

Okay, not steal. Borrow. I'd return it the next day.

I was looking for one that wasn't so covered with grease and burned food that I didn't want to touch it. Finally, I spied a grate that looked to be the right size and fairly clean. With a little wrestling, I managed to dislodge it from the concrete it rested on. With a confident smile, I walked the rest of the loop with Dash, acting for all the world as though I was officially supposed to be carrying a grill grate when other walkers and bikers passed by.

No one batted an eyelash.

Back in the distilling area of the Enchanted Garden, I piled together the oak twigs, then topped them with the lengths of larger branches. I set flat rocks on either side and placed the grate on top. Lastly, I brought out my copper distiller and tested to see if it sat evenly over the fire.

"Bingo," I said to Dash.

He woofed.

I set the jug of spring water out and a box of matches. By then, the sun was beginning to set.

It won't be long now.

CHAPTER 22

I WAITED until the moon rose above the horizon and got to work. The fire lit from a single match as if doused with kerosene, the flames crawling along the wood with eerie efficiency. It burned merrily for a while, painting the back of the garden with flickering orange light. I sat on the ground next to it until white ash had begun to dust the hardwood oak kindling. I fitted the grate over the top and went to gather the raw ingredients for tonight's perfume.

Ingredient. One.

Eschewing gloves, I selected a pair of deadheading shears, and took the copper pot and the onion-shaped condenser that served as its lid over to the mnemosyne plant. With my eyes narrowed in the dim light, I held the first pot below the plant, carefully snipped one of the blooms at the base of its stem, and let it drop into the vessel. I did the same thing with four more flowers, then set that pot aside. One by one, I clipped the final two blossoms and caught them inside the condenser.

When I'd harvested the final bloom without having touched any of them with my bare hands, I breathed a sigh of relief and carried the alembic back to where the fire had burned down to glowing coals. Filling the pot with water, I set it on the grate, then filled the condenser with more water and waited for the first one to come to a boil. The air began to grow heavy with the intoxicating aroma I'd become so familiar with over the last four days.

Breathing it in, I sat cross-legged by the fire and waited. I concentrated on the flames and on the water in the pot beginning to shimmer as the temperature increased. Curiosity spread deep inside my mind like an itch I couldn't ease. Would I finally have some clear memories of my mother? Or remember more of Gamma's teachings? So much of her murmured advice was buried deep in my mind by the years that had passed. Or would I remember something completely different, something unrelated to Gamma?

I opened her journal to the page with the mnemosyne drawing again, scanning the verse and all her notes.

Hidden memory,
Unbound

Best heeded. Those words sent a shiver down my back. They felt like a warning.

Then I spied something I hadn't noticed before, the edge of a faded word written so close to the spine that I had to carefully, oh so gently, open the book further in order to see it. The elderly volume creaked ominously but didn't split. Finally, I could make out what was really two words.

For Elliana.

Stunned, I checked along the rest of the interior margin. Nothing.

Dash nudged my arm with his nose, a rumble of concern emanating from deep within his chest.

"It's okay," I whispered, and wrapped my arms around him. He snuggled onto my lap, and together we watched the water begin to boil.

As the steam rose, I moved Dash and knelt beside the distiller. I attached the condenser, and topped the flower-filled reservoir with cool water. The bird's beak tube went on next, and I uncorked the bottle I had brought to capture the essential oil.

I'd found the perfume bottle in a junk shop years before and bought it for a few cents. Many of the bottles I used for custom perfumes were fancy or scalloped, gilt with metallic paint, odd shapes and different sizes. I collected them— always had—from garage and estate sales, thrift stores and online auction sites, and also purchased them new from gift shops and aromatherapy supply houses. Now that I had Scents & Nonsense, I was able to give some of them to my customers, but I'd always kept this one, empty, tucked away for some special purpose. If there was a special purpose, I had reasoned when looking for what to collect the mnemosyne essence in earlier in the evening, this was it.

It was purple, like the petals of the mnemosyne, made of glass that looked more than old: ancient. It was uneven, slightly lopsided, certainly handblown, and plain. But for some reason I loved it. Now, as I held it up the bird's beak, the rising moon shone through it like a portal to another realm.

The first drop of oil appeared. Its scent was so strong that my eyes watered. It let go of the metal tube and fell into the mouth of the bottle. A second one began to form.

My hands were shaking. One knee on the ground, I bent the other parallel and braced my elbow on it.

The next drop became round, grew larger, fought gravity, and plummeted into the bottle.

Barely breathing and keeping the bottle steady, I watched five more drops of the precious substance distill and collect. The last began to squeeze out of the tube. It took longer than the others, and I recognized there would be no more. The seventh drop of oil finally elongated, quivering at the tip of the bird's beak. Without thinking, I capped the bottle and put it to the side.

The final drop of mnemosyne essence fell from the copper as if in slow motion.

I held out my palm and watched as it splashed onto my skin.

Looking around me, I became aware of all the *life* in the garden, in sap and cells and the blood of creepy crawlies and those who flew, but also in the granite of a rock or the shine of a beetle shell, thrumming through wood already put to use in fence and house and planter and *fire*.

Whispers. Glimmers. Invisible moans. Slithering and laughter and chimes that can be heard only in dreams.

And then I remembered.

Mr. Finder, standing on his front walk. He seemed like an impossibly tall man, even though he was thin and his shoulders slumped forward. I was three years old and barely came up to his knee. It was late in the evening, at least for a little girl who had to go to bed when it was still light in the summertime, and he had just parked his old station wagon in the driveway of their home. I'd been playing in my yard, and when he'd pulled in, I'd skipped next door. Mr. Finder's wife frowned all the time and wasn't very nice. Her mother lived with them, too, though she had to stay in bed and so was rarely seen in the neighborhood.

But Mr. Finder was a nice man, and I liked him a lot. Now he was checking the mailbox. He pulled out a pile of envelopes with addresses showing through glassine windows. I hadn't known it then, but now, as an adult in the midst of this vivid recollection, I knew they had been bills. He sighed.

Then he saw me, and his eyes crinkled in a smile.

He *felt* funny, though. He felt so tired, as though his bones were mushy.

And I knew what would help.

"Wait here," I commanded as only an imperious three-year-old girl could do, and ran back to my mother's garden bed. There I picked a sprig of lily of the valley and, little legs churning, ran back to where Mr. Finder patiently stood.

I handed him the flower. "Smell this."

Obediently, he did. His eyes opened a little wider, and his bushy eyebrows rose. He sniffed again, and I could feel a quiet vigor returning to him.

"Thanks, Ellie," he said. "That was a real nice gift."

The memory faded, and I sat beside the dying fire, stunned. That had been the first time I'd used my gift of empathy and scent. And I realized that I hadn't really *remembered* the experience until now. It had just been a story told by my grandmother and, after she passed, by

my father and sometimes even Colby. Every family has
stories like that, cute things from a child's early years that
take on the form of either myth or joke.

But it felt as if I'd just relived it, and that made all the
difference. Because now I realized that I'd truly felt his
discomfort, just as I did with clients now, and had known
how to fix it. There had been no "fine-tuning" involved.

I truly had a gift—and always had.

Without warning, another memory flooded into my
consciousness.

This time I was lying on the sliding porch swing in
Gamma's gazebo. My head was on Mama's lap, and her
fingers stroked my wild curls. Her long dark hair was held
back from her pretty face with jeweled barrettes, and the
bangles on her wrists clanked softly next to my ear as she
moved her hand. The long skirt over her leg was warm
against my cheek, and I inhaled her scent of love and
licorice.

Gamma sat on a rocker across from us. She wore her
trademark coveralls—a part of me wondered how I could
have forgotten that she always wore those shapeless,
denim coveralls with the shiny buckles and the pocket in
front that always seemed to contain a piece or two of
candy. She smelled of earth and work, and her dark braid
was speckled with silver.

I closed my eyes. There was a pair of chickadees calling to each other from opposite sides of the yard, and I
tried to imagine what they might be saying to each other.

"Is she asleep?" Gamma asked.

"I think so," Mama said.

I kept my eyes closed, listening.

"That thing she did with Bert Finder yesterday . . ." Mama said.

A pause, then Gamma said, "She has it, too. Our talent."

"We expected that, though."

"But this young? It's so strong. Far stronger than either of us, even stronger than my own mother's. It will help a lot of people."

My mother sighed. "But it can be hard. A part of me hoped it would skip her generation."

"Hush! Don't say such a thing. It is a gift. We are given it in order to help others. She is a kind child, well suited to it."

"I know, Mother. But what do the leaves say?"

Oh, the leaves. I'd forgotten how my grandmother had gathered her herbs to make tea, and then, after drinking it, had read the leaves.

Silence drew out, and I cracked an eyelid. Gamma was looking off to the side. Finally her gaze returned to my mother's face above where I lay.

"We all help keep the balance, whatever our gifts. But the spirits in the leaves tell me this daughter of yours will do it in a larger way than some. That she will bring solace to others, but also right wrongs." She looked down at me, and I clamped my eyelids shut. "And that will be triggered by violence."

I heard my mother's intake of breath. She was one I couldn't read well, but she seemed scared.

"Don't worry, Fiona," Gamma said. "We will teach her so that she's prepared. . . ."

The scene faded from my mental movie screen, and I

was left sitting beside the glowing coals. I waited, but no more memories surfaced.

I was almost glad. The sensory memories of my mother and grandmother were so precious, and they truly felt near me now. But all that stuff about a gift and righting wrongs and predictions in tea leaves had left me reeling.

Not just tea leaves. Her *tea leaves. From* her *herbs, which she claimed possessed spirits and personalities.*

I left the water that remained after distilling the flowers to steep and went to sit on the bed of moss next to the birdbath. The denuded mnemosyne seemed to welcome my presence.

Triggered by violence.

Like a murder, say?

Hidden memory, unbound, only when ready, when needed.

Was that what had caused the mnemosyne to germinate?

And however heady, best heeded.

Heeded how? My grandmother had done her best to teach me after my mother had been killed in a freak accident, but she'd also passed too soon. I didn't know what I was supposed to do with this information about possessing a special gift.

Do what I've always done, I guess. Help where I can.

Gamma had been right about one thing—I did want to help people if I could.

Sitting in the lowering moonlight, my fingers buried in Dash's fur, I tried to differentiate the life essences pulsing through the veins of the leaves, drawing sustenance from the soil and collected sunlight from the day before. Was I imagining it, or could I really sense the innocence of the daisy, the heartthrob of the rose petals, the steadfastness of the ivy, and the militancy of the nasturtiums that tumbled from the window boxes of my tiny house?

This was how Gamma had known their language, I felt. But I was still such a neophyte.

I'd thought I simply had an elevated talent for plant scents and aromatherapy.

I'd barely scratched the surface.

I AWOKE to a cold nose prodding my neck. Then my cheek. Then my neck again. Dash made a worried sound in his throat, then gave a little bark. The dream came flooding back, then the knowledge that it wasn't a dream, and I realized it was just after dawn. I was lying in the Enchanted Garden, chilled but weirdly happy.

My fingers were still clutched around the tiny bottle of mnemosyne oil.

I laid my head back, watching the pastel tendrils of sunrise streak across the sky and fade, my body warming in the brightening sunlight with the rest of the garden. Sighing deeply and settling into my bed of moss, I drifted off again.

Apparently satisfied, Dash lay down by my side.

* * *

E LLIE?"
　　I opened my eyes. Astrid loomed above me, blocking the wide blue sky. I watched a cloud float through her rusty halo of hair.

Then her eyes widened in alarm. "Ellie! What happened? Are you all right?" She knelt. "Are you hurt? Did someone do this?"

"No, no." I struggled to sit up. "I'm fine. I just, er, fell asleep out here last night." I was vaguely aware that sounded crazy.

She stared at me. "You . . ." Reaching behind my ear, she pulled a leaf out of my hair. She turned it in her fingers with a bewildered expression, then examined my face. With her thumb, she wiped away a smudge of dirt from my cheek.

"Ellie," she said slowly. "Have you been drinking?"

"Have I . . . ?" I giggled. I couldn't help it. I tried to stop, which made it worse, and I giggled harder.

Astrid grabbed my shoulders and gave me a hard shake. "Stop it! You're scaring me."

My laughter faded into a hiccup.

I said, "I'm fine. Really."

But when I stood up, I swayed and had to catch my balance.

Astrid grabbed my arm and hustled me into my house. Worry creased her face.

I stopped her. "Really. Everything's okay. I'm going to shower now, and I'll be in the shop in no time. Okay?"

She nodded. "Okay."

But sure enough, she was still sitting on the sofa when I came out of the bathroom, and she followed me up the staircase. She sat on the edge of the bed, watching me like a hawk.

I smiled. "I'm all right. I just fell asleep. And you're the best friend ever."

She blushed. "I brought pecan shortbread. Good for dunking. I'll get the coffee going in the shop."

"Well," I said to Dash after I heard the front door close. "What do you think about this whole business?"

He grinned up at me.

THE mnemosyne plant had curled into a dry spiral under the birdbath. It had done its job. Somehow I knew it would disappear altogether by the end of the day.

The scent of coffee filled the air inside Scents & Nonsense. I ran my fingers through my drying hair as I reached for a cup.

"Be right there," Astrid called from the office.

I took my steaming mug of joe and went out to the garden to wait for her. Hopefully, she wasn't in there calling the men in white coats to take me away.

I realized that no matter what I'd learned the night before, nothing had changed in my day-to-day world. The crazy was still crazy, and I was still a murder suspect. I knew now that I needed to fine-tune my powers of scent and empathy even more. I could practice more, but I felt I needed a teacher.

I wish you'd lived longer, Gamma. Mama, too.

I'd had that thought so many times it was like a prayer.

But surely there was someone, somewhere, who could help me.

Astrid came out with the shortbread cookies. I didn't mention sleeping outside, and she let it drop. Instead, I filled her in on the scene in the Enchanted Garden the evening before, including Harris' descent into violence.

"I'm not surprised by the first bit," she said, dunking a cookie into her coffee. "As for Harris being a possible murder suspect? How would you feel about an I-told-you-so?"

CHAPTER 23

❧

Astrid offered to vacuum before the shop opened. It was a job I happened to dislike, so I happily took her up on it.

In the office, I forced myself to plow through some business things that had been piling up. I opened my e-mail and sent information to the bride-to-be about her lotion bar wedding favors, along with an offer to ship them if needed, and an invoice. Dealing with e-mail reminded me of Bob Farsen.

The more I played my conversation with Josie's former boyfriend—if that part had been true—over in my mind, the more convinced I became that, while he was definitely icky and a little scary, he probably hadn't driven to Poppyville and killed her. He'd really sounded as if he didn't know where she'd been living.

On the other hand, tracking someone on the Internet just wasn't that hard. I wondered why he hadn't done that.

Unless he had. Maybe Bob was a really good liar.

Get back to work, Ellie.

I'd been paying Maggie with cash the last few days, and needed to make her employment at Scents & Nonsense all legal and official. As I went to my payroll screen, I paused.

I owed Josie for four days of work.

Her absence hit me all over again. I considered the amount I owed her. What would she have wanted me to do with it? Send it to her brother? Not hardly.

Then I remembered the Trace Foundation. They had been going to help Josie. Now I'd donate double the pay I'd owed her to them. They had a convenient form online, and in no time it was done.

I sat back, distracted by thoughts of Josie. All my options for additional suspects seemed to be fading away.

Except for Harris. He was looking more and more as if he might have done it. Could I have actually married a murderer? If I had, then I had worse taste in men than I'd even dreamed.

Still, I couldn't bring myself to believe he'd killed Josie. He hadn't had a motive, not a real one. Of course, neither did I, but that didn't seem to matter to Harris or Max.

Josie and her photography. The difference between her early work and the streamlined—and stunning—depictions of the natural world.

Those early glamour shots.

With the daisy tattoo. *Tattoos.* Could it have been Inga with Josie in the photo at the Trace's? That made my brain hurt. Or maybe it had been another employee of the Calla Club—but then why would Inga have the daisy on her shoulder?

I needed to see that photo again.

I made a decision and marched out of the office as Astrid was turning the sign in the front window from CLOSED to OPEN.

"Turn it back around," I said. "And come with me."

"Where are we going?"

"To visit the Traces again. Can you call them and let them know we're on our way?"

She tipped her head to the side, eyes narrowed. Then she gave a nod, flipped the sign back, and went to dig her phone out of her backpack.

"I'M driving," I insisted.

Astrid shrugged. "Good thing, because I'm on my bike."

"Dash, you stay here and take care of things, okay?"

If a dog could frown, he did.

"Please," I said as I plucked a late bloom from the lily of the valley in one of the patio pots.

He made a sound of disgust and trotted out, sparing me a look over his shoulder before joining Nabby by the mosaic wall. From there, he glared at me as I locked the back door.

Astrid followed me across the street to where the

Wrangler was parked and climbed in. She smoothed her cotton knit camping dress over her knees.

"Put on your seat belt."

Giving me a sidelong look, she complied.

"Are they home?"

She nodded. "And expecting us. But they don't know why we're coming—and neither do I."

I drove nearly as fast as she had in the Peugeot, and on the way I explained about the daisy tattoos.

"Really? I don't think I ever noticed it—on either of them."

"It was on their shoulders, identical spots, where it would usually be covered up. And I never would have given Inga's a second thought if I hadn't seen it on someone who worked at the Calla Club with Josie."

"So we're going back to the Trace's because you want to see that photo again?"

"Bingo."

The morning view from the angled house on the ridge was even more spectacular than it had been in the evening. Alexandra greeted us on the porch, tail whooshing back and forth. John answered Astrid's knock with a puzzled smile.

"Astrid. Ellie. What can I do for you?"

I stepped forward. "I'd like to see one of the photos you have on your wall. One that Josie took."

He nodded. "All right. If it's important. But please be quiet. Gene followed your advice about the bundle of thyme, and it really seemed to work. I'm loath to wake him."

"Quiet as church mice," Astrid said.

Slipping off our shoes in the foyer, we tiptoed into the living room. I went straight to the picture taken in the Calla Club. Astrid came to stand beside me.

"What do you think?" I asked in a low voice.

"Gosh. It's awful hard to tell. Her eyes are closed. Her makeup is almost stylized, like a costume."

I nodded, disappointed. I really had thought another look would reveal whether or not the picture was of Inga.

"Do you want to see the other ones?" John asked from behind us.

I whirled to face him. "You have more of these?"

"About a half dozen that were going to be part of the gallery show."

Astrid and I exchanged a look.

"Would you mind showing them to us?" I asked, feeling excited.

"Sure," he said. "Follow me."

He opened a door and led us down wooden slat stairs to a cool, finished basement. I detected old mildew and laundry soap.

"Over here," he said, and pulled back a sheet from several white-matted photos on a table and pointed. "These are the ones I think you're interested in."

Sure enough, they were more shots inside the Calla Club. Eagerly, I flipped through them. One showed a woman in the same outfit Josie had worn serving drinks at a table. I could tell from one glance at her nose that it wasn't Inga. There was no one on the stage. I moved to the next one.

"There," Astrid said, and lightly touched one with her finger.

I leaned down. This one was just of the woman who appeared in the picture with Josie upstairs. Full face.

Hang on.

Her hair was short and dark, not long and perfectly blond as I'd seen it just the day before. She'd lost a lot of weight in the years since this photo had been taken, but if you ignored that, it was Inga Fowler's face.

What did all of this have to do with Josie's murder? Anything? Everything?

Astrid said, "Thanks, John. This might be useful in investigating Josie's murder."

He blinked. "Oh, gosh."

"Can I take this photo?" I asked. "I'll be very careful with it."

He waved his hand. "By all means."

Lifting it, I saw the one below it. It was another of Inga, but my lips parted in disbelief as I saw who the bartender standing behind her was. Apparently Karl Evers, the redheaded cook at the Roux Grill, hadn't always been a cook. And, like Josie, he must have moved to Poppyville from Silver Wells. Maggie had mentioned that he acted as though they'd dated before—and maybe they had. At any rate, they knew each other as coworkers in the defunct Calla Club.

And they both knew Inga.

I pointed it out to Astrid. She looked surprised, and then confused.

Pretty much the way I felt, too.

"Can I take this one, too?" I asked John.

"Of course. I want to help any way I can."

"Thanks," I said. "Astrid, we need to get going."

Outside I hurried to the Wrangler, stashed the pictures safely behind the seat, and retrieved the sprig of lily of the valley I'd plucked in the Enchanted Garden. I went back and handed it to John, who was standing on the porch.

"Here," I said, thrusting at him. "When Gene wakes up, have him take a sniff of this."

Looking bewildered, he nodded. "Okay."

If it worked for Mr. Finder all those years ago, maybe it will work for him, I thought.

On the way back down to Poppyville, Astrid asked, "So what do photos of Inga and the cook and Josie have to do with anything?"

Somehow, adding new information to the mix had only muddied the waters.

Think, Ellie.

"After all, they were all taken so long ago," she said.

I guided the Wrangler around a curve. "She looked happy. At ease. Nothing like the Inga I know now." What had happened?

Brock Fowler, mover and shaker extraordinaire had happened.

Stripper or waitress back then, Inga now had a different life with a rich husband and two adorable kids.

"You've heard the rumor that Brock Fowler wants to run for office, right?" I asked.

Astrid nodded.

"How do you think it would go over with his future constituents if they found out his wife worked in a strip club?" I asked.

Her mouth dropped open. "Blackmail."

I nodded.

"Josie?" Astrid shook her head. "You think Josie was blackmailing Inga? And Inga killed her? Holy cow!"

I frowned. "I don't know. Not only would it be hard for Inga to physically overpower Josie, but she was out of town with family at the time Josie was murdered. The detectives confirmed it."

My friend blew a raspberry. "Detectives."

"Admittedly, I don't trust Max Lang to get it right, at least not in this case, but I do trust Lupe Garcia."

I continued driving and thinking out loud. "Brock Fowler must not know Inga had worked at the Calla Club. With his political aspirations, I could see how that might be a problem. But did Inga really think something like that would stay hidden if her husband entered public life? She's uptight, but she's not stupid. On the other hand, maybe Brock had already found out, and he thought he could hide his wife's past. In that case, he might have wanted to shut Josie's mouth."

"Except he had the same alibi as his wife," Astrid pointed out. "Or . . . he might have left his family in Sacramento, using some business thing as an excuse, come back to Poppyville and killed Josie, then rejoined them."

"You have a devious mind," I said.

She smiled.

"That seems pretty complicated. Still, it's possible." I swerved to avoid a pothole. "Remember when I commented that John and Gene were rich enough to have

someone kill Josie for them? Brock Fowler certainly has
that kind of money, and then some."

"Inga sure is a jumpy one," Astrid said, utterly compla-
cent about my unusually fast driving.

I nodded. "And it was really bad when she found out
about the murder. She was really upset by the news."

"Maybe because she knew her husband was somehow
responsible," Astrid said.

Only Inga could tell us that. I pulled over in a cloud of
dust and reached for my phone, then stopped. I didn't want
to alarm her if she knew something about Josie's death.
Who knew what she'd do then? Would she run? Tell her
husband?

Instead, I rooted around and found the card Detective
Garcia had given me the first time we'd met. I entered the
number, and after four rings it went to voice mail.

"Detective Garcia, it's Ellie Allbright."

Astrid gave me a look.

"Listen, I just discovered something else. It turns out
that Inga Fowler knew Josie from when they both lived
in Silver Wells." I debated. It seemed wrong to disclose
Inga's past as a stripper when she'd been trying so hard
to keep it secret. "They, um, share a past." Let Garcia
figure it out. "And Karl Evers, one of the cooks over at
the Roux Grill, knew Josie in Silver Wells, too. I don't
know if that means anything. He's the one who's dating
the waitress I told you about, Shyla. The one who hated
Josie."

Ugh. What a mess.

"Anyway, I'm going to go pop over to see Inga now.

Astrid Moneypenny is with me. I just wanted to let you know. 'Bye."

"Now?" Astrid asked.

"This feels . . . urgent, you know?"

She nodded once. "I agree."

"I don't want to try to catch her in the gym again. That's no place to talk about something like this. And I don't want to give her a heads-up that we might be suspicious about her past."

"Right," my friend said. "Because if her husband is a murderer, then he might come after us."

I blanched. She wasn't wrong.

Brock Fowler had a lot of money from a lot of ventures and investments, but I knew he worked out of his realty office in Poppyville for the most part. Still sitting on the side of the road, I looked up the number, and as a precaution, set my phone to "private" before I dialed it.

"Gold Rush Realty," a male receptionist answered in a bored tone. "How may I direct your call?"

"Is Brock Fowler in the office?"

"One moment."

A Muzak version of the Rolling Stones' "Sympathy for the Devil" entertained me for one of the longest minutes of my life before the phone was picked up with a rattle.

"Brock Fowler."

I hung up.

He was in his office, so if we wanted to talk to Inga without him around, this was our chance. Still, the Fowlers lived in the old Miller house, which was in a fairly secluded area. That had made it a terrific place to have parties as teenagers, but perhaps not so great if her husband happened to come home while I was there.

I looked over at Astrid. "Are you game?"

"Consider me your trustworthy sidekick."

Grinning, I put the Jeep in gear. "I just want to make one quick stop at my place on the way."

CHAPTER 24

"Do you know where we're going, or do you want me to navigate?" Astrid asked as we climbed back into the Wrangler.

In my pocket, a variation on the blend of essential oils I'd taken when Ritter and I went to see Josie's brother felt oddly heavy. This time I'd left out the white poppy and added a different ingredient.

Chestnut for justice.

"I know the way." Twisting the key in the ignition, I added, "Haven't been there since I was in college, though. Wonder what they've done to the inside of the place."

My friend pointedly drew her seat belt across her lap and fastened it.

The Fowlers lived in a big log home nestled into the pines. It looked like a mountain lodge, with a deep wrap-around porch, thick railings, and two smaller decks, accessible from the upper floor. The cedar shake roof looked like the layered scales of a pinecone, and the peaked dormers had been set back to fit with the rest of the architecture. The foundation was of rough mismatched rock, giving the overall impression of a wooden houseboat beached on the shoals of a mountain river.

I parked the Wrangler at the edge of the circular drive on the west side near a copse of trees. Thinking to myself that the Fowlers needed to mitigate the flammable plant material around their home in case one of the state's ubiquitous wildfires raced through this area, I got out. I grabbed the two pictures I'd borrowed from John Trace and closed the door. It was a bit after noon, and I had to admit the trees provided nice shade.

There were no bikes or toys or evidence of Inga's perfect children anywhere in the driveway. Then I spied a swing set and large play area at the end of the house, where toys had been scattered with wild abandon, and smiled.

I knocked on the door. No response. Astrid reached over and pushed the doorbell. That elicited rapid footsteps inside, and Inga flung open the door.

Her hair hung in smooth waves over both shoulders, and she was dressed in a loose men's-style shirt worn over beige Capri pants. She was barefoot, barefaced, and wide-eyed. She didn't look surprised to see us; she looked shocked.

Her gaze ping-ponged between us. "Ellie? Astrid?" Then she saw the photos I held, and her shocked expression soured to disgust and anger. "You, too? How many people has she dragged into this mess?" She stepped back to let us in. "You're early."

Astrid and I exchanged puzzled looks and went inside.

My mind raced, fitting pieces together, making connections.

When the latch had clicked behind us, I turned to Inga. "I think there's a misunderstanding—"

"Let's just get to business," she interrupted. "And then you can be on your way."

I stared at her.

"What are you standing there for? Sit down, and I'll get it. But if you think I'm going to serve you tea and crumpets while you wait, you're sorely mistaken." She turned and strode across the room, going through an arched doorway to the dining room.

Astrid looked bewildered.

"Let's just sit down," I said.

We perched together on the sofa and waited for Inga to return.

The interior of the house was quite different from the last time I'd been inside. The Millers had decorated with lodge-style everything, from deer heads on the walls to Hudson Bay blankets on the leather sofas and a faux butter churn by the fireplace. The Fowlers had spruced up the log interior with bigger windows and light wood furniture upholstered in white. The wooden plank floor was padded with two enormous sheepskin rugs, and the antler chandelier hanging from the vaulted ceiling had been replaced with a pewter affair. A wide staircase led to the second floor, and they'd kept the original rough-hewn railing. I could see white-fabric-covered dining chairs through the door Inga had gone through. They had replaced the benches that used to surround the Miller's huge barn-door table.

How did she keep all that white stuff clean with two little kids?

Ten-foot-tall French doors at one end of the room opened out to a tiered cedar deck that overlooked the sloping valley behind the house. I spied an outdoor kitchen and rows of planter boxes spilling over with trailing verbena, sweet potato vine, and creeping Jenny. One of the doors was open, and a hint of hyssop drifted in to join the breakfast smells of bananas and cinnamon toast in the house.

A rustle came from the other room. Then a door slammed.

Inga stomped back in and threw a letter-sized manila envelope on the table in front of us. Tossing her hair over her shoulder, she said, "Take it and get out."

Astrid and I looked at each other, then at her.

"Is that what I think it is?" I asked.

The woman's familiar nervous energy hovered in the background, but at the moment it was dwarfed with rage.

"Of course it is. And it's the last payment. Do you understand?"

"Um, we're not here for any money."

Her jaw set, and she started to say something. Then she paused, and doubt crept onto her face. "You're not?"

I shook my head. "Please. Sit down. We need to talk to you."

Slowly, she perched on the edge of a chair. Her eyes veered toward the staircase.

"Inga, where are the children?" I asked.

"I don't have to tell you that!" Her eyes flared, and her shoulders tensed with a fierce protectiveness.

"Oh, for heaven's sake!" Astrid said. "What do you think we're going to do?"

"We don't want to hurt anyone. I just want to know if they're safe. Are they?" I asked Inga in a quiet voice.

She nodded.

"Okay." I scooted closer to her and laid Josie's photos on the coffee table. "We know about the Calla Club. That you worked there."

Her lips pressed together.

"That you were a dancer." I was guessing, but she didn't deny it.

She looked at the envelope on the table, and her forehead wrinkled. "But you're not here for money?"

"No." I glanced at the envelope, too. "Who have you and Brock been paying off?"

"Brock. Oh, God. He's going to find out. After all this, he's still going to find out," she said. Tears welled up in her eyes. She buried her face in her hands.

Astrid shot me a helpless look.

"I'm sorry. Truly," I said. "But you have to tell us what happened."

She looked up and hiccuped a sob.

"Tell us what happened to Josie," I prompted.

"I don't know," Inga practically wailed. "We got home from Sacramento, and she'd been murdered. And God help me, I was *glad*." Her jaw set. "When you told me that someone had killed her, Ellie, I was glad."

No, you weren't, I thought, remembering the anxious energy coming off her. *You were scared.*

Astrid looked outraged, then faded into thought. "But you didn't kill her."

"No!" Inga said.

"And your husband didn't do it," Astrid said, slowly, working it out.

"No! Why would he? He didn't . . . know about . . ." She blinked back tears again. "But he's going to find out now. Worse than that, the kids will know."

And that, I realized, was what she was really worried about.

I shook my head. "I'm sorry, but I'm confused. Are you saying you gave Josie money? And that's why you were glad she was dead?"

Chin quivering, she nodded. "I didn't give the money to her, but she had to have been behind it. And now that she's out of the picture, it's still going on. It'll never stop!"

Astrid and I exchanged a look.

"Who did you give the money to?" I said, pretty sure I knew the answer.

"Are you sure he didn't send you?" she asked with a bewildered expression.

"No one sent us." I looked at Astrid. "I think she means Karl."

Astrid blinked. "The cook at the Roux Grill?"

"He worked at the Calla Club, too, after all. Didn't he, Inga?"

Inga nodded, looking thoughtful. "Uh-huh."

"Tell us what happened."

Inga looked between us, then seemed to make a decision. "I got a letter."

"A letter or an e-mail?" I mentally kicked myself. *Let her tell you.*

"A hard copy letter."

"Who was it from?" Astrid asked.

Inga said, "It must have been from Josie, right? It didn't have a name on it, but she'd already told me she had some pictures that I was in. 'Art photos,'" she said, glancing down at the pictures on the coffee table. "She threatened to make them public."

"How?" I asked.

"She was going to show them in a gallery in Sacramento."

"The pictures are brilliant photography," I said. "But I never in a million years would have recognized you in them. Just look."

"You wouldn't?" she asked in a small voice, and leaned forward.

I smiled. "Except for your daisy tattoo I happened to see the other day."

Her fingers fluttered to her shoulder. "But the letter . . ."

"What did it say?" Astrid asked.

"It came right out and said if I didn't pay a hundred thousand dollars, she'd tell Brock I was a stripper at the Calla. That there were pictures. I thought she was my friend." Tears threatened again, and I was relieved when she took a deep breath and seemed to force them back. "He's very conservative. Brock, I mean. I met him at a fund-raiser where I was waitressing." Defiance flashed in her eyes when she looked at me. "I worked for a caterer during the day."

I nodded but managed to keep my mouth shut.

She went on. "We hit it off. He liked me, even though I was a waitress and he was an important businessman. He lived in San Francisco—didn't know anything about the Calla Club. He'd only been in Silver Wells to help support some political candidate when I met him." She sighed, and her expression turned dreamy for a moment. "I quit the Calla and moved to San Francisco when things started getting serious. Once we got married, though, he wanted to get out of the city. For the"—her throat worked—"for the kids. So we moved to Poppyville."

She looked down at her hands, now twisting in her shirttail. "It was perfect." Her gaze rose to ours. "I had the perfect life. I love Brock, I really do. He's good to me and kind, and we have Molly and Ethan." Her face collapsed. "They're going to hate me."

"No, they won't," Astrid said. "You're their mama."

"Tell us about the blackmail," I said.

"After the letter, I knew Josie was serious. So I got the money together," she said simply. "When Karl showed up, it kind of surprised me, but, then again, not really. They'd been friends at the Calla, so he already knew about my past. When I asked if Josie had sent him, he said she had. So I gave him the money. I dared to hope that would be the end of it. I really thought it was, once I heard someone had killed Josie." She looked down at the pristine rug at our feet. "But now Karl wants another payment."

"Wait a minute." Astrid stood. "What do you mean, 'now'?"

I rose as well, alarm bells clanging in my brain.

Inga gazed up at us. "He's coming this afternoon." She looked at her watch. "In about ten minutes."

"Inga!" I reached for her arm and pulled her up from the chair. "I don't think Josie sent Karl here. You were the one who mentioned her name to him, right?"

She gave a small nod.

"Josie never wanted to blackmail you. She just wanted to show her photos in a real art gallery. She was proud of them, and she wanted you to know." I paused, thinking. "I bet she told Karl, too—maybe even showed him the pictures. And bingo, he saw an opportunity and decided to make a quick buck. But Josie wasn't like that."

I remembered how the redheaded cook had assumed I didn't want Harris to know I'd been in his office, and that I'd want to sneak out the back way.

"But Karl *is* like that. And worse, I think when you asked if Josie sent him, he saw her as a rival for the blackmail money he was planning to milk from you for a long, long time." I looked at Astrid, whose eyes had gone wide as she put it together.

"And he killed her," she breathed.

Inga turned white and grabbed the back of the chair.

My friend had already moved toward the stairway. "Get your kids, Inga," I said. "Astrid, will help you. We're going to the police station. Right now."

At the mention of her children, Inga regained her balance and ran past Astrid. My friend followed her up the stairs, two at a time.

I pulled out my cell and called 911. The call failed, and I realized there were no bars on the phone. How could cell reception be so terrible this close to town? I went out to the deck, tried again, and got through. Relieved, I said, "This is Ellie Allbright. I'm at the Fowler's home. The old Miller place, you know?"

The response was garbled nonsense.

"Nan? Nan Walton, is that you? Can you hear me?"

More cellular gobbledygook.

"Darn it!" I hung up and called Lupe Garcia's number. I couldn't hear anything on the other end of the line, but the call didn't end, so I said, "It's Ellie. I'm at Inga Fowler's. Karl Evers killed Josie. I'm sure of it. We're coming to the station."

I hung up and ran inside, casting around the room for evidence of a landline. With cell reception this horrible, the Fowlers had to have one. I spied a cordless handset tucked behind a vase on a console table across the room.

"Hurry up, you guys," I called, taking a step toward it. "We have to get out of here!"

"And why is that?"

I whirled around to see Karl Evers had walked right in as if he owned the place.

CHAPTER 25

A LARM turned to fear, winging through my veins.
Then the fear turned to terror as I saw his freckled
smile drop into a sociopathic sneer. "Why, Ellie Allbright.
I sure didn't expect to see you here."

The smell of the aftershave I'd thought my ex had
started using wafted through the air, acrid and sour. I'd
smelled it on Josie's body, and in Harris' office. Now I
realized it had been a barely there undercurrent of the all
the kitchen smells at the Roux Grill, and I'd put that down
to Harris, too. But I didn't remember smelling it on Harris
when he came to Scents & Nonsense to complain about
my hiring Maggie.

It had been Karl all the time.

"Inga!" he called. "Where are you? Get out here."

"No!" I yelled. "Lock the door and call the police!"

Karl grabbed my arm. "Shut up." His gaze flicked to the stairway.

Inga stood looking down at us with her hand on the rail. She was so pale that her face shone white in the semidarkness at the top of the stairs.

"Ah, there you are. Good." He looked back at me. "She knows better than to call the cops. Don't you, dear?"

He sneered down at me. I tried to pull away, but he tightened his grip. "You're not going anywhere. Now sit down." He pushed me back, and I landed on the sofa.

"Good girl," he said softly. "Inga, come down here." His gaze rose over my shoulder. "Now, please."

I heard her footsteps on the stairs behind me. I realized Karl was older than I'd originally thought. The red hair and Howdy Doody demeanor gave him a boyish air, but the lines around his eyes and mouth told a different story. Karl Evers was pushing forty.

Oh, and those eyes. Now that I was so close, I could see the deep-seated and carefully nurtured resentment in them.

And fear. There was so much fear in the room . . . Oh, wait. Even though I recognized Inga's trademark disquiet, the fear that was making my hands tremble wasn't something I was picking up from her or Karl.

That was all mine.

Karl smiled at me again. He liked how scared I was. Then the smile dropped. "Why are you here, Ellie? Did you think you could horn in on the money like Josie did?"

"I don't know what you're talking about," I began.

"Of course you do." He looked down at the photos on the table. "I have one of those, too, you know."

I tipped my head to the side, remembering the blank

spot on Josie's living room wall. "But you stole yours, didn't you, Karl? You stole Harris' key to Josie's apartment. The manager there heard you going through her things next door."

He smirked. "And where did you get yours?"

I was silent.

He looked up at Inga. "Come on over here."

She walked around the edge of the sofa and sat down next to me. Then her trembling finger pointed to the envelope on the table. "Take it and go."

He crossed his arms. "Well, now thank you very much for your installment, but it appears that now I have a little more to think about than what do with all that cash, don't I? For example, what am I going to do with you ladies?"

"The police are on the way," I said.

"Hmm. You know, I don't think they are. I think you came here looking for a payoff from the golden goose here, just like me. And I don't think you'd invite the cops to the party."

I was getting pretty sick of everyone thinking I was either a murderer or a blackmailer. "You're an idiot," I said, still scared but now angry, too.

He blinked.

"Not everyone in the world is as money-grubbing as you are. Not everyone is as evil or walks around with a big chip on their shoulder, thinking the world owes them something."

My words must have struck a chord, because his jaw set and his nostrils flared.

"Josie never wanted any money from Inga." I jumped to my feet and backed toward the front door.

"Sit down," he grated.

"But you were so sure she was as horrible as you are that you killed her, didn't you? Josie didn't want Inga's stupid money, and she didn't know anything about what you were doing. You lured her to the park and killed her for nothing!"

Karl took three steps, grabbed my arm, and yanked me into the kitchen. I slipped on the tile floor, but he pulled me to my feet and reached for the wooden knife block on the shiny granite counter. He selected a utility knife with a nine-inch-long blade, turned, and jerked me after him. In front of the sofa, he pushed me. I staggered. The sofa hit the back of my knees, and I sat down with a thump. Beside me, Inga, who hadn't budged, sucked her breath in between her teeth.

A charged silence filled the room. I turned to glare at Inga. While Karl and I had been in the kitchen, even so briefly, she could have run out the front door. She looked at the stairway, and I got it. No way would she leave her children.

Who were upstairs. *With Astrid.*

And Karl had no idea Astrid was in the house. I thought of the balconies overlooking the front drive. Would it be possible for her to climb down from one of those?

He began to pace back and forth in front of us, swinging the knife in time with his steps. When he turned away, my gaze shot over to the phone I'd seen on the console. Maybe I could get to it long enough to punch in 911.

I shifted in my seat. Karl paused midstep and pointed the knife at me. "Stop fidgeting, and let me think. As you know, I'm perfectly willing to use this if you try anything stupid."

Wide-eyed, I fell still. He resumed pacing.

My hand was in my pocket, though. Moving as slowly as possible, I uncorked the bottle of bittersweet, heather, and chestnut oils.

Truth, protection, and justice. The volatile oils immediately rose into the air.

Suddenly Karl stopped. I saw him sniff the air. Then he paused in front of me.

"I didn't lure Josie to the park. I made her go with me."

"She fought you."

Regret flickered across his features. "She did. And she got away."

And came to the first building on that end of town.

He blinked, then narrowed his eyes at me. "Enough with the interrogation."

Except I hadn't asked him any questions.

Truth: check. Now for protection and justice.

"Where are your kids?" he suddenly asked Inga.

Anxiety cascaded off Inga, but there was that ferocious mother-bear protectiveness, too. She would do anything to protect her children. Her eyes narrowed, and she glared at him.

"Where?" he demanded, sounding desperate. He pointed the knife at her.

"Where you can't get to them," she said, her eyes shifting for a split second to the stairs. She couldn't seem to help herself.

Karl saw it, and his lips thinned. "All right. Here's what

we're going to do. I know there's a safe in the house." His eyes flicked to me, and he smiled. "Josie told me that before I killed her."

I felt the blood drain from my face.

"So we are going to go up to your bedroom, and you are going to open that safe, Inga. You are going to give me everything inside of it, and then I'm going to leave. Easy as pie."

"You'll really go?" Inga asked in a small voice.

He nodded. "Yep. Far away."

She stood.

"Inga," I said. "He's lying."

"Oh, Ellie. You clever thing." He motioned me up with the knife. "Come along."

Having no choice, I shuffled toward the stairs. As I passed the console, I looked down at the portable phone handset. It was glowing orange.

Someone was using another handset. *Astrid.*

We began to climb. I said, "He's going to kill us, Inga."

We just have to stay alive long enough for help to arrive.

"We know he killed Josie." I looked over at her. Understanding passed between us. Whatever she had in mind, Inga wasn't giving up yet.

"True!" Karl crowed from behind us. "I never said I wasn't going to kill you. In fact, I'm thinking you'll be found with the knife in your hand, Ellie. According to the ranting of your ex-husband, the police already think you killed Josie. They won't be surprised to find you killed Inga, too."

"I called them before I came," I said. "They'll know it was you."

"Nice try, honey."

We'd reached the upstairs hallway. Five doors opened off it, two on each side, and at the end, double doors led to the master bedroom. Where was Astrid?

Inga stopped and turned to face Karl. "I'm not opening any safe for you."

He reached out and pushed her. She stumbled against the wall.

"Yes, you are."

Her chin came up. "Why should I, if you're just going to kill us?"

"Because if you do what I ask, I won't start opening all these doors until I find your children. I'll do what I have to do, and then I'll walk away."

She closed her eyes for a moment, then opened them as if she'd made a decision. "You'll leave them alone?"

He nodded.

She turned and looked at me, then put her hands on my shoulders and squeezed. "I'm sorry, Ellie. I don't have a choice."

And then, very slowly, she winked.

Inga turned and walked to the end of the hallway. "The safe is in here."

But instead of opening the doors to the master suite at the end, she opened the door on the right.

Karl's eyes narrowed. "Josie said the safe was in your bedroom."

"It is," Inga said. "This is our bedroom." She walked in.

At first I thought she was trying to trick him, but when I got a good look at the books on the nightstand, the mussed coverlet on the king-size bed, and the tray on the dresser that held a phone charger, keys, and loose change, I changed my mind. The scent of the custom perfume I made for Inga confirmed it: This was where she and Brock slept.

Karl pushed me into the room behind Inga and waited in the doorway.

I turned to look at him, and saw Astrid standing behind the door. I looked away again, not wanting to give her away, but in that brief glimpse I saw she was absolutely livid.

Livid was good. Astrid kicked butt when she was livid.

Inga went to a tapestry on the wall and moved it aside. The wall safe was right behind it. Karl seemed to relax when he saw it.

"Open it."

Inga moved to stand in front of the safe, twirling the combination forward, back, and forward again so none of us could see the combination. Karl smiled, seeming to find her secrecy amusing. After all, we'd both be dead soon.

It took all my effort not to look at Astrid. I carefully kept my attention on Inga, exactly where Karl expected it to be, while trying to see what my friend was doing from the corner of my eye. The tiny bottle of oil was still clenched in my fist. Casually, I upended it and let the oil dribble out on the floor.

Karl looked confused, but the two women didn't seem to notice.

Inga twisted the handle, and the door of the safe silently opened. "What do you want me to do now?" she asked, without turning around.

A satisfied smile spread on his face, and Karl stepped into the room.

And slipped in the puddle of oil. The klutzy cook went sprawling. The knife flew out of his hand and clattered against the wainscoting. He groaned, the wind knocked out of him, and Astrid and I both jumped on him to try to pin him down.

He grunted and was still.

We relaxed and gave each other a grin.

Suddenly, he twisted, and pushed me off. He took a swing at Astrid, and his fist glanced off her shoulder.

"Ow," she grunted, struggling with him.

"Karl, be still," Inga said.

I looked up at her, gaping.

She stood in front of the safe, training a gun down on Karl.

Astrid and I scrambled out of the way. Karl stared at her, his bravado and arrogance shriveling as he tried to sit up.

A banging came from downstairs, then voices.

"Ellie? Astrid? Inga?"

"Up here, Detective Garcia," I called, holding my hand out for the gun.

Inga relaxed and handed it to me. "I think I might need a new perfume from you in the next few days."

"Come by the shop," I said. "I'll see what I can do."

Lupe Garcia looked around the edge of the doorframe and took in the tableau. I motioned her into the room and handed her the gun.

"This is Inga's." I pointed to the knife on the floor. "So is that, but Karl was planning to use it on us the same way he killed Josie Overland."

Detective Garcia grinned at me. "Nice job, Ellie."

Out in the hallway, I saw Max Lang redden and look away. I tried very hard not to feel self-satisfied—and utterly failed.

I tipped my head at Karl, who was still lying on the floor. "He grabbed the knife from the Fowler's kitchen. You know, I wouldn't be surprised if the knife that killed Josie came from the Roux Grill kitchen."

His glare told me I was right. I smiled at him.

"I have to check on my kids," Inga said, pushing out of the room.

I looked in the safe, expecting to see a sheaf of cash, or at least a jewelry box. But there was nothing in it except for another even larger gun.

CHAPTER 26

‡

DASH jumped to the ground from the seat of my Wrangler, and I picked up the paper plate of raspberry thumbprint cookies with both hands. I closed the door with my foot, and walked across the parking area toward the barn. The *bock-bock*ing of a chicken echoed from the far side of the paddock, and three sturdy quarter horses watched me walk by with interest. One ambled over and tossed his head over the low fence.

"Sorry, buddy. These cookies are spoken for."

Dash looked up at him with a grin and jogged after me.

I found Gessie in her combination office–tack room in front of the stables, hunched over paperwork. Halters hung along the back wall, and the single saddle stand in the corner held her fancy silver-studded show saddle that I'd seen her sitting on in last year's July Fourth parade.

She looked up when I blocked the sunlight in her

doorway. "Hey, Ellie!" She stood and gave me an awkward hug around the plate of cookies. "Heard you had a little excitement recently."

"A little. Things are going to get back to normal now." *At least they'd better.*

"Good to hear it. So what can I do you for?"

Lifting the plate, I said, "I don't suppose Pete Grimly is around, is he?"

"Bongo Pete? Probably."

"I brought him some cookies."

She smiled. "Well, that's awful nice. He likes cookies."

"Where would I find him?"

"Let me show you." Gessie led me outside and around to the back of the barn. Pointing to a line of trees a few hundred feet away, she said, "You can see where the river is there. He's usually down that way, to the right. Away from the rest."

"Really?" I asked in surprise. "He doesn't camp with the others?"

She shook her head. "Not usually. He's kind of, well, sensitive, I guess you'd say. Being around other people makes him nervous."

I looked down at the cookies.

"Oh, don't worry. He likes visitors. Go on."

After thanking her, I made my way down the dirt path that had been worn through the bunchgrass. Dash bounded through the field, scaring up grasshoppers, collecting seed pods in his fur, and having a great time.

A figure sat in a foldout camp chair next to a tent. He smoked a pipe, and I smelled the enticing aroma of cherry tobacco.

"Pete?" I called, not wanting to frighten him.

He turned and saw me. His broad face lit up, and his grin grew even larger when Dash ran up to him and started wiggling his tailless behind in greeting. He bent to pet him, and the corgi lapped at his hand.

"Hi," Pete said shyly. "I remember you." He wore canvas pants, boots like Ritter's work boots, and the T-shirt that said KING OF THE BONGOS.

"From the park?" I asked, coming to sit beside him. The river murmured at our feet, tumbling over rocks and boulders and releasing the scents of wet soil and fish scales into the air around us.

"Nah," he said. "From the other day. And you always say hi to me on the street."

I nodded. "And you say hi back. But you don't remember seeing me in the park the other night?"

"Oh! Sure?"

"How late was it?" I asked.

He shrugged. "I don't know. Dark?"

It didn't matter. I held out the covered plate. "Do you like raspberry thumbprints?"

"Mmm. I love them! You made these for me?"

"Well, my friend did. She's a better cookie baker than I am."

He took a delicate bite. "This is delicious. Would you like one?" He held out the plate.

I took a cookie and nibbled it while looking at the river. "It's peaceful here," I said.

"That's why I like it so much," he said. "The water washes away the stuff."

Surprised, I asked, "What stuff?"

He waved his hand. "All the extra stuff. The sounds

of the grass growing and squirrel's heartbeat and how hungry the trout get by the time the sun goes down."

I stared at him.

"Sorry." His head ducked down. "Gessie says I shouldn't say stuff like that. She says they'll put me away if I do. No one knows what I'm talking about." He met my eye. "I'm not trying to scare you."

I wondered if he could hear my heartbeat right then. I cleared my throat. "Pete, you're not scaring me."

"Really?"

I nodded. "Really."

He smiled. "Would you like another cookie?"

M ORE champagne?" Ritter asked.

I grinned, already feeling kind of silly after just one glass. We were sitting in the dining room of the Sapphire Supper Club. A jazz quartet played quietly in the corner, and we'd already plowed through the gravlax appetizer. The champagne was in celebration of my no longer being a murder suspect.

"Get this," I said to Ritter. "Lupe told me they found the murder weapon in Karl's kitchen. Once they knew who killed her, they got a warrant for the restaurant and Karl's house. He'd taken it from the Roux Grill."

"Talk about hiding in plain sight," he said with a grimace. "I wonder why he didn't just bury it in the woods someplace, or dump it in the river."

I pointed my fork at him before snagging the last piece of yummy salmon. "Karl is one arrogant guy. I wouldn't be surprised if he liked the idea of keeping it close." I chewed for a moment. "Shyla was horrified to find out her boyfriend killed someone—even if she was jealous of Josie. Karl wasn't what anyone at the Roux thought." I looked around at the dark leather booths. "Maggie told me he used to work here before cooking for Harris."

A speculative look crossed Ritter's face. "Huh. I wonder why he left?"

"Me, too. Maybe someone here found out what kind of guy he really was. Not that it matters anymore. He's going to prison for a long, long time."

"You'll have to testify at his trial."

"Better than having to listen to Bongo Pete testify against me. I went and saw him, you know."

"Really?" He took a sip from his champagne flute. I silently admired the way his long fingers held the glass so delicately.

"Yep. And you know what?"

He raised his eyebrows.

"Pete didn't remember telling Lang he'd seen me in River Park—that night or any other."

"You don't think Max lied, do you?"

I shook my head. "I think that would be a stretch even for him. Lupe put in a request to work alone from now on. I hope the chief grants it."

"Lupe, huh."

"I like her," I said. "And I'm helping her to remember some things for a memoir she's writing about growing up in Albuquerque." An idea that occurred to her after she'd made the *champurrado* from her childhood.

Ritter's forehead wrinkled. "How are you helping her to remember?"

I twiddled my fingers. "Oh, you know. With scents and nonsense." And a teensy, tiny bit of mnemosyne oil.

The waiter brought our entrees. Ritter tucked into his seared scallops with bacon and leeks, and I savored my mussels steamed with tomatoes, fennel, and ouzo. We ate in silence for a little while, listening to the jazz and simply enjoying each other's company. For a first date, it was pretty good.

I took a break from the deliciousness and sat back. "Inga was wrong about her husband, you know. Maggie, the font of all knowledge, told me he's not worried about his wife's past being bad for his political career. Apparently infamous is as good as famous these days."

Ritter snorted.

After dinner, we ordered a piece of lemon cheesecake to share. "A girl could get used to this," I said.

Ritter's smile lit up his face. "I hope so. Plenty more where this came from."

He hadn't mentioned leaving Poppyville when a new grant came through, and I wasn't going bring it up, either.

"How about a dance?" he asked.

I held up my hand. "Oh, no. You need to know something right off the bat. I can't dance."

"Elliana—"

"No, I mean it. I *really* can't dance."

Shrugging, he stood. "That's okay. What are you going to do, bruise my feet? You're light as a feather." He held his hand out to me.

I tried to protest again, but the words died in my throat when I saw the expression on his face. Heart pounding, I took his hand. He led me out to the postage-stamp dance floor and wrapped me in his arms. I leaned my cheek against his chest as we swayed to the mellow music.

"This isn't so bad, is it?"

Feeling utterly content, I murmured, "No."

The band started in on a livelier tune, and my nervousness returned. As I turned to go sit down, Ritter slowly spun me out, around, and back into his arms.

I laughed.

He did it again, a little faster, and then again with an extra twirl at the end. Nuzzling my hair, he said, "I don't know who told you that you can't dance, but you're a natural."

We sipped our champagne and danced and nibbled on cheesecake for the next hour. Finally, I said, "I need to get back. Early day tomorrow."

"Okay," he said easily.

As he drove me back in Thea's Terra Green truck, he reached over and took my hand. I looked down, but didn't pull back. He parked and walked me to the gate.

"I'm going to stop here," he said. "Don't want to be too pushy."

"Thanks," I whispered, overwhelmed and giddy and still a little scared.

"This is for you." He reached into this pocket and withdrew a small bouquet. Even without seeing it I knew it was lavender. *Lavandula stoechas*, to be precise. Ritter placed it in my hand, curling his fingers around mine to hold it, and kissed me on the cheek.

I watched him drive away before opening the gate. Dash was waiting for me.

In the Enchanted Garden, I whispered to the corgi, "Do you think Ritter knew what lavender is supposed to mean?"

The acknowledgment of love.

I was answered by light breeze moving through the wind chimes.

Inside, I turned on the light by the love seat in the living room and reached for the purple leather-bound blank book I'd purchased at Rexall Drugs earlier. I opened the package of colored pencils that had been part of my little buying spree as well. Opening the journal to a random page, I began to sketch a picture of a topped lavender bloom.

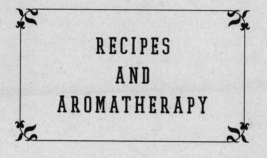

RECIPES
AND
AROMATHERAPY

Astrid's Chewy Double Chocolate Chunk Hazelnut Cookies

Makes approximately 48 cookies.

1¼ cups butter
2 cups sugar
2 large eggs
2 teaspoons vanilla extract
2 cups flour
¾ cup cocoa powder
1 teaspoon baking soda
½ teaspoon salt
1 tablespoon espresso powder or instant coffee
1 cup dark chocolate chunks (or large chips)
1 cup hazelnut pieces

Preheat oven to 350 degrees F.

In a large mixing bowl, cream together butter and sugar. Add eggs and blend until smooth and fluffy. Thoroughly mix in vanilla extract. In another bowl, sift together the flour, cocoa powder, baking soda, salt, and espresso powder. Add flour mixture to the creamed mixture and blend well. Fold in chocolate chunks/chips and hazelnuts.

Mound cookies on parchment-lined baking sheets, two inches apart, using about two tablespoons of dough for each cookie. Bake for 10–13 minutes. Remove and allow to cool on baking sheet for 3–4 minutes before moving to a rack to cool further. The cookies will be very pliable at first (so chewy later!). Delicious served slightly warm with coffee or milk.

Aromatherapy Tips

In order to achieve the most benefit from aromatherapy blends, it is important to use real, high-quality essential oils. Unlike Elliana, you don't have to distill them yourself! Many common oils are available in natural-food stores and even some grocery chains. However, buying them online can be more cost-efficient, especially for larger quantities. Two reputable online sources are From Nature with Love and Camden-Grey Essential Oils.

To check the quality of an essential oil, put a single drop on a piece of brown paper. After twenty-four hours there should hardly be any sign of the oil. If the spot still looks oily, then it is likely that another oil has been added to extend the essential oil. Pure essential oils are extremely volatile, meaning they evaporate very quickly (which is why their scent can fill a room so fast).

If you plan to apply an essential oil or essential blend to your skin, it is imperative that you use a carrier oil to dilute the oil. Using undiluted oils directly on skin can be harmful, causing reddening and even burning the skin. A good rule of thumb is to use twelve drops of essential oil to each ounce of carrier oil. A carrier oil can be any unscented oil, but jojoba oil is best because it most closely resembles the oils in human skin. Close seconds are almond and avocado oils.

Aromatherapy Blends

These are for use in a diffuser and are *not* to be applied directly to the skin.

RELAXATION
5 drops lemon
5 drops lavender
10 drops clary sage

MUSCLE FATIGUE
5 drops thyme
10 drops rosemary
5 drops cypress
10 drops grapefruit

CREATIVITY
3 drops rosemary
2 drops coriander
3 drops cypress
5 drops lemon

SLEEP
2 drops lavender
2 drops lemon
2 drops chamomile

CONFIDENCE
6 drops lemon
2 drops basil
3 drops bergamot
1 drop lavender

THIS was a grand adventure, I told myself. The ideal situation at the ideal time. It was also one of the scariest things I'd ever done.

So when I rounded the corner to find my aunt and uncle's baby blue Thunderbird convertible snugged up to the curb in front of my new home, I was both surprised and relieved.

Aunt Lucy knelt beside the porch steps, trowel in hand, patting the soil around a plant. She looked up and waved a gloved hand when I pulled into the driveway of the compact brick house, which had once been the carriage house of a larger home. I opened the door and stepped into the humid April heat.

"Katie's here—right on time!" Lucy called over her shoulder and hurried across the lawn to throw her arms around me. The aroma of patchouli drifted from her hair as I returned her hug.

"How did you know I'd get in today?" I leaned my tush against the hood of my Volkswagen Beetle, then pushed away when the hot metal seared my skin through my denim shorts. "I wasn't planning to leave Akron until tomorrow."

I'd decided to leave early so I'd have a couple of extra days to acclimate. Savannah, Georgia, was about as different from Ohio as you could get. During my brief visits I'd fallen in love with the elaborate beauty of the city, the excesses of her past—and present—and the food. Everything from high-end cuisine to traditional Low Country dishes.

"Oh, honey, of course you'd start early," Lucy said. "We knew you'd want to get here as soon as possible. Let's get you inside the house and pour something cool into you. We brought supper over, too—crab cakes, barbecued beans with rice, and some nice peppery coleslaw."

I sighed in anticipation. Did I mention the food?

Her luxurious mop of gray-streaked blond hair swung over her shoulder as she turned toward the house. "How was the drive?"

"Long." I inhaled the warm air. "But pleasant enough. The Bug was a real trouper, pulling that little trailer all that way. I had plenty of time to think." Especially as I drove through the miles and miles of South Carolina marshland. That was when the enormity of my decisions during the past two months had really begun to weigh on me.

She whirled around to examine my face. "Well, you don't look any the worse for wear, so you must have been thinking happy thoughts."

"Mostly," I said and left it at that.

My mother's sister exuded good cheer, always on the lookout for a silver lining and the best in others. A bit of a hippie, Lucy had slid seamlessly into the New Age movement twenty years before. Only a few lines augmented the corners of her blue eyes. Her brown hemp skirt and light cotton blouse hung gracefully on her short but very slim frame. She was a laid-back natural beauty rather than a Southern belle. Then again, Aunt Lucy had grown up in Dayton.

"Come on in here, you two," Uncle Ben called from the shadows of the front porch.

A magnolia tree shaded that corner of the house, and copper-colored azaleas marched along the iron railing in a riot of blooms. A dozen iridescent dragonflies glided through air that smelled heavy and green. Lucy smiled when one of them zoomed over and landed on my wrist. I lifted my hand, admiring the shiny blue-green wings, and it launched back into the air to join its friends.

I waved to my uncle. "Let me grab a few things."

Reaching into the backseat, I retrieved my sleeping bag and oversized tote. When I stepped back and pushed the door shut with my foot, I saw a little black dog gazing up at me from the pavement.

"Well, hello," I said. "Where did you come from?"

He grinned a doggy grin and wagged his tail.

"You'd better get on home now."

More grinning. More wagging.

"He looks like some kind of terrier. I don't see a collar," I said to Lucy. "But he seems well cared for. Must live close by."

She looked down at the little dog and cocked her head. "I wonder."

And then, as if he had heard a whistle, he ran off. Lucy shrugged and moved toward the house.

By the steps, I paused to examine the rosemary topiary Lucy had been planting when I arrived. The resinous herb had been trained into the shape of a star. "Very pretty. I might move it around to the herb garden I'm planning in back."

"Oh, no, dear. I'm sure you'll want to leave it right where it is. A rosemary plant by the front door is . . . traditional."

I frowned. Maybe it was a Southern thing.

Lucy breezed by me and into the house. On the porch, my uncle's smiling brown eyes lit up behind rimless glasses. He grabbed me for a quick hug. His soft ginger beard, grown since he'd retired from his job as Savannah's fire chief, tickled my neck.

He took the sleeping bag from me and gestured me inside. "Looks like you're planning on a poor night's sleep."

Shrugging, I crossed the threshold. "It'll have to do until I get a bed." Explaining that I typically slept only one hour a night would only make me sound like a freak of nature.

I'd given away everything I owned except for clothes, my favorite cooking gear, and a few things of sentimental value. So now I had a beautiful little house with next to no furniture in it—only the two matching armoires I'd scored at an estate sale. But that was part of this grand undertaking. The future felt clean and hopeful. A life waiting to be built again from the ground up.

We followed Lucy through the living room and into

the kitchen on the left. The savory aroma of golden crab cakes and spicy beans and rice that rose from the take-out bag on the counter hit me like a cartoon anvil. My aunt and uncle had timed things just right, especially considering they'd only guessed at my arrival. But Lucy had always been good at guessing that kind of thing. So had I, for that matter. Maybe it was a family trait.

Trying to ignore the sound of my stomach growling, I gestured at the small table and two folding chairs. "What's this?" A wee white vase held delicate spires of French lavender, sprigs of borage with its blue star-shaped blooms, yellow calendula, and orange-streaked nasturtiums.

Ben laughed. "Not much, obviously. Someplace for you to eat, read the paper—whatever. 'Til you find something else."

Lucy handed me a cold sweating glass of sweet tea. "We stocked a few basics in the fridge and cupboard, too."

"That's so thoughtful. It feels like I'm coming home."

My aunt and uncle exchanged a conspiratorial look.

"What?" I asked.

Lucy jerked her head. "Come on." She sailed out of the kitchen, and I had no choice but to follow her through the postage-stamp living room and down the short hallway. Our footsteps on the worn wooden floors echoed off soft peach walls that reached all the way up to the small open loft above. Dark brown shutters that fit with the original design of the carriage house folded back from the two front windows. The built-in bookshelves cried out to be filled.

"The vibrations in here are positively lovely," she said. "And how fortunate that someone was clever enough to place the bedroom in the appropriate ba-gua."

"Ba-what?"

She put her hand on the doorframe, and her eyes widened. "Ba-gua. I thought you knew. It's feng shui. Oh, honey, I have a book you need to read."

I laughed. Though incorporating feng shui into my furnishing choices certainly couldn't hurt.

Then I looked over Lucy's shoulder and saw the bed. "Oh." My fingers crept to my mouth. "It's beautiful."

A queen-sized headboard rested against the west wall, the dark iron filigree swooping and curling in outline against the expanse of Williamsburg blue paint on the walls. A swatch of sunshine cut through the window, spotlighting the patchwork coverlet and matching pillow shams. A reading lamp perched on a small table next to it.

"I've always wanted a headboard like that," I breathed. "How did you know?" Never mind the irony of my sleep disorder.

"We're so glad you came down to help us with the bakery," Ben said in a soft voice. "We just wanted to make you feel at home."

As I tried not to sniffle, he put his arm around my shoulders. Lucy slipped hers around my waist.

"Thank you," I managed to say. "It's perfect."

Lᴜᴄʏ and Ben helped me unload the small rented trailer, and after they left I unpacked everything and put it away. Clothes were in one of the armoires, a few favorite books leaned together on the bookshelf in the living room, and pots and pans filled the cupboards. Now it was a little after three in the morning, and I lay in my new bed, watching the moonlight crawl across the ceiling. The silhouette of a magnolia branch bobbed gently in response to a slight breeze. Fireflies danced outside the window.

Change is inevitable, they say. *Struggle is optional.*

Your life's path deviates from what you intend. Whether you like it or not. Whether you fight it or not. Whether your heart breaks or not.

After pastry school in Cincinnati, I'd snagged a job as assistant manager at a bakery in Akron. It turned out "assistant manager" meant long hours, hard work, no creative input, and anemic paychecks for three long years.

But I didn't care. I was in love. I'd thought Andrew was, too—especially after he asked me to marry him.

Change is inevitable . . .

But in a way I was lucky. A month after Andrew called off the wedding, my uncle Ben turned sixty-two and retired. No way was he going to spend his time puttering around the house, so he and Lucy brainstormed and came up with the idea to open the Honeybee Bakery. Thing was, they needed someone with expertise: me.

The timing of Lucy and Ben's new business venture couldn't have been better. I wanted a job where I could actually use my culinary creativity and business know-how. I needed to get away from my old neighborhood, where I ran into my former fiancé nearly every day. The daily reminders were hard to take.

So when Lucy called, I jumped at the chance. The money I'd scrimped and saved to contribute to the down payment on the new home where Andrew and I were supposed to start our life together instead went toward my house in Savannah. It was my way of committing wholeheartedly to the move south.

See, some people can carry through a plan of action. I was one of them. My former fiancé was not.

Jerk.

Lucy's orange tabby cat had inspired the name of our new venture. Friendly, accessible, and promising sweet goodness, the Honeybee Bakery would open in another week. Ben had found a charming space between a knitting shop and a bookstore in historic downtown Savannah, and I'd flown back and forth from Akron to find and buy my house and work with my aunt to develop recipes while Ben oversaw the renovation of the storefront.

I rolled over and plumped the feather pillow. The mattress was just right: not too soft and not too hard. But unlike Goldilocks, I couldn't seem to get comfortable. I flopped onto my back again. Strange dreams began to flutter along the edges of my consciousness as I drifted in and out. Finally, at five o'clock, I rose and dressed in shorts, a T-shirt, and my trusty trail runners. I needed to blow the mental cobwebs out.

That meant a run.

Despite sleeping only a fraction of what most people did, I wasn't often tired. For a while I'd wondered if I was manic. However, that usually came with its opposite, and despite its recent popularity, depression wasn't my thing. It was just that *not* running made me feel a little crazy. Too much energy, too many sparks going off in my brain.

I'd found the former carriage house in Midtown—not quite downtown but not as far out as Southside suburbia, and still possessing the true flavor of the city. After stretching, I set off to explore the neighborhood. Dogwoods bloomed along the side streets, punctuating the massive live oaks dripping with moss. I spotted two other runners in the dim predawn light. They waved, as did I. The smell of sausage teased from one house, the voices of children from another. Otherwise, all was quiet except for the sounds of birdsong, footfalls, and my own breathing.

Back home, I showered and donned a floral skort, tank tops and sandals. After returning the rented trailer, I drove downtown on Abercorn Street, wending my way around the one-way parklike squares in the historic district as I neared my destination. Walkers strode purposefully, some pushing strollers, some arm in arm. A ponytailed man lugged an easel toward the riverfront. Camera-wielding tourists intermixed with suited professionals, everyone getting an early start. The air winging in through my car window already held heat as I turned left onto Broughton just after Oglethorpe Square and looked for a parking spot.

From *New York Times* bestselling author

Bailey Cates

The Magical Bakery Mystery Series

Katie Lightfoot helps her aunt and uncle run the
HoneyBee Bakery in Savannah's quaint downtown
district, where delicious goodies, spellcasting, and the
occasional murder are sure to be found...

Brownies and Broomsticks
Bewitched, Bothered, and Biscotti
Charms and Chocolate Chips
Some Enchanted Éclair

"An attention-grabbing read that I couldn't put down."
—*New York Times* bestselling author Jenn McKinlay

"Charming and magical."
—*Kings River Life Magazine* "

"A top-notch whodunit."
—*Gumshoe*

OM0161